the strange and beautiful sorrows of ava lavender

the strange and beautiful sorrows of ava lavender

LESLYE WALTON

WALKER
BOOKS

This is a work of fiction. Names, characters, places and incidents are either the product of the author's imagination or, if real, used fictitiously. All statements, activities, stunts, descriptions, information and material of any other kind contained herein are included for entertainment purposes only and should not be relied on for accuracy or replicated as they may result in injury.

First published in Great Britain 2014 by Walker Books Ltd
87 Vauxhall Walk, London SE11 5HJ

2 4 6 8 10 9 7 5 3 1

This book has been typeset in Granjon and CG Carmine Tango

Printed and bound in Great Britain by Clays Ltd, St Ives plc

British Library Cataloguing in Publication Data:
a catalogue record for this book is available from the British Library

ISBN 978-1-4063-4808-8 (Hbk)
ISBN 978-1-4063-5445-4 (Trade pbk)

www.walker.co.uk

To Anna,
my partner in crime and fellow survivor,
who flies with her own wings

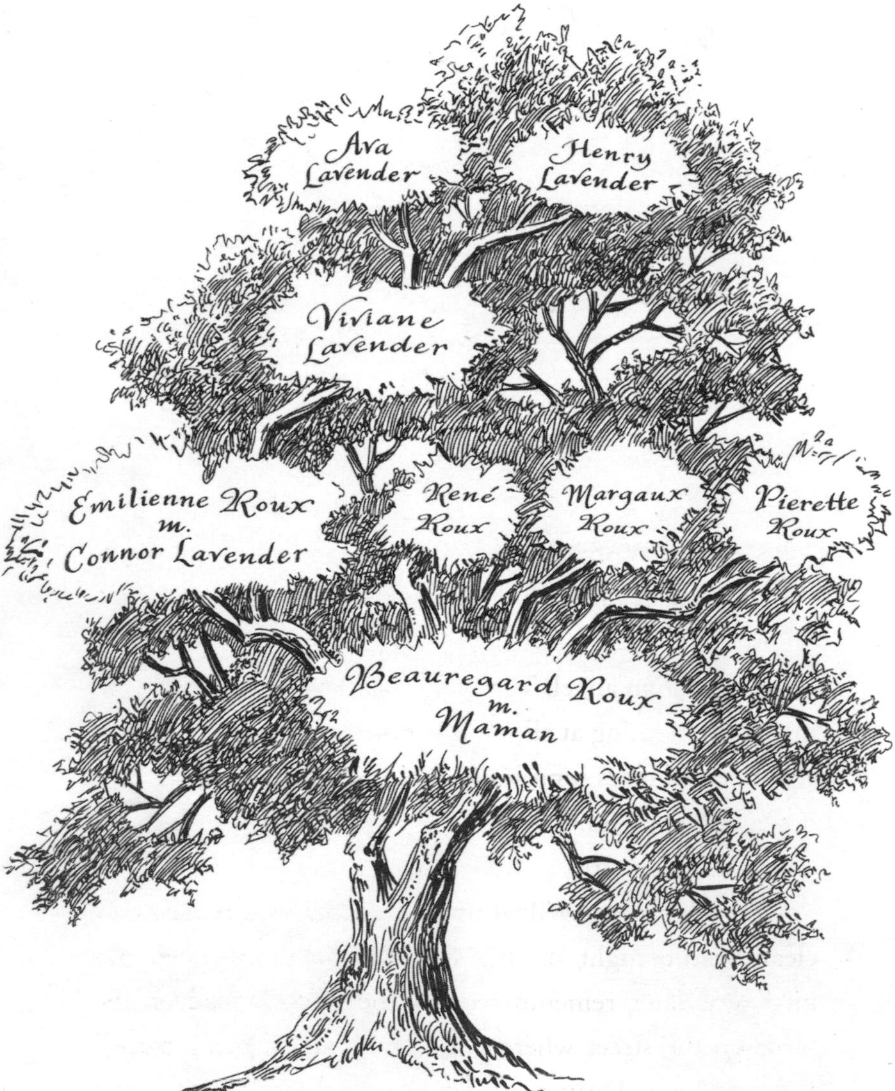
Ava
Lavender
Henry
Lavender
Viviane
Lavender
Emilienne Roux
m.
Connor Lavender
René
Roux
Margaux
Roux
Pierette
Roux
Beauregard Roux
m.
Maman

Prologue

TO MANY, I WAS MYTH INCARNATE, the embodiment of a most superb legend, a fairy tale. Some considered me a monster, a mutation. To my great misfortune, I was once mistaken for an angel. To my mother, I was everything. To my father, nothing at all. To my grandmother, I was a daily reminder of loves long lost. But I knew the truth—deep down, I always did.

I was just a girl.

I was born Ava Wilhelmina Lavender on a remarkably clear Seattle night on the first of March in 1944. My birth was later remembered for the effect it had on the birds on the street where I lived, the auspiciously named Pinnacle Lane. During the day, as my young mother began experiencing labor pains, the crows collected mounds of tiny cherry pits in their beaks and tossed them at the house windows. Sparrows perched on women's heads and stole loose strands of hair to weave into their nests. At night nocturnal birds gathered on the lawns to eat noisily, the screams of their prey sounding much like my own mother in hard labor. Just before slipping into a deep twilight sleep — relief granted by a nurse and a cold syringe — my mother opened her eyes and saw giant feathers fall from the ceiling. Their silky edges brushed her face.

As soon as I was born, the nurses whisked me away from the delivery room to explore a matter that was later described on an anonymous medical report only as *a slight physical abnormality.* It wasn't long before the devout gathered in the light from the hospital windows, carrying candles and singing hymns in praise and fear. All because when I was born, I opened my eyes, then unfolded the pair of speckled wings that wrapped around me like a feathery cocoon.

Or so the story goes.

Where the wings came from, no doctor could ever determine. My twin (for there was a twin, Henry) had surely been born without them. Until then, no human being on record had ever been born with animal parts — avian or otherwise. For many in the medical field, the case of Ava Lavender produced the first time science had failed them. When the religious masses gathered below my mother's hospital room window with their fevered prayers and flickering candles, for once the doctors considered the devout with jealousy, rather than with pity or disdain.

"Imagine," said one young intern to another, "believing the child is divine." It was a musing he uttered only once. Then he wiped his tired eyes and went back to his medical books before returning to my mother and claiming what every other specialist had already concluded—there was nothing they could do. Not medically, at least.

"I've never seen anything like it," he said, shaking his head to show my family that he sympathized. It was a practice he would master in time.

My entire muscular, skeletal, and circulatory systems were irrevocably dependent on my wings. The option of removing them was quickly deemed out of the question. I would lose too much blood. I could end up paralyzed. Or dead. It seemed there was no separating the girl from the wings. One could not survive without the other.

Later the young intern wished himself audacious enough to interview the family. But what would one ask? *Is there a history of winged beings populating the family tree?* In the end, the intern instead made his rounds to other patients with ailments that did not evoke such complex questions. But let's pause and imagine if he had. What might have happened if he had turned to the sullen young mother with the unnaturally red lips, or to the stern but beautiful grandmother with the strange accent, and asked them the two questions that would haunt my every winged step:

Where did I come from?

And even more important: *What would the world do with such a girl?*

Perhaps my mother or my grandmother would have had an answer.

And perhaps then my life would have turned out much differently. For the sake of the intern, it was probably best that he convinced himself that there was nothing he could do and left it at that. For what could he have done? Foreseeing the future, I would later learn, means nothing if there is nothing to be done to prevent it. Which just proves that my story is much more complicated than just the story of my birth. Or even the story of my life. In fact, my story, like everyone's, begins with the past and a family tree.

The following is the story of my young life as I lived it. What started out as a simple personal research project as a young woman—a weekend in 1974 spent at the Seattle Central Library compiling information about my birth—led me down a road that took me from one coast to the other. I have traveled through continents, languages, and time trying to understand all that I am and all that has made me such.

I will be the first to admit that certain facts may have been omitted, long forgotten over time by myself or by other involved parties. My research has been scattered, dropped, neglected, then picked up, shuffled, and reorganized time and again. It cannot be considered a holistic document. Nor is it unbiased.

The following is the story of my young life as I remember it. It is the truth as I know it. Of the stories and the myths that surrounded my family and my life—some of them thoughtfully scattered by you perhaps—let it be said that, in the end, I found all of them to be strangely, even beautifully, true.

A. Lavender

March 2014

Chapter One

MY MATERNAL GRANDMOTHER, Emilienne Adou Solange Roux, fell in love three times before the eve of her nineteenth birthday.

Born on March first in 1904, my *grand-mère* was the first of four children, all born on the first day of the third month, with René following Emilienne in 1905, Margaux in 1906, and ending with Pierette in 1907. Since each child was born under the sign of the fish, it would be easy to assume that the Roux family was full of rather sensitive and remarkably foolhardy individuals.

Their father, Beauregard Roux, was a well-known phrenologist whose greatest contributions to his field were said to be the curls of goldenrod hair atop his head and on the backs of his hands—and the manner in which his French was laced with just a hint of a Breton accent. Thick and large, Beauregard Roux could easily carry all four of his children dangling from one arm, with the family goat tucked under the other.

My great-grandmother was quite the opposite of her husband. While Beauregard was large, grandiose, mountainous even, his wife was small, indistinct, and walked with the blades of her shoulders in a permanent hunch. Her complexion was olive where his was rosy, her hair dark where his was light, and while every head turned when Beauregard Roux stepped into a room, his wife was best known for her capacity to take up no capacity at all.

On nights they made love, their neighbors were kept awake by the growls Beauregard made upon climax—his wife, however, hardly made any noise at all. She rarely did. In fact, the doctor in the small village of Trouville-sur-Mer who delivered their first child, my grandmother, spent the length of the delivery looking up from his duties just to be sure the mother had not perished during the act. The silence in the room was so disturbing that when it came time for the birth of their next child—my great-uncle René—the doctor refused at the last minute, leaving Beauregard to run the seventeen kilometers in his stocking feet to the town of Honfleur in a rush to find the nearest midwife.

There remains no known history of my great-grandmother before her marriage to Beauregard Roux. Her only proof of existence lay in the faces of her two oldest daughters, Emilienne and Margaux, each with her dark hair, olive complexion, and pale-green eyes. René, the only boy, resembled his father. Pierette, the youngest, had Beauregard's rich yellow curls. Not one of the children ever knew their mother's first name, each believing it was Maman until it was too late for them to even consider it could be anything else.

Whether or not it had anything to do with his large size, by the dawn of 1912 the small French village had proven much too *petit* for Beauregard Roux. He dreamed of places full of automobiles and buildings so tall they blocked the sun; all Trouville-sur-Mer had to offer was a fish market and Beauregard's own phrenology practice, kept afloat by his female neighbors. His fingers ached for skulls whose bumps he hadn't read time and time again! So, on the first of March of that year—which was eldest daughter Emilienne's eighth birthday, son René's seventh, Margaux's sixth, and Pierette's fifth—Beauregard began to talk of a place he called Manhatine.

"In Manhatine," he'd say to his neighbors while pumping water from the well outside his home, "whenever you need to take a bath or wash your face, you just turn the faucet, and there it is—not just water, *mes camarades*, but *hot* water. Can you imagine? Like being greeted by a little miracle every morning right there in your own bathtub." And then he'd laugh gaily, making them suspect that Beauregard Roux was perhaps a little more unstable than they might have wished for someone so large.

It was to the dismay of the women in Trouville-sur-Mer—and the men, for there was no other character they liked better to discuss—that Beauregard sold his phrenology practice only one month later. He secured six third-class tickets aboard the maiden voyage of the SS *France*—one for each of his family members, with the exception of the family goat, of course. He taught his children the English words for the numbers one through ten and, in his enthusiasm, once told them that the streets in America were unlike anything they'd ever seen before—not covered in dirt like the ones in Trouville-sur-Mer, but paved in cobblestones of bronze.

"Gold," my young grandmother, Emilienne, interrupted. If America was really the impressive place her father thought it was, then certainly the streets would be made of something better than bronze.

"Don't be foolish," Beauregard chided gently. "Even the Americans know better than to pave their streets in gold."

The SS *France*, as I've come to learn in my research, was a marvel of French engineering. Over twice the size of any ship in the French merchant fleet, she would set a new precedent for speed, luxury, service, and cuisine for the French Line. Her maiden voyage departed from the bustling port of Le Havre, forty-two kilometers from Trouville-sur-Mer.

Le Havre of 1912 was a place clearly marked by the distinctions of class. Surrounded on the east by the villages of Montivilliers, Harfleur, and Gonfreville-l'Orcher, the Seine River separated the city from Honfleur. In the late eighteen hundreds, when the neighboring villages of Sanvic and Bléville were incorporated into Le Havre, an upper city developed above the ancient lower city with two parts linked by a complex network of eighty-nine stairs and a funicular. The hillside mansions of rich merchants and ship owners, all of whom had made their fortunes from Le Havre's expansive port in the early nineteenth century, occupied the upper part. In the city's center were the town hall, the Sous-Préfecture, the courthouse, the Le Havre Athletic Club, and the Turkish baths. There were museums and casinos and a number of lavish and expensive hotels. It was this Le Havre that gave birth to the impressionist movement; it was where Claude Monet was inspired to paint *Impression, soleil levant.*

Meanwhile, the suburbs and old districts of Le Havre, where the working-class families lived, and the flat quarters near the port, where the sailors, dockworkers, and laborers worked, were neglected. Here dwelt the effects of grueling and unreliable employment, poor sewer systems, and unsanitary living conditions. Here the cemeteries were overwhelmed with the dead from the cholera outbreak of 1832. It was where consumption found its victims. Here were the bohemians, the red-light district, the cabaret with the effeminate master of ceremonies where a man could pay for a drink and a little entertainment without having to take off his hat. And while the rich Havrais in the upper part of the city raised a toast to many more blissful and successful years, those living in the slums rotted away in a toxic smelly mess of insalubrity, shit, promiscuity, and infant mortality.

To the Roux children, the dock where the ship was moored was a melody of interesting sights, smells, and sounds, an unsettling concoction of the exotic and the mundane: the oceanic air, the sharp bite of coffee beans mixed with the acidic tang of fish blood, mounds of exotic fruits and burlap bags of cotton from the surrounding cargo ships, stray cats and dogs scratching their ribs for mange, and heavy trunks and suitcases marked with American addresses.

Among the crowd of news reporters, a photographer stood documenting the ship's maiden voyage with his imposing folding camera. As the first-class passengers made their way to their private cabins, the Roux family waited with the rest of steerage to be inspected for lice. Beauregard lifted Emilienne onto his tall shoulders. From her perch, the cheering onlookers looked like a sea of broad-brimmed boater hats. A photograph printed in the Paris newspaper *Le Figaro* showed the grand ship at this moment—by squinting, a reader could just make out the shadowy shape of a girl balanced eerily above the crowd.

Embarking only one week after the implausible sinking of Britain's Unsinkable Ship, the *Titanic*, the passengers aboard the SS *France* were keenly aware of the cold waters below as they gravely waved good-bye to the crowd on the distant dock. Only Beauregard Roux ran to the other side of the ship, wanting to be the first to greet the land of opportunities, bronze streets, and indoor plumbing.

The Roux family's quarters contained two tiny bunk beds built into the cabin walls and a washbasin in the center. If Beauregard inhaled too deeply, he could suck all the air out of the room. Maman claimed that the ship's ceaseless vibrations gave her palpitations. The children, however, loved the tiny cabin, even when Beauregard's snoring left them with little oxygen some nights.

The SS *France* opened up a world they'd never imagined. They spent their evenings waiting for the sound of a lone fiddle or set of bagpipes that announced the start of that night's impromptu celebration in steerage. Later still, they waited in hushed anticipation for the sounds of their neighbors making their own entertainment. The children spent hours listening to the noises resounding through the walls, stifling their wild laughter into scratchy pillows. Days were spent exploring the lower decks and trying to sneak their way into the first-class sections of the boat, which were strictly off-limits to third-class passengers.

When American soil could be seen from the ship, the passengers breathed a collective sigh of relief so strong, it caused a change of direction in the winds, which added a day to their trip, but no matter. They had made it—forever squelching the fear that the *Titanic*'s fatal end was a harbinger of their own disastrous fate.

As the SS *France* approached the dock in west Manhattan, my grandmother received her first glimpse of the United States. Emilienne, who had no idea that *La liberté éclairant le monde*—the Statue of Liberty—was as French as she was, thought, *Well, if this is America, then it is certainly very ugly indeed.*

The Roux family was quickly declared lice-free and so set off to begin their new lives of prosperity and delight—the likes of which only America could provide. By the time Germany declared war on France, they were finally settled in a squalid two-room apartment in Manhatine. At night Emilienne and Margaux slept in one bed, Beauregard and Maman in the other, René under the kitchen table, and tiny Pierette in a bureau drawer.

It didn't take long for Beauregard to learn how difficult it would be to sell himself as a skillful phrenologist—especially since the phrenology craze in America had died with the Victorian period. How was a French immigrant with a thick rolling accent and no skill but reading skulls expected to support his family? *It's hard enough for the Irish micks down at the docks to get a decent pay,* my great-grandfather confided to no one, *and they speak perfect English. Or so they claim.*

Beauregard's own neighbors had no use for his talents. They already knew their own dismal futures. So instead he took to the streets in Yorkville and Carnegie Hill, where many prominent German immigrants lived in country estates and lush town houses. Toting his rolled-up charts, metal calipers, and his china phrenology head, Beauregard was soon invited into the parlors of these villas to run his fingertips and palms over the skulls of the *Frauen und Fräulein* of the house, proving yet again that Beauregard Roux was destined to serve women, regardless of what country he was in.

New York, in all of its fast-paced glory, did nothing to dissuade Beauregard from his belief that it was the most magnificent place in the world. Maman, however, found her husband's beloved Manhatine most disagreeable. The tenement where they lived was small and cramped; it smelled distinctly of cat urine regardless of how many washings of lye soap she applied to the floors and walls. The streets were a slew of slaughterhouses and sweatshops, and were not paved in bronze but lined with garbage and piles of horse dung awaiting the unsuspecting foot. She thought the English language harsh and ugly, and the American women shameless, marching through the streets in their white dresses and sashes, demanding the ridiculous right to vote. To Maman, America was hardly the land of opportunities. Rather, it seemed to be the place where children were brought to die. Maman watched in horror as her neighbors lost their children, one after the other. They died with the pallor and fever of consumption, the coughing fits of pertussis. They died from mild bouts of the flu, a singular encounter with a cup of sour milk. They died from low birth weight, often taking their mothers along with them.

They died with empty bellies, their eyes vacant of both dreams and expression.

Maman fed her family meals of low-quality meat and limp carrots because this was what they could afford—barely. She inspected the children every time they returned home—searching the crevices behind their knees and elbows, the soft places in between toes, behind ears, and under tongues for the mark of a pox or a tick.

Beauregard hardly shared his wife's concerns. At night, as the couple lay in bed, their children asleep in the bed across the room and cramped under the kitchen table and tucked into a bureau drawer, Maman tried to persuade her husband to leave the city so that they might raise their children in the light French air of their former home.

"Oh, *mon cœur*, my heart," he answered lightly, "you worry much too much." Then he rolled over and fell into a deep sleep while Maman fretted the night into morning.

Then one otherwise unremarkable evening in the spring of 1915, garishly handsome Beauregard Roux did not return home to his wife and their four children. Nor did he arrive the next night or in a month's time. A year later the only tangible memory of Beauregard Roux was in the person of René, who had a penchant for carrying the couch around the apartment balanced on his forearms.

It was rumored that Beauregard left his family for a Germanic woman blessed with infertility and a convex along the back of her head, which, as every good phrenologist knew, meant Beauregard had found himself a complaisant woman, one who was likely to give him loud affection any night he pleased. It was a tale so creative that even Maman believed it. This belief later led to the development of a small hole in the top chamber of her heart, which her doctors falsely ascribed to her diet and her unknown ancestry.

In truth, the disappearance of Beauregard Roux was a case of mistaken identity. Beauregard, for all his rugged beauty, was also the very image of another man caught sleeping with the wife of a local butcher. How unfortunate for Beauregard that the butcher's thugs found him first. The discovery of his body, found floating in bloated and unidentifiable pieces along the Hudson River, was briefly mentioned in a side column of the *New York Times.* This unfortunate mix-up had its own ironies: Beauregard Roux had loved his wife immensely; he found her quiet tendencies refreshing and never strayed from her once in all the time they were married.

Upon realizing that her husband had performed a permanent disappearing act, Maman took to her bed and spent the next three months wrapped in the sheets that still retained her husband's pungent scent. The children were cared for by their neighbor, a pygmy named Mrs. Barnaby Callahoo whom they called Notre Petit Poulet, Our Little Chicken, due to a habit the tiny woman had of clucking her tongue against the roof of her mouth. It was a nickname Mrs. Barnaby Callahoo found most agreeable.

Eventually Maman pulled herself from her bed and

took a job as a bookkeeper at the dry cleaner's down the street. In time she made enough money to serve the lowest quality of horsemeat to her family three times a week. She also moved Pierette out of the drawer.

All the while, it grew apparent that Maman was slowly making her own disappearance. Emilienne was the first to notice this when, on a busy street corner, she reached out to take hold of her mother's hand. Her fingers slipped right through, as if passing through a wisp of steam.

In 1917 Emilienne was thirteen years old and living with her three siblings and Maman in a crowded city block of apartment buildings. Each tenement came with its own problems of sanitation, crowding, and desiccated stairwells. The Roux children were so accustomed to their neighbors' voices permeating the thin walls that each child could eventually speak in several languages—all four in French and English, Emilienne in Italian, René in Dutch and German, and Margaux in Spanish. The youngest, Pierette, spoke only in what was later identified as Greek until her seventh birthday, when in perfect French she declared, *"Mon dieu! Où est mon gâteau?"* which meant "My God! Where is my cake?" and made them all suspect that Pierette had many tricks up her sleeve.

It was on this city block that my grandmother met the first love of her life. His name was Levi Blythe, a runt of a boy with black hair and ill-fitting shoes. A gang of boys from the next block repeatedly called Levi a faggot before pelting his forehead with rocks. He was the first boy Emilienne ever saw cry, not counting her brother, René, who had a surprisingly low tolerance for pain.

After a particularly gruesome beating, an event to which most of the neighborhood children were witness, Emilienne and her younger sister Margaux followed Levi Blythe to a back alley, where they watched him bleed until Levi turned to them and yelled, "Get lost!"

So they did. Momentarily.

Emilienne climbed the stairs to her family's apartment, shadowed closely, as always, by Margaux. She tore a triangle out of the bottom sheet of the bed she shared with her sister, took the bottle of iodine from her mother's drawer, and ran back to where Levi sat slumped against the alley wall. After watching him wince from the sting of iodine against his cuts, Emilienne let him touch her bare bottom. It was an offering she rationalized later to Margaux, saying with a sigh, "Love can make us such fools."

Emilienne never saw Levi Blythe after that day, nor did anyone else. Many believed that the sordid affairs that regularly took place in his mother's apartment had finally caught up to her, and that perhaps Levi and his two sisters had become wards of the state. But then again, no one was ever really sure—in those days, many people disappeared for lesser reasons; it was difficult to keep track of them all.

It took three years for my grandmother to forget poor

Levi Blythe. At sixteen, she fell hopelessly for a boy she knew only as Dublin, a nickname derived from the place of his birth. Dublin taught her how to smoke cigarettes and once told her she was beautiful.

"Beautiful," he said with a laugh, "but strange, like everyone in your family." He then gave Emilienne her first kiss before running off with Carmelita Hermosa, who was just as lovely as her name implied. And quite unfairly so.

In 1922, when Emilienne was eighteen, the Roux family underwent a number of transformations that confirmed they were, indeed, a little strange. Pierette, who did in fact have many tricks up her sleeve, was now fifteen years old and had fallen in love with an older gentleman with a fondness for bird watching. After failing every other attempt to get the ornithologist to notice her — including a rather disastrous event where she appeared on the stoop of his apartment building wearing nothing but a few feathers plastered to an indiscreet place — Pierette took the extreme step of turning herself into a canary.

The bird-watcher never noticed Pierette's drastic attempt at gaining his affection and instead moved to Louisiana, drawn by its large population of *Pelecanus occidentalis.* Which only goes to show, some sacrifices aren't worth the cost. Even, or perhaps most especially, those made out of love. The family gradually became accustomed to Pierette's cheery morning songs and to the tiny yellow feathers that gathered in the corners of the rooms and stuck to their clothes.

René, the only boy in the Roux family, had surpassed his father's good looks at the tender age of fourteen. By seventeen, he was considered a god among mortals. With simple phrases like *Could you please?* and *Would you like?* René caused young girls' faces to flush with hysteria. On the street, otherwise reputable women walked into walls at the passing by of René Roux, distracted by the way the sun moved through the hair on his knuckles. This was a frightening phenomenon in and of itself, but René found it most upsetting because, unlike Levi Blythe, René *was* in fact fonder of the boys on his street than the girls and took to sharing his bare bottom with some of them, though certainly not while any of his sisters were around.

Aside from Pierette, Emilienne was considered the strangest Roux of them all. It was rumored that she possessed certain unlikely gifts: the ability to read minds, walk through walls, and move things using only the power of her thoughts. But my grandmother hadn't any powers; she wasn't clairvoyant or telepathic. Simply put, Emilienne was merely more sensitive to the outside world than other people. As such, she was able to catch on to things that others missed. While to some a dropped spoon might indicate a need to retrieve a clean one, to Emilienne it meant that her mother should put the kettle on for tea—someone was coming to visit. An owl hoot was an omen of impending unhappiness. A peculiar noise heard three times at night meant death was near. To receive a bouquet was a tricky one since it depended on the flowers—blue violets said,

I'll always be true, but a striped carnation, *Sorry, I can't be with you.* And while this gift proved useful at times, it could also make things quite confusing for young Emilienne. She struggled to distinguish between signs she received from the universe and those she conjured up in her head.

She took up the harpsichord for this very reason—when she pressed her hands to the keys, its complex voice drowned out everything else. She played nightly renditions of Italian love sonnets, which some later attributed to a correlating rise in the neighboring population. Many children were conceived under the amorous music of Emilienne Roux, accompanied by the harmonious voices of her siblings—René's soft tenor, Pierette's sharp chirp, and Margaux's haunting alto. Margaux wasn't strange, but she wasn't beautiful like the others either. This made her strange in her own way. And Maman continued to grow more transparent, enough so that her children could reach right through her to place a milk bottle in the icebox, often without thinking much about it.

Around this time a man called Satin by his friends and Monsieur Lush by everyone else was seen carousing through the streets of lower Manhattan in a silk-lined jacket and wearing rich cologne. They said that he came from somewhere up north—Quebec or Montreal—for his French was impeccable, though oddly accented, and that Manhattan was a usual stop in a circular trek he made every few months. The reason for his visits wasn't apparent, but it was easy to assume that it was nothing good based on the rough sort of men with whom he kept company and the way his left leg clinked from the flask he wore in his trouser leg.

The day Emilienne met Satin Lush, she was wearing her cloche hat, newly painted with red poppies. Her hair was curled and peeked lightly out from under the hat to cup the curve of her chin. There was a rip in her stocking. It was May and heavy wet lines of spring rain streamed down the windows of the café where Emilienne had just spent her day serving black coffee and sticky buns to dreamless Irishmen. The smell of glazed sugar and folded pride still lingered on her clothes. As she waited for the rain to let up, the bells of Saint Peter's chimed five times and the water fell only harder upon the awning over her head.

She was thinking of the loveliness of such moments, admiring the rain and the graying sky the way one might admire the painting of an up-and-coming artist, one whose celebrity seems presaged by the swirls of his brush marks. It was while she was in the midst of such thoughts that Satin Lush walked out of the café, the clink of his leg disturbing the rhythm of the rain against the awning. Emilienne was immediately transfixed by the circle of light green in one of his eyes, the way it deliciously clashed with the cerulean blue of the other. She found that she did not mind losing the previous moment, for this one was just as lovely.

As they made their way through the borough, Satin holding an umbrella over their heads and the lip of

Emilienne's cloche hat periodically hitting Satin's right ear, the lovers were unaware of the worsening weather. They didn't notice how the clouds gathered and the rain fell in such torrents that the rats of the city flipped the cockroaches onto their backs, stepped aboard, and floated down the streets on tiny arthropod rafts.

That night Emilienne introduced Satin to her family as her *betrothed*, and he spent the evening praising the half-moons of Emilienne's fingernails. Satin quickly became a favorite in the Roux apartment. Emilienne would often return home from work to find Maman and Satin locked deep in discussion, a fast procession of vivid French spilling from their lips. And when René disappeared for three days, it was Satin who knew where to find him. The two returned, René with a chip in one of his front teeth and Satin missing his right earlobe. When asked, the only response given was a vague *You shoulda seen the other guy* and a look between men when one has a secret the other is willing to protect.

The strangest development during this time, however, was the remarkable transformation of unlovely Margaux. After months of living in strained denial, the Roux family could no longer hide from the fact that sixteen-year-old Margaux was pregnant.

This was a particularly confusing time for Emilienne. Until then each of the two sisters had stuck to her predestined role—Emilienne was beautiful, mysterious. A tad strange at times, yes. But Margaux? Margaux was only a pale shadow of the art form that was Emilienne. There was a time when it was Emilienne with the secrets and Margaux who ached to learn the reason behind the devilish smile and lovely arched eyebrow. But, now, now it was Emilienne who ached. And how she did! Especially when it was no longer Emilienne but Margaux—what with that glowing complexion, those rosy cheeks, that effervescent twinkle in her eyes—that everyone considered the beauty of the family.

Margaux never spoke the father's name. Only once, in a moment of weakness—after a particularly grueling interrogation by her older sister—Margaux ran a finger over her own lovely arched eyebrow and said, "Love can make us such fools," sending a chill up Emilienne's neck. She left the room to fetch a sweater. That was the last time anyone asked Margaux about the father of her child. Instead, her siblings took to playing the "Is that the rat fink?" game while watching men pass by on the street.

The day the child was born, Emilienne was walking home from some errand no one remembered in the end, Pierette perched on her collarbone. The thing remembered was Emilienne's cloche hat—the one painted with red poppies—blowing into the street and being retrieved by an exuberant boy of ten. Emilienne dug a penny out of her purse to reward the boy. As she placed the shiny coin in the child's outstretched hand, she looked up into his dirt-smudged face and noticed his eyes were different colors. One was green, the other blue. On impulse, Emilienne asked the child who his father was, to which the boy answered with a shrug and ran off, holding his penny to the light.

Making their way through the street, Emilienne paid closer attention to the children in their path and came across another child with mismatched eyes, another child who didn't know his father. On the next block over, they came across another one. And another. Racing from one block to the next, Emilienne counted seventeen such children in twelve blocks.

By the time they made their way back to the family apartment, Pierette was in such a twitter that Emilienne had to stuff her poor sister-bird into the pocket of her jacket. In her haste to get inside, Emilienne knocked over Mrs. Barnaby Callahoo, who, after she'd been helped back onto her feet, announced that Margaux had given birth.

"It's a boy," Notre Petit Poulet said, her tiny fingers fluttering with excitement, "with black hair. But his eyes! One's blue, and the other? The other's green!"

Emilienne walked into the apartment and found Satin Lush, the man she would never call her *betrothed* again, sitting on the sill of an open window, smoking a cigarette. He shrugged when he saw her. "You know how it goes," he said.

In disgust, Emilienne charged toward him and, with an angry shove, pushed him out the window as she screamed, "Eighteen children!"

Satin Lush bounced off the pavement, sprang to his feet, and ran away, never to be seen again.

Whether it was the arrival of Margaux's child or Satin Lush's betrayal that led to the downfall of the Roux family remains unresolved. But it was only a few hours later that young Margaux was found in the community bathroom down the hall. She'd carved out her own heart using a silver knife and laid it with care on the floor by the bathtub. Below the red mass of sinew and blood was a note addressed to Emilienne:

Mon cœur entier pendant ma vie entière.

My whole heart for my entire life.

The child died soon after. Margaux was a mother for approximately six hours. The date was March 1, 1923.

Love, as most know, follows its own timeline, disregarding our intentions or well-rehearsed plans. Soon after his sister's demise, René fell in love with an older married man. William Peyton wept the day he met René Roux. It was in a rather compromising embrace that William's wife caught René and her husband in the bed where she herself had been turned away night after night for two decades. In his haste to flee the unpleasant scene, René ran out into the street, forgetting to take his clothes with him.

As he ran through the shop-lined blocks toward his family's apartment, he was followed by a growing crowd of women (and a few men), all wrought with hysteria over the sight of René Roux's naked buttocks. The frenzy quickly escalated into a full-fledged riot that lasted four and a half days. Several kosher businesses were burned to the ground and three people were trampled to death, including tiny Mrs. Barnaby Callahoo. *Bonsoir, Notre Petit Poulet.*

Once the panic finally subsided, René's lover sent a message to the Roux apartment, begging René to meet him at the docks along the Hudson River that night. The next morning the Roux family — what was left of them — awoke to find René's body on their doorstep, a handkerchief covering the place where William Peyton had shot him in his handsome face.

Chapter Two

IN THE MID-1920s, a small, inconsequential neighborhood sat in the blossoming city of Seattle, Washington. The neighborhood, some three thousand miles from Beauregard Roux's Manhatine, was later overshadowed by the Fremont bohemians in the 1960s and was mostly remembered for the house that sat on the hill at the end of Pinnacle Lane. It was remembered because I lived in that house.

The house was painted the color of faded periwinkles. It had a white wraparound porch and an onion-domed turret. The second-floor bedrooms had giant bay windows. A widow's walk rested on top of the house, its balcony turned toward Salmon Bay.

A Portuguese ship captain built the house in the late 1800s, its dollhouse charm inspired by a favorite childhood relic of his younger sister. Fatima Inês de Dores was still a child when, after the passing of both parents, she was sent to Seattle to live with her brother.

For many years neighbors could remember her tiny face on that day she arrived—her lips chapped and her thick dark brows partially hidden by the hood of her green cloak. They remembered with distaste how her brother's face flushed with desire and how his fingers burned red as he helped her down from the carriage.

Throughout the months her brother was at sea, Fatima Inês lived less like a child and more as a woman awaiting the return of a husband or lover. She never left the house, refusing to attend school with other children her age. She spent her days on the roof of the house with the doves she kept as pets. Wrapped in her hooded green cloak, she watched the sea from the widow's walk until forced inside by the dark-skinned housemaid, who cooked the child's meals and prepared her for bed.

In the spring, when the captain returned home from long voyages at sea, he brought his sister elaborate gifts: a hand-carved marionette from Italy with leather boots and a metal sword; a domino set made of ivory and ebony; a cribbage board etched into a walrus tusk bartered from the Eskimos; and, always, a bundle of purple lilacs.

Throughout his stay, the purple blooms scented the air with their heady perfume, and the house was said to pulse with an eerie golden hue at night. Years later, even after the ship captain and his sister no longer lived in the house at the end of Pinnacle Lane, the smell of lilacs could send impious ripples through the neighborhood.

During those spring months, the church pews were unusually full.

The entire neighborhood was built with little Fatima Inês in mind. Captain de Dores was the benefactor behind the post office, where he sent his younger sister packages from other ports. And he helped fund the elementary school, even after Fatima refused to attend.

Following a rather peculiar incident involving the priest from the nearest Catholic parish, Fatima Inês was also the reason they built the Lutheran church. At his sister's request, Captain de Dores had arranged for a visit from a priest to administer her First Communion. He commissioned a local seamstress to make her dress—a long white gown with tiny buttons up the back and a veil trimmed with pearls. He had the house filled with white roses for the occasion, and the petals from the blooms caught in Fatima's lace train when she walked.

When the priest set the host upon the rose of the young Fatima Inês's tongue, however, the holy wafer burst into flame.

Or so the story goes.

The priest refused ever to return to the house at the end of Pinnacle Lane. A few months later, the new Lutheran church was holding its first service.

The captain's only request, if the neighborhood wanted the patronage to continue, was a yearly public celebration of Fatima's birthday on the summer solstice.

No one knew what to expect the first year. And then the gold-embossed carriages of emerald green, fuchsia, and tangerine appeared on the dirt path leading up Pinnacle Lane. Driven by small men in blue satin top hats and pulled by dappled ponies, the carriages were windowless except for the last. Through its windows the gathering neighbors caught a glimpse of the ringmaster and the contortionist twins of Nova Scotia. The impossible postures on display by all turned out to be the most talked-about part of the entire celebration, even after the elephants arrived.

The celebrations grew all the more lavish and indulgent as the years went by: there were acrobats shipped in from China for Fatima's tenth birthday; a gypsy woman with wrinkled hands and a crystal ball when she turned eleven; white tigers that lapped up giant bowls of cream when she turned twelve. The summer solstice soon became a holiday that was anticipated with as much excitement as Christmas or the Fourth of July, with attendants arriving from miles away to dance around the bonfire with white daisies woven in their hair.

Fatima never attended the event herself. Occasionally someone — drunk on wishful thinking and mead — would insist that they saw her cloaked form perched on the roof with her birds, watching the festivities below with interest.

But this was quite unlikely.

Then one spring the captain didn't return from sea. The summer solstice was celebrated with as much fervor as in previous years, but there were no white tigers, no gypsy psychics, no displays of sexual prowess by the contortionist twins of Nova Scotia.

And no one had seen Fatima Inês in months.

The day she was finally brought out of the house would later be remembered as a day when shadows seemed blacker, as if something more lingered in those darkened spaces. Curious neighbors came out to stand in the street and watch as Fatima Inês, wearing nothing but a tattered white dress covered in bird droppings and feathers, was taken from the house at the end of Pinnacle Lane.

The young girl whose birthday they had celebrated for nine years had not aged a day since her arrival, that first day when the ship captain's fingers had burned red at her touch.

The doves Fatima Inês had kept as pets freed themselves from their hutches on the roof and bred with the local crows. Their monstrous young—ugly, mangled half-forms of both birds—plagued the neighborhood with their haunting calls and meddlesome intellect.

What happened to the child, no one knew. Many believed she was taken to the Hospital for the Insane in Steilacoom.

"Well," the neighbors asked one another, "what else could they have done with her?"

The summer solstice remained a celebrated event in the small Seattle neighborhood throughout the years. The house had few subsequent inhabitants — a family of gypsies lived there one fall, in 1910, and it was briefly used as a meeting place for the local Quaker chapter — but on the whole, it remained empty until the day my grandfather, Connor Lavender, turned his face to the Seattle sky.

After the death of her siblings, Emilienne gave up her chic cloche hat. She grew her hair unfashionably long and pulled it into a tight spinsteresque bun at the nape of her neck — a failed attempt at suppressing her beauty as much as possible. She wore light dabs of face powder on her cheeks to hide the permanent track marks left by so many tears. Maman, her poor heart made all the more fragile by the loss of her children, soon disappeared completely, leaving behind only a small pile of blue ashes between the sheets of her bed. Emilienne kept them in an empty tin of throat lozenges.

Then, one hot August day in 1924, while waiting in line at the local drugstore to purchase her powder, Emilienne took notice of the man behind her. He was leaning heavily on a dark wood cane.

His name was Connor Lavender. He was thirty-one years old and had contracted a severe case of polio at the age of seven. He was bedridden for more than eight months, and, regardless of the number of chamomile compresses his mother applied to his little body, the disease crippled his left leg, forcing him to depend on a cane to walk. Whether this illness was a blessing or a curse, it exempted him from the draft, and Connor Lavender never served his country in the First Great War. Instead, he leaned on his cane and served customers at the corner bakery where he worked. His condition was the very reason my grandmother married him.

Emilienne looked at Connor Lavender's withered leg and his mahogany cane, and decided that such a man would have trouble leaving anywhere, or anyone for that matter. As sweat collected in the crease behind her knees and underneath her arms, she decided on her life with Connor Lavender. If he agreed to take her far away from Manhattan, she would be willing to give him one child in exchange. She would close her eyes as he made love to her so that she wouldn't have to look at his misshapen leg.

My grandparents married three months later. Emilienne wore Maman's wedding dress. Just after the ceremony, Emilienne glanced in the mirror. She saw not her own reflection but a tall empty vase.

Emilienne figured a loveless union was the best option for each of them. Best for Connor since, until meeting the desolate Miss Emilienne Roux, he had considered himself doomed to a life of perpetual bachelorhood, with single-serving soups and a widowless deathbed; and best for Emilienne because, if the past had taught her anything, it was that as long as she didn't love someone, he wasn't as likely to die or disappear. When they were pronounced man and wife, Emilienne silently promised she'd be good to her husband, as long as he didn't ask for her heart.

She no longer had one to give.

As per his promise, exactly four months after Connor Lavender married Emilienne Roux, he gathered his new bride, collected their few belongings—including a rather finicky pet canary that Emilienne refused to leave behind—and boarded a train bound for the great state of Montana. But when it came time to bid the train *adieu*, Connor's wife took one look at the rolling tumbleweeds and monotonous flat plains and simply said, "No," before heading back to the stuffy, cramped sleeper car they'd called home for the last several days.

"No?" Connor repeated, following her as he pushed his way past the rest of the passengers, whose wives, he noted silently, had not refused to leave the train. "What do you mean, no?"

"I mean, no. I will not live here."

And with that began a conversation that would repeat for several hundred more miles as Emilienne rejected Billings, Coeur d'Alene, Spokane, and all the towns in between. Connor Lavender was so exasperated that he hadn't spoken to his wife since they'd left the train station in Ellensburg, a town that had once famously burned to the ground completely. Emilienne took one look outside and said, "Whatever made them want to rebuild it?"

I believe that by the time the train had reached Seattle, my grandmother knew she had run out of options. It was either here or continuing on alone. So when they reached King Street Station, Emilienne mutely gathered her things and finally departed from the train.

In their quest for a home, my grandparents looked first at a Craftsman bungalow in Wallingford with a low-pitched roof and exposed rafters, but that proved far too expensive, even with the raccoon infestation in the basement. Then there was an old Victorian on Alki Point, but Connor worried that the nearby lighthouse would keep them up at night.

It was a stone Tudor with a swooping roof and crumbling foundation that brought them to a small neighborhood in central Seattle. The house stood across the street from a school where someday, Connor imagined, their children would attend classes, where their tiny handprints in thick-colored paint would be among the ones covering the windows. Connor looked up at the sky just as a light rain started to fall. It was bewildering; the Seattle rain felt so different. The misty raindrops clung to every part of him, soaked his eyelashes, and seeped into his nostrils. It was while noticing this that Connor first saw the house on the hill.

It stood alone on a hill at the end of the neighborhood's main street, Pinnacle Lane, where the cobblestones gave way to a dirt and pebble road. The house was painted the color of faded periwinkles; it had a white wraparound porch and an onion-domed turret. The second-floor bedrooms had giant bay windows. A widow's walk rested on top of the house, its balcony turned toward Salmon Bay. The cherry tree along the side of the house was in bloom; pink blossoms, their edges browned and withered, scattered across the porch.

There were only two neighboring homes. One belonged to a man named Amos Fields, and the other closeted the Widow Marigold Pie's black dresses. Overgrown rhododendron and juniper bushes obscured each house from view.

The little annexed neighborhood was barely a stopping point for travelers on their way to the more established town of Ballard. On the right side of Pinnacle Lane stood the post office, the drugstore, and a brick elementary school; on the left there was the Lutheran church, with its austere walls and hard wooden pews. There was also an abandoned shop that had once sold wedding cakes and where hungry customers would soon find fresh bread and rolls hand-kneaded and marked by Connor Lavender.

Moving was a quiet affair for the Lavenders since the only earthly possession they truly needed was Connor's cane. There was also a tin of throat lozenges filled with blue ashes and a shoe box containing the remains of a tiny yellow bird. Pierette, who'd never been emotionally stable even in human form, hadn't survived the weary cross-country train ride. Both were buried in the empty garden bed behind the new house, marked only by a large river stone.

Emilienne walked through the house, her steps swaying under the girth of her swollen belly. She hadn't thought it possible to get pregnant so quickly—she'd only been with her husband once before leaving Manhattan, and, with the limited space and bathing options available on the train, neither had initiated anything while aboard.

It wasn't until they'd reached Minnesota that Emilienne began to consider the possibility that she was pregnant. Halfway through North Dakota, Emilienne was able to put into words how she felt about it. Words like *disappointed*, *infuriated*, and *trapped.* When she finally told Connor, somewhere between Coeur d'Alene and Spokane, she chose words different from those in her head. He'd cried with joy.

Emilienne ran her hand along the edge of the cast-iron sink before moving on to the dining room, with the built-in cabinets with lead-glass doors. She listened to the creak of the wood floors as she walked from dining room to foyer, hallway to stairwell. In a corner of the parlor stood the harpsichord that Connor had shipped from Manhattan; Emilienne planned to leave the instrument untouched. She wanted to watch as it acquired dust and the keys yellowed with age. The stubborn thing rudely refused and instead kept its glossy sheen, the keys always remarkably in tune.

The neighbors regarded Emilienne the way most do when confronted with the odd. Of course, this was a tad more complex than an aversion of the eyes from an unseemly mole or a severely scarred finger. Everything about Emilienne Lavender was strange. To Emilienne, pointing at the moon was an invitation for disaster, a falling broom the same. And when the Widow Marigold Pie began secretly suffering from a bout of insomnia, it was Emilienne who arrived at her door the next morning with a garland of peonies and an insistence that wearing it would ensure a restful sleep that night. Soon the quiet whispers of *witch* began following Emilienne wherever she went. And to associate with the neighborhood witch, well, that would be an invitation for a disaster much more dangerous than anything the moon might bring. So her neighbors did the only thing that seemed appropriate — they avoided Emilienne Lavender completely.

Fortunately, they found no fault with Connor — his strange wife hardly spent any time at the bakery — and the little shop began to thrive. Connor's success could have been ascribed to a number of things. The location was certainly part of it — no passing parishioner could help but make a stop at the bakery on the way home from church, particularly on those Sundays when Pastor Trace Graves bestowed the congregation with the Holy Communion. Body of Christ or not, one torn piece of stale bread was hardly satisfying after a morning of Lutheran hymnody. If anything, it made those freshly baked loaves of sourdough and rye, displayed in the bakery window like precious gems, all the more enticing.

Many preferred not to acknowledge it, but Emilienne certainly played a part in the bakery's success, if only behind the scenes. She had impeccable taste and an eye for appealing design, for flattering fabrics and colors (of course she did — she was French). She used her natural talents in choosing the butter-yellow paint for the bakery walls and the white lace valances for the windows. She arranged wrought-iron tables and chairs across the black-and-white-tiled floor, where customers sat to enjoy a morning sticky bun and the wafting scents of cinnamon and vanilla. And though all these ingredients helped build the bakery's recipe for success, Connor's bakery did so well because Connor was an exceptional baker.

He'd learned from his father, who took his crippled son under his wing and taught him all there was to know about feeding the New York masses: how to make black-and-white cookies, sponge cake, rum-and-custard-filled crème puffs. When Connor married Emilienne Roux and moved to Seattle, he brought with him those same recipes and served them with panache to the people of Pinnacle Lane, who claimed to have never before tasted such decadent desserts.

So, naturally, Connor spent most of his time at the bakery, which for Emilienne meant whittling the hours away in the big house, walking her restless womb from one room to the next, waiting for her husband to return home. For night to fall. For time to go by. As the months passed, Emilienne watched the yellowed leaves of the cherry tree in the yard rot in the autumn rain. She watched mothers walk their children to school, watched her own body change—morphing daily into something foreign and abstract, something that no longer belonged to her.

Pregnancy proved to be a very lonely time for Emilienne even though she was never alone: not on the day she married Connor Lavender, or when she refused to leave the safe haven of the cramped sleeper car, or even when murmurs of *witch* drifted up from the neighborhood and through the house's open windows. *They* were always there. Him with his urge to speak despite his face having been shot off, and her with a cavern in the place where her heart once beat, sometimes with that child on her hip—that phantom child with mismatched eyes. And then there was the canary.

Only when she daydreamed that she was back in that dilapidated tenement in Beauregard's Manhatine—when the high notes of Pierette's effervescent laugh still echoed through the hallways, when René's beauty still rivaled her own, before Margaux had betrayed her—could Emilienne attempt to understand them. But Emilienne could rarely bring herself to think of her former life and all the pain that existed there. She'd moved across the country to get away from it—how dare they insist on following her! Her unwelcome guests—for unwelcome they were!—provided her little comfort. She refused to decipher the frantic gestures her dead siblings made and never stopped long enough to make sense of the silent words that poured from their lips. No matter how desperately they tried, she was determined not to listen.

During her daily explorations, Emilienne discovered relics of Fatima Inês de Dores still littered a number of rooms in the large house: the gifts her brother brought home from his trips overseas. There was the marionette, the chess set, the glass marbles, and hundreds of porcelain dolls. Dolls with blinking eyes, with jointed arms and legs. Dolls with bonnets, dressed in saris, wrapped in kimonos printed with dragons and with tiny fans tied to their tiny hands. There were cowboy dolls riding saddled toy Appaloosas, Rajasthani dolls sent from India, Russian nesting dolls, fashion paper dolls. There was a giraffe the size of a small sheepdog and a rocking horse, its runners creaky with age. No one had had the courage to rid the house of them. Their watchful unblinking eyes might well have been the reason so few people had ever wanted to occupy the house.

If Fatima Inês, apparition or otherwise, still existed in the house, Emilienne would be the one to know. After all, she was the woman with whom the flowers seemed to converse, whose three deceased siblings mutely followed her around the house instead of fading into the afterlife. But Emilienne knew better than to believe the house was haunted by the young girl's restless spirit.

On one particularly frustrating day, when words much worse than *witch* came floating in through the window and René persisted in trying to talk with her, Emilienne took the antique toys out the front door and smashed them one by one, until the porch was covered in tiny flecks of colored glass, fabric, and porcelain.

Ashes to ashes. Dust to dust.

Emilienne did everything she promised herself she would do as a wife, though she could hardly be confused with any of the other wives in the neighborhood—the sort of women who, before marriage, had spent their high-school years practicing their penmanship by signing their first names with their future husband's last. Wives who spent their days cleaning and going to the market and collecting interesting tidbits for a dinner *tête-à-tête.* Wives who met their husbands at the door with freshly painted lips and a conversation as thoughtfully prepared as the meal. Wives who did not begin their married lives as empty vases.

To her credit, Emilienne kept a clean house and fed her husband nightly meals of pot roasts and red potatoes; she fussed over the creases in his trousers, and she took diligent care of his cane, polishing it nightly so that the mahogany shone with a reddish hue. But neither Emilienne nor Connor ever once stopped to ponder the miracles love might bring into their lives. Connor because he didn't know such things existed, and Emilienne because she did.

And then my mother was born.

She came into the world a screaming, demanding red nymph with a full head of black hair—all stick-straight but for one perfect ringlet at the back of her head—and infant blue eyes that would later darken to a brown so deep they sometimes seemed to have swallowed the iris whole. They named her Viviane.

When they brought her home, Emilienne carried her through the house and grimaced at her husband as he announced each room with the zest and gusto of a circus ringmaster. *And on your left, what is this you ask? This grand stretch of carpeted interior space? Why it's the second-floor hallway!* He introduced Viviane to the kitchen's cast-iron sink, the built-in cabinets with lead-glass doors that stretched along the dining-room wall and above the stove. He watched Viviane's face to see if she loved the creak of the wood floors as he did. They took her into their bedroom, where he pointed out the tiny wicker bassinet where she would sleep and the rocking chair in which Emilienne would rock her every night until the floor under it was marked with wear. He showed her the garden, where a solid river rock marked a small burial site, and the parlor, where a harpsichord sat unused yet remarkably in tune. He showed her everything but the third floor, since no one went up there anyway.

There were times when Emilienne thought it possible to love the crippled baker with his sure hands and unsteady gait. She would feel her heart unclench and stretch its tightly coiled legs, preparing to leap into the path of yet another love. She'd think, *This time could be different. This time it could last.* Maybe it would be a longer, deeper love: a real and solid entity that lived in the house, used the bathroom, ate their food, mussed up the linens in sleep. A love that pulled her close when she cried, that slept with its chest pressed against her back. But then Emilienne would think of Levi Blythe or Satin Lush, or steal a glance at the ghostly shapes of her siblings in the far-off corner of the room, and she'd bury her heart under handfuls of dirt once again.

Connor, for his part, did the best he could, considering. Considering he had no past experience to help him make sense of the woman he married. Connor Lavender had been a bachelor in every sense of the word until the day he came across Emilienne Roux. The only naked woman he'd ever seen before his wife had been a picture on a tattered set of trading cards he'd once found tucked behind the counter of his father's bakery. The picture was of a full-figured brunette—her back arched in a way that was surely uncomfortable. It was the woman's breasts that Connor remembered most, the areolas the size of small dinner plates, the nipples high and pointed. To his adolescent mind, it looked as if she had small teacups and saucers balanced atop each breast.

Connor was thinking of just this woman as he closed up the bakery for the night. He wiped down the counters, straightened the wrought-iron tables and chairs, and checked the yeast he'd left to rise for the morning. Just like every other evening. The only difference on this particular evening—on December 22, 1925—was that while he was locking the bakery door, a sharp twinge shot down his left arm.

It was felt so briefly, Connor hardly took note. In fact, the time Connor spent considering the pain in his arm added up to approximately three seconds—just enough time to clench and unclench the fingers before his mind moved on to more important matters. His infant daughter, for example—Had she eaten yet? Had Emilienne already put her to bed?—and his perpetually unhappy wife. So Connor forgot about his arm (and all its connotations) and rushed to return home, where he bathed the baby and struggled through a stagnant conversation with his wife before going to bed. He slept soundly that night, dreamed a baker's dreams of flour and egg whites, until the next morning, when his heart stopped beating. And then, in shocked disappointment, and stunned horror, I'm sure, Connor Lavender realized he was dead.

The morning of December 23, Emilienne woke from the kind of hard, heavy sleep known only to soldiers, drunks, and mothers of newly born children. Thinking at first that she'd been awakened by her child's cry, her fingers immediately moved to untie the loose knots along the front of her nightgown, and she swung her legs over the side of the bed. But when Emilienne's feet touched the cold floor, she saw that the baby still lay sleeping in her crib and discovered that what had pulled her from slumber was the sound of her husband's last breath escaping his body.

Emilienne called for an ambulance, whispering to the operator, "Though there isn't any need to hurry."

Emilienne pulled her husband's finest clothes—the very ones he'd worn for their wedding just one year earlier—from the closet and laid them on the bed next to his body. When she saw that the dress shirt was wrinkled, she starched and ironed it. When she saw that the red velvet vest was missing one of its large black buttons, she got down on her hands and knees and searched the floor until she found it. Then she set to dressing him. The pants were particularly difficult. She polished his cane one last time and slicked his hair back with grease from a tin he kept beside the bathroom sink. And only then was she satisfied, for it meant she'd kept the promise she'd made when she married poor Connor Lavender. That she would be a good wife to him. Up to, and even after, the bitter end.

She put her hand against his cheek. It felt cold and stiff under her touch, as if her husband's skin had been wrapped around a rock.

With the efficiency of a woman in denial, she found his key to the bakery and hung it from a leather cord around her neck. At a quarter to five, having been a widow for not yet an hour, Emilienne carefully wrapped her baby daughter in a thick cocoon of blankets and carried her the three and a half blocks to the bakery. Emilienne walked through the shop in the dark, her shoes squeaking against the black-and-white linoleum floor. By this time Viviane was ready to be fed. Emilienne brought the baby to her breast, but both were startled when no milk would come. Suddenly the sole owner of a bakery, Emilienne thought of all the mouths she was now responsible for. If she couldn't even feed her own child, how could she feed anyone else?

Emilienne went to the pantry and pulled out a giant bag of sugar. She spooned a tiny amount into a bowl of warm water and dipped in the rubber teat of Viviane's pacifier before sticking it into the baby's mouth. Then she lined a cardboard box with her jacket, scarf, and sweater and nestled the infant inside. When she fired up the oven,

Emilienne dismissed any ideas she might have had for pastries or other sweets. What she would make was bread. Hearty sustainable bread, warm from the oven and crisp on the outside, soft on the inside.

It didn't take long for the shop to fill with the aroma of rising breads: the thin-crusted *pain au levain*; dense, hard-crusted *pain brié*; *pain de campagne*, chewy and perfect for dipping in soups and thick stews; and *pain quotidien* for sandwiches and toast in the morning. After displaying the new goods in the window and cleaning the smudges from the glass, my grandmother opened the bakery doors to let the air carry the scent of freshly baked bread into the street. Then she stepped back, patted the white flour smudges on her apron, and, with a dread so fierce and strong it left a taste of nickel on her tongue, realized that no one would ever buy anything from her.

Chapter Three

THE NEWS OF Connor Lavender's death spread throughout the neighborhood, quickly followed by a thick and tangled web of gossip, tall tales, and lies. Some said he died of a brain aneurysm. Others insisted it was a tumble down a flight of stairs that did him in. Almena Moss, who lived with her sister Odelia in one of the rented rooms above the post office, claimed to have seen Emilienne purchase a rather large bottle of rat poison at the drugstore, which only bred rumors more fantastic than before. But whatever happened to Connor Lavender, there was one thing everyone in the neighborhood agreed on: no one would ever again step foot in that bakery. Not with *her* in charge.

So the shop remained empty, and Emilienne learned to live on the leftover loaves of bread that no one came to buy. That is, until an early February windstorm brought Wilhelmina Dovewolf to Pinnacle Lane.

Exactly where Wilhelmina came from very few people knew. A direct descendant of an infamous Seattle chief, Wilhelmina was a member of the Suquamish tribe—her lineage obvious by her prominent cheekbones, bronzed complexion, and the thick black hair she wore in a long braid down her back. Wilhelmina was twenty-two years old—only five months older than Emilienne. She'd spent her formative years at an Indian boarding school, where she was repeatedly beaten for speaking her own language. As an adult, she carried with her the air of someone forever displaced—not quite part of the white race, yet no longer fitting in with the members of her tribe. In other words, Wilhelmina was a very old soul in a young body. The people of Pinnacle Lane regarded her much in the same way they regarded Emilienne, meaning, of course, that they didn't regard her at all.

The scent of Emilienne's bread coaxed Wilhelmina inside. Emilienne was in the back, her fists deep in a lump of white dough—what would soon be another loaf of unsold bread—when the bells above the door rang through the shop. The sound gave both Emilienne and Viviane such a start that the baby, once content in the cardboard box, began to wail in fright. Emilienne quickly ran her palms together to dust off the flour.

"I'll be right there," she called, making her way to the front of the shop. She caught only a fleeting glimpse of Wilhelmina's back, her braid a swinging tail behind her, as she ran out the door. A loaf of rye bread had been taken from the front window, and in its place sat a small cedar basket.

Ignoring the crying baby in the back of the bakery, Emilienne cupped the basket in her still-doughy hands and watched as her first customer disappeared down Pinnacle Lane.

It took a few weeks for Wilhelmina to return. By then Emilienne had been surviving on bread alone for three months, and Viviane had begun to roll over and to babble in the incoherent way that infants do. When Emilienne heard the bells on the door, she only peered out from the back of the shop and watched as Wilhelmina stealthily took one of the loaves from the display window and left another basket in its place. She scurried from the shop and Emilienne followed her.

The woman paused in the shelter of the three birch trees in front of the bakery. Keeping her distance, Emilienne watched the woman tear a piece from the loaf of bread, place it in her mouth, and, closing her eyes, thoughtfully chew then swallow before wrapping the rest in her scarf and tucking it under her arm.

A week later Emilienne was ready. As soon as she spotted the long braid swinging over Wilhelmina's shoulder as she made her way down Pinnacle Lane, Emilienne wrapped a loaf of freshly baked bread, still warm from the oven, in white paper, tied it with string, and left it on the counter.

From her hiding place in the back, Emilienne could see Wilhelmina approach the package cautiously and sniff, as if checking the air for the scent of danger. Then, with a scowl, she pulled out a tiny purse and began rummaging around for what Emilienne assumed was a string of beads, which just goes to show how little Emilienne knew about the world.

"Take it," Emilienne said, stepping out from the back. "I'm giving it to you."

"I don't take handouts," Wilhelmina replied gruffly.

Emilienne's cheeks burned with embarrassment. "Fine, then." She drew herself up to her fullest height, making her a few inches taller than the Indian woman. "That'll be twenty-five cents." She held out her hand.

Wilhelmina brushed Emilienne's hand aside and opened the package of bread. She tore pieces from the loaf and stuffed them into her mouth. "Got something better," she replied. "I'll make you a deal."

Emilienne folded her arms. "I'm listening."

Wilhelmina took another bite of the bread. "Rumor has it you're the neighborhood witch."

Emilienne raised her eyebrows.

Wilhelmina chuckled. "Now, don't get me wrong. I ain't the type to resort to name-calling, plus I tend to make up my own mind about such things. Got my own way of figuring stuff out."

Emilienne nodded. So did she. For example, Emilienne could tell that Wilhelmina had been born in October from the opal pendant that hung from the woman's neck. *October,* Emilienne mused, *a Libra. Balanced. Diplomatic. Even-tempered.*

Wilhelmina cocked her head, eyeing Emilienne thoughtfully. "There is something about you. I can't quite put my finger on it . . ." Her voice trailed off. "I am sure about one thing, though. You've seen a lot of death. I'm right, ain't I?"

Death. Emilienne winced. Of that she had seen her fair share.

"That's what I thought. It wasn't just the husband, was it?" Wilhelmina sighed when Emilienne didn't answer. "Death just seems to follow some of us, don't it? Death's been following me for years. It's easy to spot your own kind. That kind of sorrow you can't just wash away; it sticks to you. And people, they can tell. They can *feel* it. And ain't nobody likes the feel of death—especially in a place where he eats. What you need is a cleansing ritual."

Wilhelmina finished the bread and pulled two bundles of dried herbs tied with red cotton string out of her pocket.

"Burn them as you walk through the shop. Pay special attention to corners and places behind doors."

Emilienne took the smudging sticks of sage and hyssop from the Indian woman. Reluctantly, she rolled the herbs in her hands before dropping them to the counter. "And doing this will accomplish what exactly?"

"Clean the air. Rid the place of any curses, illnesses, bad spirits. Burn these herbs, and people won't be thinking about death every time they walk by the shop. Or by you, for that matter." Wilhelmina paused. "Listen, you seem like a smart woman. Do like I say, and, I promise you, business will change." She wrapped her scarf tighter around her shoulders and turned to leave. "Then you can give me a job."

Emilienne snorted. "You want to work here? I barely have enough money to buy flour. I can't afford to hire you."

Wilhelmina smiled. "Trust me, you'll be needing the help."

Whether it was out of curiosity or sheer desperation, Emilienne burned the bundles of dried herbs per Wilhelmina's instructions—making sure the spiraling smoke touched every corner, reached behind every door of every room.

The very next morning, she arrived to a line of customers waiting at the bakery door. The line stretched all the way to the drugstore down the street, some four doors away.

Most claimed that the scent of rising yeast and freshly baked bread had drifted into their dreams the previous night. As the years went by, the people of Pinnacle Lane found that a day wasn't well spent if their meals didn't include a slice of bread or a roll from Emilienne's bakery. There were Almena and Odelia Moss, who always dressed the same and came into the bakery for a loaf of cinnamon bread every Monday afternoon. There was Amos Fields, who was partial to the heavy *pain brié.* There was Ignatius Lux, who would become principal of the local high school many years later. There was Pastor Trace Graves and Marigold Pie, a war widow and a good devoted Lutheran one at that. There were the Flannerys, the Zimmers, the Quakenbushes. And then there was Beatrix Griffith.

It was Beatrix's husband, John, who fueled the neighborhood's initial isolation of the widowed Emilienne Lavender. He considered her strange and, as such, unwanted. It was John who first implied—loud and often—that Emilienne Lavender was a witch. Soon after the Lavenders moved onto Pinnacle Lane, he informed his wife, Beatrix, that they would have nothing to do with *her.* And John Griffith was not a man who changed his mind.

Unbeknownst to her formidable husband, Beatrix secretly came into the bakery every week anyway for three loaves of sourdough bread. When the bakery began to thrive under Emilienne's and Wilhelmina's talented hands,

John Griffith sneered at his neighbors, "Any day now you'll all be traveling by broom."

Not knowing that with each morning breakfast of toast and eggs, he, too, was making his own contribution to Emilienne's success.

Chapter Four

MOTHERHOOD PROVED bewildering for Emilienne. At only twenty-three years of age, she had already lost her parents, all three siblings, and a husband. She was the sole owner of a now-successful bakery and the sole parent of a little girl whose exhausting exuberance seemed to double with each passing day.

By the time Viviane turned two, Emilienne realized that she'd given birth to a child unlike herself in every way. Whereas Emilienne was dark like her *maman*, with long black hair that she kept wrapped in a thick chignon, Viviane was pale like her father, with wispy thin brown hair framing her cherubic face. To Emilienne, seeing a spider spinning a web was a sign of good luck; to Viviane, a spider was a reason to fetch a jar, preferably one with holes hammered into the lid. There was nothing Roux about Viviane, as far as Emilienne could tell.

Occasionally, Wilhelmina Dovewolf stepped in to take care of my mother—typically when she was sick. It was Wilhelmina's long braids Viviane reached for in comfort when struck with a case of the stomach flu or a bout of bronchitis. Viviane would later come to connect Wilhelmina's woodsy scent of dry leaves and incense with a feeling of safety and security.

In the end, Viviane all but raised herself—meals were yesterday's pastries; baths and bedtimes were rarely enforced. Her childhood was spent amid the scents and sounds of the bakery. It was her sticky fingers that topped the Belgian buns with glazed cherries, her hands that warmed the pie dough. As a toddler, she could easily whip up a batch of *profiteroles*, standing on a chair and calmly filling each *choux* pastry with cream. With barely a sniff of the air, Viviane Lavender could detect the slightest variation in any recipe—a talent that she would perfect in later years. Yes, Viviane spent many hours in the bakery. Her mother barely acknowledged she was there.

The summer before her seventh birthday, Viviane found an old white dress in one of the many forgotten closets in the house at the end of Pinnacle Lane. The dress resembled a child-size wedding gown. Emilienne assumed correctly that the dress once belonged to the young Portuguese girl for whom the house had been built. The

First Communion dress was by then yellowed with age and had an inexplicable burn mark down the front. Through the course of the summer, Viviane refused to wear much else. It was subjected to many stains and tears—a blotch of raspberry jam on the collar, a rip along the seam.

It was while wearing this dress that Viviane met her best friend, Jack.

The day they met, Viviane climbed into the branches of a large birch tree in front of the bakery to watch a boy dig a hole in the wild overgrown patch that was his father's lawn. It was a hole the boy believed would eventually lead him to the remains of King Tut. Burdened by shovels and buckets, the boy woke early each morning to take on what he considered a serious project, one full of routines and hours of dedication and more than anything else, of belief. His day began with a survey of the previous day's work, a solemn walk around the site, a measuring of the depth of the hole. Buckets went to the left, shovels to the right. Rocks were separated from the dirt; worms and other insects were spared and collected tenderly into one of the buckets reserved solely for such sensitive things. At the end of the day, upon the collapse of the sun, the boy transported each insect from the bucket and placed it gently into the churned ground of his mother's compost pile.

Of that summer, Jack best remembered the feel of the cool dirt beneath his fingernails and the weight of potential discovery brought on by each bucket of dirt. Viviane remembered how her muscles ached from spending so many hours perched in the tree's branches. She remembered the smudges of the darkest brown dirt across Jack's cheekbones and his grimace as he lifted large rocks from the deepest part of his excavated hole. She remembered his hair, slick with sweat, wet against his forehead. And she remembered, more than anything else, the twinge in her stomach that compelled her to leap down from that tree, ripping the hemline of the pint-size wedding dress as she did, and walk to the edge of that large hole.

The boy standing at the bottom of the hole peered up at Viviane, his eyes squinting in the sunlight. "Want to know what I'm doing?"

"Yes," Viviane said, trying not to knock more dirt into the hole.

"Okay. But you have to wait. Until I'm done, that is. Then you'll be able to see it for yourself." He picked something out of the dirt, cupped it lightly in one of his hands before placing it in one of the buckets near his feet. "You don't mind waiting?"

Viviane shook her head. No, she didn't mind.

He smiled then, bringing back that twinge in her stomach, something that she only later recognized as the pangs of desire.

I often wish I knew my mother as she was then—wild and unruly and running, always running with her hair trailing behind her and her mouth open in a gleeful scream. And I wonder what her life might have been had she never met Jack Griffith, the son of Beatrix and John

Griffith. Would she have developed a talent for baking, as my grandmother had?

I've been told things happen as they should: My grandmother fell in love three times before her nineteenth birthday. My mother found love with the neighbor boy when she was six. And I, I was born with wings, a misfit who didn't dare to expect something as grandiose as *love*. It's our fate, our destiny, that determines such things, isn't it?

Perhaps that was just something I told myself. Because what else was there for me — an aberration, an untouchable, an outsider? What could I say when I was alone at night and the shadows came? How else could I calm the thud of my beating heart but with the words: *This is my fate*. What else was there to do but blindly follow its path?

Viviane and Jack were inseparable throughout the rest of the summer and well into the school year. The neighborhood boys teased Jack mercilessly until learning that Viviane Lavender could outrun and outspit any one of them. She also came up with the best games to play — it was my mother's ingenious idea, for example, to wage a schoolyard battle against the kids who were bused down from Phinney Ridge. It was a rivalry that would last for seven years — until America entered the Second Great War. The teams were then briefly recast as American soldiers versus the Japs, but that was deemed little fun since the grown-ups were playing their own version of that game.

The neighborhood girls barely acknowledged the

friendship between Jack and Viviane Lavender. Viviane was hardly the type other girls sought for a friend. She never seemed to do any of the things other girls did. She had never thrown an imaginary tea party, would not, in fact, have known what to do at a tea party where there wasn't any actual tea. Their interest in Jack grew with time. By that point, they hardly wanted him as their *friend*, and each figured she could easily pull him away from Viviane Lavender—if it came down to that.

Chapter Five

IN REGARD TO Emilienne Lavender, John Griffith had made up his mind long ago. And John Griffith was not the kind of man who changed his mind. If anyone had paid closer attention, they would have guessed that John Griffith's feelings toward Emilienne Lavender maybe stemmed from something much more potent than hatred.

It was the way he watched her. At the post office, in her yard, through the window of the bakery with her hands deep in dough, a smudge of flour on each cheek and her hair tied into a thick chignon at the nape of her neck. For seventeen years, John Griffith's lust for Emilienne Lavender pumped through his veins, bled from his gums. It was the red that polluted the whites of his eyes, the pink that flushed his cheeks. It was the jealousy that burned the back of his throat whenever he saw his son with Emilienne's daughter, Viviane.

John Griffith was an angry, prideful man who believed he deserved much more than life had given him. He worked as a delivery-truck driver for a small laundry in Pioneer Square. Most of his meager wages were spent in the opium-filled dens of Seattle's Chinatown. So, since 1925, the year the Lavenders moved onto Pinnacle Lane, his wife, Beatrix, cleaned houses on First Hill much grander than her own. His son's lengthy newspaper route took three hours to complete. It was only through Beatrix's and Jack's combined hard work that the Griffith house was kept from the edge of squalor.

"You're a disappointment, Jack," John Griffith once told his son. "You always were." At the time, John and Jack were sitting at opposite ends of the kitchen table. Jack was watching his father finish off another bite of chocolate cake.

Beatrix would often think back on this moment, but neither her son nor her husband would even remember that she had been there, too. Only a few months earlier, more than two thousand American sailors had launched the United States into the Second World War. Going to war meant many things, but for Beatrix Griffith, whose son was only seventeen and, thankfully, too young to be drafted, it meant only one: food rations. It was hard enough trying to keep peace at the dinner table, what with a husband who insisted on meals of choice-cut steak when the

Griffiths could barely afford the vegetables Beatrix grew in her own garden. With the looming disappearance of eggs, sugar, and butter, finding ways to appease John Griffith at mealtimes was going to be harder than ever. She'd have to hide food stamps from him in order to make sure she and Jack had enough to eat. It was perhaps because of this guilt that Beatrix had given in to her husband that particular night: he'd demanded his favorite dessert, and she'd used the last four eggs to make it.

John Griffith rarely let anyone watch him eat, said it gave other people the impression he was weak. (*Or human,* Beatrix had thought at the time. Not that she'd said so. Not that she would ever dare to say such a thing to John Griffith.) But tonight was an exception. Tonight John Griffith's wife and son would be granted the honor of watching him enjoy every delicious bite.

John Griffith pointed his fork at Jack. "Amos Fields's boy is captain of the football team," he said. "Roy Zimmer's will be taking over the family business when he gets back from the war."

"I have a job—" Jack started.

John jumped up from his chair and flew across the table, knocking the plate of chocolate cake to the floor. He froze with his fork poised at the Adam's apple in Jack's throat.

"You want a medal?" he asked, his voice like ice. "Think you're some kinda hero for having a paper route?"

Jack winced in spite of himself, causing a cold smirk to appear on his father's frosting-covered lips. John stabbed at another piece of cake while his wife wiped the other mess off the floor. "Then there's John Griffith's son, *my* son," he said between clenched teeth, "who will only ever be remembered for fucking the daughter of the neighborhood witch." John snorted. "That *will* end, Jack. It's about time you start being useful around here."

He glared at his son until Jack was forced to look away, embarrassed by his wretched need to blink. John gave a quick wave with his large hand, dismissing Jack from the table. As he rose to leave, Jack was crushed by the realization that while his father considered himself to be a great man, in his father's eyes the best Jack could ever hope to be was *useful.*

In January 1942, a new theater opened in West Seattle. The gala opening of the Admiral Theater was a grand affair and was attended by most everyone in the area. In a photograph printed in the *Seattle Post-Intelligencer*, a large crowd of movie patrons gathered below the brightly lit marquee and the words *Seattle's Finest Theater* glowing in iridescent script. At one edge of the crowd stood a girl and a boy of about the same height, the boy's hand resting affectionately on the square of the girl's back.

Viviane stood on her tiptoes to get a better look at the people around her. It looked to her like almost everyone from the neighborhood had decided to come: there was Ignatius Lux, one of Viviane's and Jack's favorite teachers at the high school, and Mr. Lux's bride-to-be, Estelle Margolis. There were the old Moss sisters. There were Constance Quakenbush and Delilah Zimmer, whose brother Wallace—as well as Mart Flannery and Dinky Fields—had dropped out of school and joined the navy the moment they turned eighteen. It seemed the war was under everyone's skin. Viviane reached over and laced her fingers through Jack's, happy that it hadn't yet reached them.

When the doors to the theater finally opened, Viviane and Jack quickly made their way inside—marveling at the walls splashed with oceanic scenes and the usherettes and doormen dressed in nautical uniforms. Jack examined the innovative push-back seats, throwing Viviane an occasional *Can you believe these?* look, to which Viviane smiled back. Jack had an eye for things new and shiny. Viviane took off her coat and shoved it into the seat behind her. The theater smelled like fresh paint and new carpeting, like expectation and hope. Viviane leaned her head back and breathed deeply, taking in all at once the wet, salty smell of the theater popcorn, the heavy musk of perfume, the sharp spice of cologne. And the light scent of soap and Turtle Wax—Jack.

To say Viviane had a keen sense of smell was an understatement. She could detect what people had eaten for dinner from a mere whiff of their breath. Not even the strongest toothpaste could hide the sharp tang left by onions and garlic, the buttery aroma of chicken noodle soup. The smell of unwashed hair was unbearable to Viviane, as were infected wounds and cooked meat. But her strange talent went even further. She could tell when a woman was pregnant—even before the woman herself might know—just from the way she smelled: a combination of brown sugar and Stargazer lilies. Happiness had a pungent scent, like the sourest lime or lemon. Broken hearts smelled surprisingly sweet. Sadness filled the air with a salty, sea-like redolence; death smelled like sadness. People carried their own distinct personal fragrances. Which was how she could tell when Jack was near, and how she knew that the two conspiring heads in front of her belonged to best friends Constance Quakenbush and Delilah Zimmer. They were classmates of Viviane's and Jack's. As if on cue, the two girls tossed a synchronized glance at Viviane, then went back to another round of furtive whispering.

Viviane shifted in her seat, trying not to overhear what they must be saying. Why would she even want to, for that matter? It was obvious to everyone that Constance had her eye on Jack and wasn't about to let anything get in her way. Even, or perhaps especially, Viviane. For the most part, Viviane wasn't concerned—after all, beneath the fumes of her excessive perfume, Constance smelled like sour milk and cat urine—but she wouldn't be concerned at all if Constance wasn't so goddamn pretty.

At seventeen and a half, Jack was a good-looking young man with an angular jawline, thick, unruly eyebrows, and a lock of wavy dark hair that fell in his eyes due to a favorably situated cowlick.

Viviane, for her part, was attractive. The particular components of her face were nothing special—just a pair of brown eyes, a nose, a set of lips—but Jack thought her beautiful, and that was enough, for Viviane and most everyone else. Most were content to leave the two of them alone, free to follow the blissful path fate seemed to have set before them. Everyone, that is, except for Jack's father and Constance Quakenbush.

Constance turned around again, bouncing a little as she did, her long blond hair swinging prettily across her shoulders. She threw Jack a bright smile. "Hi, Jack," she said.

Jack looked up, distracted. He blinked twice before offering an awkward "Oh, hi, Constance."

"I'm sorry I didn't say hello earlier," Constance said. "I didn't know you were there."

Viviane rolled her eyes.

"Delilah dear and I were just trying to decide which Hollywood starlet I look like the most," Constance continued, "Veronica Lake or Rita Hayworth."

"A *blond* Rita Hayworth," Delilah interrupted, turning around and giving Viviane a smug look. Delilah wasn't nearly as pretty as Constance, but her drab looks and constant need for approval helped her play the part of Constance's sycophant perfectly.

"Naturally, when I realized *you* were sitting behind us,

I thought, well, surely Jack will know. You always have the answer to everything," Constance purred. "Delilah thinks Rita Hayworth, but I'm not so sure." Constance leaned toward Jack. "Did you know Veronica Lake's real name is Constance? Isn't that spooky?"

Jack stood and brushed off his knees before sitting back down. "Not really," he said. "I am pretty sure there was a Sicilian queen named Constance sometime in the twelfth century."

Constance and Delilah shared a delicious glance. "Really?"

"I bet she was beautiful," Delilah gushed.

Jack shrugged. "Actually, Constance of Sicily wasn't married until she was thirty. Some say that the reason was because she was so ugly. No one wanted her for a wife."

Constance's face fell, and a glorious shade of red bloomed from her chin to her hairline. She turned around after muttering something about the movie starting. Delilah shot Viviane a dark look. "It's a lie," they heard her whisper. "I bet her name wasn't Constance. Bet it was Viviane."

Jack draped his arm across Viviane's shoulders.

"Well, Constance is right about one thing," Viviane said, leaning into him.

"What's that?"

"You certainly do have the answer to everything."

Jack gave Viviane a sideways glance, a playful smirk on his lips. "Are you calling me a know-it-all?"

"Who me? Never."

The film was *Week-End in Havana* and starred not Veronica Lake or Rita Hayworth, but the exotic Carmen Miranda. After the movie Jack drove Viviane to their favorite spot: the town reservoir.

The reservoir was located on the highest point of the neighborhood—the hill at the end of Pinnacle Lane came in a close second—and was hidden by a grove of maple trees. The caretaker and his wife lived in a little white house near the reservoir's edge and spent autumn days scooping five-pointed leaves of orange, gold, and red from its still waters. At night when young lovers came to park at the water's edge, they smiled at one another, turned the radio up, and closed the curtains against the darkness. Jack and Viviane had discovered the place in daylight years ago—they'd even built a secret fort in the trees. They'd only recently started coming at night and were amazed by how different everything looked when bathed in the silvery light of the moon.

Jack parked and turned the engine off. "Did you like the movie?"

Viviane nodded, thinking of the colorful costumes and the lively dance numbers. "I wish I could dance," she mused.

"I can teach you," Jack said.

Viviane looked at him. "You don't know how to dance."

Jack smiled. "I do. I know how to waltz; I can do the foxtrot. I even know how to tango."

Viviane's eyes grew wide. "Where did you learn that?"

"Must have read how somewhere." Jack opened his door. "Come on, I'll show you."

As she stepped from the car, a cold draft of January air ran up Viviane's bare legs. She wrapped her coat tighter around her.

Jack grabbed Viviane around the waist and pulled her close, so close that she could feel his breath on her face as he spoke. "It's believed," he said, "that the tango was born in the brothels of Buenos Aires." He moved his right hand to the middle of her back. "I think it stems from the Latin word *tangere*, which, of course, means 'to touch.' "

"Of course."

Jack took her left hand and placed it on his shoulder, then took her right hand with his left. In spite of the cold, their palms were slick with sweat. Jack cleared his throat. "Okay, I'm going to take two slow steps forward. Just follow my lead."

So they danced as Jack counted out the beat—T-A-N-G-O!—until Viviane could move in his arms as naturally as an Argentinean *prostituta.* It was hardly a fast dance, but perhaps because it came from the Latin word for "to touch," both Viviane and Jack were soon breathless. They broke away and collapsed onto the grass, watching their breath make clouds above their lips.

Jack turned to Viviane. "Are you cold?"

"Freezing," she lied, and turned to wrap her hands around his neck. She pulled his face to hers, and he met her smiling mouth with his.

Their kisses grew deeper. Jack moved on top of her, propping himself up with his elbows, his body hovering a few inches above hers. That was where they usually stopped. Then Jack would take Viviane home, her cheeks flushed, her eyes only able to make out a hazy outline of Jack's face, regardless of what else might be in front of her — a hot stove, a dinner plate, a mother asking, *What's wrong with you?*

But on this night, before Jack could move away, Viviane reached up and let her fingers trip along the buttons of his shirt. With fast fingers, she unbuttoned the top two, then left him to finish the rest while she moved on to her own, watching his face as she revealed the lace hidden under her clothes.

Jack leaned down and kissed her bare neck. When his mouth passed across her collarbone, she shuddered. Lightly, his fingertips circled her exposed navel. He reached for her waist —

"Stop!" Viviane yelped, grabbing at his hands.

Jack sat up, breathless. "Viviane, you're being silly," he said. "I've known you since you were six. I was there when you were sick. Come to think of it, you threw up on my shoe."

When Viviane was nine, she suffered what she remembered as the worst stomachache she'd ever had. She did throw up several times, actually, and once on Jack's shoe. She was diagnosed with appendicitis and rushed to the operating table, where she received quite a scar. Not just any scar, but a deep crevice about the width of Jack's ring finger that ran the length of Viviane's right side. When she was younger, she loved that scar—it was hideous and grotesque and perfect for pretending to be a battle-scarred soldier. But now, at sixteen, Viviane hated it—it was hideous and grotesque.

Viviane brought her hands to her face. "It's ugly," she moaned.

"It's not," Jack said, "but if you want to see something ugly, take a look at this." Jack held out his hand to display a jagged white line between his thumb and forefinger. "Can opener," he said.

Viviane took a closer look at Jack's tiny scar and smiled. "That's nothing," she said, sitting up and pulling off one of her shoes. "I dropped a hot skillet on my foot." She showed him the mark. "And . . ." Viviane held up her elbow, pointing out a thick pucker of scar tissue. "I was six. Learning to ride a bike and I crashed. I had to pick the rocks out of my skin. I think I missed one, though. Here, feel it."

Jack laughed. "I don't need to feel it. I believe you."

"Jack, I need you to feel it," Viviane said in mock seriousness. "It's very important that you do."

He pressed his fingers gingerly against Viviane's skin. "Yeah, okay. I think there's something in there. Or it might just be your bony elbow."

Viviane made a face. "Ha-ha."

Jack then revealed the place where he'd cut his ankle on the runner of a sled one winter, the circular scar from a childhood vaccination, and the pockmark along his nostril left over from the time everyone in second grade came down with the chicken pox. "So, see? I'm much more scarred than you'll ever be. Probably always will be."

There were other scars—from wounds that leave the skin unmarred. Of those, Jack certainly had many more than Viviane. Each pondered this in their own silent way as they lay side by side, the air around them growing colder still and the moon moving higher in the sky.

"Sometimes I think my dad must hate me," Jack said after a moment.

"He doesn't hate you," Viviane whispered, too quickly to be convincing. She didn't actually believe that John Griffith had the capacity to care about anyone other than himself. Even if he tried. Even if he wanted to. Viviane could count on one hand the number of times she'd heard her own mother say *I love you*, and she'd still have a few fingers left over. But that didn't mean Emilienne wasn't capable of love. It just meant, for a reason Viviane had yet to understand, she preferred to hide it.

"Sometimes," Jack started, "I think he wouldn't hate me as much if only—"

"If only what?"

Jack turned and gave her a sad smile. "If only you and I weren't together."

Viviane closed her eyes and pushed down the small ball of panic growing in her stomach. She groaned and gave

Jack a nervous, playful jab. "You breaking up with me, Griffith?"

Jack paused just long enough for the ball of panic to bounce back up into Viviane's throat. "No," he finally answered. "That's something I could never do."

He stared into the dark shadows around them. "He thinks I'm useless," he murmured.

Viviane pulled him to her. "Shush," she said. With a sigh of defeat, Jack let his head drop against the lace exposed by her open shirt. His breath grew deep and heavy while Viviane tried to draw comfort from the rhythmic beat of his heart against her pelvic bone.

Chapter Six

JACK AND VIVIANE sat parked on the dirt road at the bottom of the hill on Pinnacle Lane in John Griffith's 1932 Ford Coupe. It was September and Viviane had just turned seventeen, making her one year and two months younger than Jack.

Jack tapped his foot in rhythm to a song playing in his head. The cuff of his pants had inched up his leg, exposing his sock and a section of his calf. His socks were navy blue; the hairs on his leg were unusually pale and silky. Viviane couldn't see them, but she knew what they looked like. The hairs on her own legs stuck out like sharp pins. She didn't know whether to be self-conscious about this or not—it wasn't her fault there was a shortage of razor blades—so she pulled her feet away from the humming floor and tucked her legs under the skirt of her dress, just in case. The sole of her left shoe grazed Jack's thigh.

Jack got up early every Saturday to wash and wax his father's Coupe after those Friday nights when he took Viviane out for a movie at the Admiral Theater or for a five-cent bottle of Coca-Cola at the drugstore. Jack's father watched for his son not on Friday nights but on Saturday mornings, to be sure the car was thoroughly taken care of. Jack never missed a washing. Neither knew what would happen if he did.

Just like everyone else in the world, Jack and Viviane were both thinking about the war, but each for different reasons. Unbeknownst to Viviane, Jack had been eagerly counting down the days until he turned eighteen. As soon as he did, he went to enlist but was rejected due to his flat feet and poor eyesight.

When Jack told his father that he'd failed the physical exam for military combat, Jack knew John Griffith would let him know exactly what he thought. And he was right.

John had laughed—a hollow and empty bark—and jeered at Jack. "You never cease to amaze me, Jack. Just when I think you couldn't disappoint me more, you always seem to find a way."

"It's not my fault," Jack said.

"What about the Lavender whore? You're still screwin' around with the witch's daughter, aren't ya?" John released the laugh again. "Probably cast some spell on you—wouldn't be hard, weak-minded son of a bitch that you are."

"Dad—" Jack started.

John dismissed him with a wave of his meaty hand. "Whatever you got to say ain't worth hearing."

"Do ya know what kind of fellas go to college these days?" Jack asked Viviane suddenly, hitting the Coupe's steering wheel with his open hand. "The quacks. The ones with deformities or syphilis. No girl would be caught dead with an F-er."

Jack was right. Most girls wouldn't be caught with a boy deemed unfit for combat. Lucky for Jack, though, Viviane wasn't most girls. The idea of Jack fighting in the war had always terrified her—she'd barely slept the week before his birthday. She'd never tell him, but she thanked God every morning for blessing Jack with lovely flat feet. Instead of going to war, the next morning Jack would be leaving to attend Whitman College in Walla Walla. Even if it was two hundred seventy miles away, at least it wasn't across a whole ocean.

Viviane grabbed Jack's hand and pressed it to her lips. "You looking to meet some girls in between your studies, college man? Because if that's the case, you won't find me waiting here for you to come back."

"Oh yeah?" Jack smiled, revealing the slight gap beside one of his incisors. "What're you gonna do instead?"

"I'll follow you," Viviane answered simply.

For a very long time, Viviane and Jack lived in that

world people inhabit *before* love. Some people called that place friendship; others called it confusing. Viviane found it a pleasant place with an altitude that only occasionally made her nauseous.

The light from the windows of the Lavender house cast a soft glow across the front seat of the Coupe. Jack brushed his thumb along the hollowed dimple in Viviane's left cheek. "You don't have anything to worry about," he said. "I love you, you know."

Viviane let the words hang in the air between them for a moment, like a sweet pink cloud. Then she inhaled the words in whole, turned them over in her mouth, relished their solidity on her tongue.

Viviane raced up the hill to her house. Before she went inside, she turned back toward Jack and the idling Coupe and yelled, "We're in love! We're in love! We're in love!" Even her neighbor, the sourly Marigold Pie, awakened by Viviane's declaration, had to smile at that.

Chapter Seven

THE MORNING OF THE SUMMER SOLSTICE found Viviane in the bathtub, her arms wrapped around her knees. The water splashing from the silver faucet was scalding hot. She filled the bathtub as high as she could, nonetheless, watching her breasts and the rounded points of her knees turn bright pink in the steam.

She let herself slip under the water and opened her mouth, thinking she might swallow the bathwater in one gulp and sink to the bottom. It was a weak moment and only lasted until her cheeks filled. She sat up, choking on mouthfuls of hot, body-soiled water.

It had taken only two dismal months for Jack's promised daily letters to falter to three a week, and then two, and then none at all. By June Viviane hadn't heard from Jack in five months, one week, and three days. The one time Viviane tried phoning him, she was told Jack Griffith was out, but the dorm mother swore to tell him she'd called. Whether she actually did, Viviane never got the chance to ask. Jack never called.

She spent her days trying to forget the sound of his voice, and her nights trying to remember. She spent her hours standing by the mailbox waiting for letters that did not come, sitting by a telephone that would not ring. Her mother banned her from the bakery—everything Viviane touched made the customers weep.

Yet in spite of the circumstances, Viviane was optimistic. Jack had to leave in order to come back, didn't he? And she knew he would be back, just as she knew that some of the stars that shone bright in the sky were already dead and that she was beautiful, if only to Jack. And that's just the way it was.

Viviane pulled the plug from the drain and wrapped the chain around the faucet, counting in her mother's French with each turn.

"Un, deux, trois, quatre, cinq, six." Viviane could only count to ten, but no matter; it didn't take so many turns. She stepped out of the bathtub. As she wrapped a towel around her hair, Viviane glanced through the bathroom's small window to where her mother's newest houseguest was busy working in the yard.

Emilienne had started taking in houseguests just after

the start of the war. It was the only patriotic thing she ever did. The house on the hill became a carousel of ever-changing men, women, children, and animals, all needing a place to rest, sometimes for the night, sometimes longer. The longest to stay was a family of black cats. It was later rumored that these cats and their ancestors had inhabited the rooms and hallways of our house for thirty years, which only further supported speculations that my grandmother was a witch in *pâtissier* clothing. The longest-staying resident of the human variety, however, was Gabe.

Gabe was unusually tall, so had to be careful where he stood, for if he blocked the sun, his shadow could cause flowers to wither and old women to send their grandchildren inside to fetch their sweaters. Because of his height, many thought Gabe to be much older than he was. This was both a blessing and a curse.

Like most other new arrivals, Gabe's first stop in the neighborhood was the bakery. He was drawn by the sharp scent of sourdough bread, but also by the girl standing in the shop's open doors, the wind swirling her brown hair around her head. Viviane hadn't been blessed with her mother's thick black hair or green eyes. She was hardly the obvious beauty her mother was. To think Viviane was beautiful required a certain acquired taste. It was the kind of beauty perceived only through the eyes of love.

When Gabe learned that the girl from the bakery lived in the house at the end of Pinnacle Lane, he walked right up to that house with every intention of offering up his soul in return for a room. Fortunately, he didn't have to make the offer. Emilienne took one long look at Gabe and easily decided she needed a tall handyman who could reach the light fixture on the front porch when the bulb needed changing.

He quickly proved himself to be more than just a tall man able to reach things in high places. At Emilienne's request, he fixed the broken banister on the front porch and retiled the kitchen counters. He spent a full month sanding and waxing the wood floors — he had welts on his knees to prove it. He was told to leave the third floor as it was; no one went up there anyway.

During the first few months Gabe lived with the Lavenders, he could barely manage to be in the same room as Viviane without knocking the butter dish to the floor or breaking out in itchy red hives.

If asked, he would have shyly admitted that every improvement he made to the house he made for Viviane. Fortunately for Gabe, no one asked.

Gabe's mother had come from a long-removed line of Romanian monarchs. She was an olive-skinned beauty with thinly fashioned eyebrows and a sturdy, hooked nose. She told her young son lavish tales about their ancestry while sitting at her vanity table and applying careful circles of rouge to her cheeks and thick swipes of blue to her eyelids.

She had moved to Hollywood with dreams of acting for Paramount Pictures alongside Clara Bow and Estelle Taylor. Instead, she found herself living near Los Angeles in a tiny studio apartment with a black widow spider infestation. How Gabe had come into the picture he never knew. On the nights she went out, she would remind Gabe to chain the door, then leave him to his empty dreams amid a fog of her velvety black perfume. When she returned, she'd rap on the door three times and Gabe would smooth his imprint from the sheets of her bed and place a sultry jazz recording on the turntable that sat in the corner of the room.

On those nights she came home, Gabe slept in the closet on a bed of moth-ridden coats and shawls, his long legs curled to his chin. He knew it was okay to come out when she switched the record to a more melancholy song. He'd emerge to find his mother sitting at her vanity, painting a red-lipsticked smile on her face before leaving again.

"Just remember, *inimă mea*, my heart," she would say, "royal blood flows from our wounds."

In the morning they'd go down to the diner on the corner, where she'd smile at the waitress and order Gabe the biggest stack of pancakes, and a coffee—black—for herself. These breakfasts always made Gabe sick, but he always managed to choke them all down. Every last bite.

Then one night the turntable never switched its tune. When Gabe finally crawled out from the closet, he found his mother in a broken heap, her royal blood in congealed pools around her head. A handful of dollar bills had been thrown to the floor, half of them sticky and red. The room filled with static as the needle on the turntable bumped again and again into the end of the record.

Gabe wrapped his mother in his arms and lifted her onto the bed. He had to swallow the vomit that rose in his throat when her head lolled unnaturally to one side. He tucked her between the sheets, propped her neck with a pillow, and curled up beside her.

He stayed with her for days. When the corpse began to smell and the putrid air of the apartment wafted out into the hallway, the other tenants started complaining and covering their noses with handkerchiefs when they passed by. After a final glance at his dead mother, Gabe finally left one night, taking nothing with him but the resolve to remember her only as she looked when she was alive. He ignored the money on the floor. He was ten years old.

Over the next few years, Gabe moved around a lot. His incredible height made people believe he was fifteen when he was ten and eighteen when he was twelve. As such, he was able to easily find work and spent a few months at a goat farm in Florida, loading grand pieces of art for a gallery in Queens, and collecting pond samples in central Oregon. For an entire year, Gabe worked as an assistant to a carpenter in New Hampshire. He lived with the carpenter and his family — two young children, a dog, and a wife.

If Gabe had been the age he looked, he would have caught on to the carpenter's wife's intentions: the way she offered to make him breakfast in the morning with her hand on his upper thigh, how the children always had an early bedtime the nights her husband played poker with his buddies, the laughter, the glances, the sighs. If he'd been more worldly, he wouldn't have been so utterly shocked the night she entered his room and climbed on top of him. And he probably would have suspected something by the time she removed her robe, revealing her naked skin in the moonlight. And when she took him in her mouth, he probably wouldn't have burst into tears, crying, "I'm thirteen!" and run out of the house, his pajama pants wrapped around his ankles.

Gabe spent the next couple of years waiting for the war to hit U.S. soil, and after December 7, 1941, he was the first to enlist, figuring the beaches of Hawaii were close enough. Once again his remarkable height and build allowed him to lie about his age without question. If asked, not one of his fellow soldiers would have guessed the tall quiet guy was only fifteen. His superiors, however, found him to be much too sensitive for battle, as well as too weak-stomached to be a medic, so they let him fight the good fight the only way he could—in the mess hall. While he served canned meat and soluble coffee, Gabe observed his fellow soldiers composing love letters to girls whose creased pictures they carried in their helmets and listened to them speak of their mothers in voices that cracked with longing. He wept every time one of them died. Gabe was discharged with fatigue after just a year in the service—it proved too exhausting to mourn so many lives.

When Gabe appeared at the Lavenders' front door, his clothes wrinkled and two sizes too small, Emilienne encouraged him to stay as long as he liked. It wasn't just because she needed a handyman who could reach the light fixture on the front porch. It wasn't just because she suspected he was clearly younger than he wanted her to believe he was—a speculation that was later reinforced when she noted the way he dipped his head when someone said something appreciative to him and how he shuddered in Viviane's presence. No, Emilienne welcomed him in because, upon opening the door, she heard a birdsong rising from the east, announcing good love's arrival.

Viviane paid little attention to her mother's new houseguest. She failed to notice his youthful gaze and mannerisms. She assumed—as everyone did—that he was much older (and certainly not younger!) than herself. She once called him *sir* and was confused and embarrassed by his crestfallen face. He was always polite, offering her the last piece of blackberry pie, and it was nice that he fixed the dripping bathtub faucet. And though he was hardly Jack, Viviane would even go so far as to say he was handsome. If you liked that tall, dark sort of thing.

But Viviane's mind was hardly on her mother's houseguest right then; rather, it was on the fact that the solstice celebration was that evening, an event that no neighborhood resident dared to miss. Most especially Jack. Or so she hoped.

The yearly celebrations of Fatima Inês de Dores's birthday had changed since the days when the child had lived at the end of Pinnacle Lane. The gypsy woman and Chinese acrobats were a thing of the past, but the celebration hadn't lost its magical, sumptuous ways. At night the celebration came to a grand *apogée* with a giant bonfire in the school parking lot. It was where exhausted children fell asleep—the warmth of the flames against their cotton-candied faces—where high schoolers snuck off to neck in the shadows, where forlorn lovers scribed their woes on blue-lined paper and burned them in the flames. It was a fitting place, Viviane believed, for fate to bring her and Jack back together again.

Perhaps in anticipation of the festivities, this year's dahlias had bloomed early in a splendid array. Their maned faces filled every garden, like a parade of dancing children in their Sunday best, but none were more glorious than those in Emilienne's garden. She created her own hybrids in fanciful colors unseen anywhere else: the deepest cerulean blue, fiery reds that faded to yellow or orange or the richest purple, a green so pale they looked white at first glance. They dwarfed the surrounding fruit trees; their colorful blooms arched over the first-floor windows of the house. But hidden by those large blooms was Emilienne's real garden: white chrysanthemums for protection, dandelion root for a good night's sleep, eucalyptus and marjoram for healing. There was foxglove, ginger, heather, and mint. The poisonous belladonna. The capricious peony. And lavender. One could never have enough lavender.

Emilienne watched her daughter come into the garden through the rusted iron gate. As Viviane made her way down the path toward her mother, she ducked under the swaying blossoms and batted at them playfully. She was wearing a white lace dress, and in her hair was a garland she'd made in preparation for *la fête*. She'd spent hours carefully weaving the stems together and tying strands of ribbon to hang down her back.

Viviane looked, Emilienne noted silently, like a bride on her wedding day.

"What are you dressed up for?" Emilienne was troubled by the faraway look in Viviane's eyes. Lately the only expression Viviane wore was one of misery and longing. This was a different look, Emilienne noted. There was some excitement there, some hope.

Viviane smiled. "Solstice."

"Ah." Emilienne stood, brushing the dirt from her knees. "You should ask Gabe to go with you." Emilienne cringed at her attempt to speak casually with her daughter—it was a skill she'd never mastered.

Viviane was too distracted to notice. "Who?"

"Our guest," Emilienne pointed to where Gabe was sanding the new railing he'd recently installed on the back porch. "Go ask him," Emilienne commanded. "It would be polite."

"Fine." Viviane sighed. "But I'm going there to meet Jack."

Emilienne raised her eyebrows. "And you know he'll be there, how?"

"I just know."

The glow in her daughter's eyes left a taste like metal in Emilienne's mouth.

She reached out and tucked a sprig of lavender into the crown of flowers on Viviane's head. "For luck," she said, a bit more gruffly than she meant to.

Without another word, Viviane dreamily skipped back up the path and through the garden gate.

Viviane noticed the way the neighbors looked at her mother when they went into the bakery to buy a loaf of bread, noticed how they flinched if her hand touched theirs when she gave back their change. She knew the neighbors thought her mother was strange.

Well, Viviane thought, *I guess they could think the same thing about me.*

Viviane tilted her head back and breathed in deeply, trying to decipher the concoction of smells in the air. The wet, earthy one was the dahlias—all flowers smelled that way, even the ones with their own pungent odor, like roses and gardenias. Her mother's scent was that of fresh-baked bread, tainted by a slight brackish tone, as if the bread had been salted with tears. Viviane took in another deep breath, trying to figure out the source of the last of the aromas.

It was a rich smell, like cedar or pine. Viviane always found woodsy scents comforting. They reminded her of Wilhelmina, but there was a hint of sweetness in this particular scent that Wilhelmina didn't have.

For a moment, Viviane allowed herself to admire the muscles in Gabe's back, glistening with sweat, as he worked. She blushed when he looked up, embarrassed that he'd caught her watching him. "I'm supposed to ask if you want to come to the solstice celebration," she said.

He set down his tools and squinted down at her. "Supposed to, huh?" he teased.

She rolled her eyes. "So, you want to go or not?"

"How can I refuse such an offer?" Gabe left his tools and lumber scattered across the porch and followed her down the hill. She pretended not to notice as he threw his shirt back on. She wasn't sure how she felt about how easily his slow ambling gait matched her quick pace.

They made their way quietly through the festivities. The streets were lined with booths offering oversize ears of yellow corn dripping with butter and garlic, Norwegian treats of *pannekaken*, *krumkake*, and *fattigmann* served by the women from the next town over. There were tents of sheer turquoise and white where dark-skinned women danced with scarves, the wooden bangles on their wrists knocking together in tune to their circling hips. The girls from the high school's Kiwanis Key Club offered face painting for local children, and their mothers sold pies for the benefit of the Veterans Hospital downtown. Musicians played mandolins, accordions, creaky violins, xylophones, clarinets, and sitars from street corners. The poorer families from the other side of the bay sold kittens, chicks, and baby ducks for a nickel.

Gabe waited politely when Viviane stopped to buy a chocolate truffle from one of the booths lining the streets. She wasn't sure how she felt about the way he looked at her. How he seemed so content just to be in her presence.

"I've been meaning to ask you something, Vivi," he said.

Viviane raised an eyebrow at him. "Vivi? I have a nickname now?"

He smiled, puzzled. "What's wrong with Vivi?"

"No one calls me Vivi."

He peered down at her. "Maybe I do."

She laughed and as she did, she caught sight of the young man standing watching her from across the street. Viviane remembered the slight gap in his smile wistfully, the way one might recall the illustrations in a favorite childhood picture book.

Viviane raised the sweet to her lips, but instead of the sharp tang of dark chocolate and coconut—her favorite—she tasted only her own smile. She glanced absently at Gabe. "I'll catch ya later."

She walked away before he could reply.

"Tell me one thing you couldn't live without." Jack stepped onto the low cement wall of the reservoir. His reflection in the water seemed pale compared to the brightness of the moon.

"Bathtubs." Viviane walked neatly beside Jack, her shoes dangling from one hand. The cement felt rough and cool against her feet.

Jack jumped back off the wall. "It would be hard to live without you," he said, and looked at Viviane in a way that made her realize the seriousness of the conversation.

"You've done all right." Viviane surprised herself by saying this matter-of-factly, without any trace of bitterness on her tongue. She knew that Jack had to leave in order for him to come back. That was just the way things worked.

"Nah. See, 'cause you were always with me." Jack pointed to his head. "In here." He pointed to his chest. "And here, of course."

"Of course," she murmured.

"Are you cold?" A pale glow from the white house illuminated his face.

Viviane shook her head, happy for the occasional cool gust against her neck and the way it ruffled the garland in her hair.

A song rose into the air; the music surely coming from a radio inside the white house. Jack took Viviane's shoes from her and set them on the ground. Then he took her hand in his, letting her fingertips rest lightly in his palm. "Remember how to tango?"

Viviane laughed. "I do."

They danced, and all around them the leaves fell from their branches, some landing in the water to float on the moon's shimmering silver reflection. Jack looked down at Viviane through the curved arc of their joined arms. "Are you actually letting me lead?"

"Stranger things have happened," she replied. She was surprised by how much could change in a year, wondered if she felt as foreign in his arms as he did in hers. The music changed over to a slow jazz tune and they stood frozen. After a moment, they pulled apart.

"I have to tell you something," Jack said while Viviane searched for her shoes.

"What's that?"

Viviane used Jack's shoulder for balance. She slipped a shoe on one foot, then the other. He rested his hand on the small of her back, almost timidly. The golden heat of his palm caused a ripple to run up her spine.

Viviane placed her chin on his shoulder. "I think I can handle it," she said into his ear, hoping she sounded coy.

"I met someone." And the leaves fell from the trees, landing to float in the calm black waters.

Viviane stood with her chin still resting dumbly on Jack's shoulder. The music stopped. The moon disappeared from the sky. The couple in the white house had gone to bed, taking the warm light with them. Jack dropped his hand from her back, and all Viviane could think was *Where did the moon go?*

Jack asked if she wanted to meet her, this someone

he had met, and Viviane found herself nodding yes and being led away from the reservoir and back into the midst of the celebration to where a girl stood nervously twisting her copper-colored hair between two fingers. The left ring finger was encircled by a thin gold band, the diamond a tiny pinpoint only noticeable when caught by the light.

As Viviane watched this girl take Jack's arm, and she saw this girl's hand meet Jack's, Viviane was hit by the extraordinary thought that this girl, this Laura Lovelorn—which was, horribly, her name—had bought Jack a birthday present that year, that she had bought him other presents as well: little knickknacks from vacations taken over school holidays, romantic gifts for anniversaries, little tokens of affection for *just because.* Viviane could see Laura Lovelorn making her way through various department stores and specialty shops, maybe bringing along a friend or two—her future bridesmaids. Viviane could picture the moment Laura found it, this thing, this item that *her* Jack—because he was no longer Viviane's Jack but Laura Lovelorn's Jack—would treasure. Viviane could imagine Laura Lovelorn's pleasure that she had found her future husband the perfect present, that she knew him that well. Upon imagining all of this, Viviane had the sudden impulse to run, to run until she reached, say, Topeka, Kansas, where she could shed this life and live in quiet refuge as a waitress at a roadside diner. Or something like that.

So she did.

She ran past the booths of *pannekaken*, *krumkake*, and *fattigmann*, and the overcooked ears of yellow corn. She ran past the tainted tents of turquoise and white, the plain-faced girls of the high school's Key Club and their mothers selling overcooked pies for the Veterans Hospital downtown. She ran past the drunken musicians, the boxes of flea-bitten kittens, the wretched inferno in the school parking lot.

She ran until the night was a blur of blue and black and watery reflections and copper-colored hair. She ran until she reached her mother's garden behind her house, and there she discovered that Jack had been keeping up behind her the whole time.

Jack stood panting with his hands on his knees.

"This isn't what was supposed to happen," Viviane said quietly. "You were supposed to come back *for me.* Not come back with someone else."

Jack looked away, squinted up at the glare of the streetlight. He opened his mouth to speak, then closed it, reconsidered what he was going to say. "She's nice. You'd like her—"

Viviane stood and turned away from him, looking up at the glow from a window in her house. "I'm giving you to the count of ten to leave," she said. *"Un, deux."*

He stepped closer. She could feel his breath on the back of her neck.

"Trois, quatre, cinq." She bit the inside of her lip.

"Six, sept, huit." She closed her eyes at the kiss Jack placed on her neck.

"Neuf, dix." Viviane could only count to ten in French. She allowed herself ten tears, one for each step it took for her to lay down beneath her mother's dahlias, her face to the sky. She removed her crown of flowers and threw it on the ground.

She was only vaguely surprised when Jack sat down beside her, smashing the garland she'd spent hours making.

Jack winced. "I'm sorry," he said, pulling it out from under him and trying to straighten the bent flowers.

Viviane grabbed it from him and flung it back to the ground. "It doesn't matter," she said.

What happened next neither of them could ever fully explain. Viviane felt as if she were watching it happen to someone else, someone else's clothing being undone, someone else's lips on Jack's skin, someone else's hands on his chest. Her thoughts were consumed only with the taste of his mouth and his fingers catching in the knots in her hair. And when he rolled over the garland for the second time that night, she straddled his hips with her own and arched her neck to the sky.

The mulch of the garden felt cool beneath Viviane's head. It gave off a rich, potent stench that clung to the inside of her nostrils. The largest dahlia in her mother's collection was called the Dauntless, a bright red flower shaped like a pom-pom and the size of a dinner plate. Viviane reached up and snapped it off at the stem—then tossed it back and forth, amazed by how big it was, yet so fragile she could so easily pluck it right off with her fingers.

Viviane's white dress hung loosely off her shoulders, leaving her breasts exposed to the moonlight. The skirt had twisted around her waist. She traced the smudges of dirt on her shoulders and fingered the ripped lace on the hem, noting without emotion—how could she possibly feel anything now that she'd lost Jack?—that she was dressed as a bride both the first time she saw Jack, as well as what would probably be the last. There must be some irony in that, though it did little to soothe Viviane's downtrodden heart.

Viviane could still see the orange flames of the bonfire against the dark sky. If she closed her eyes, she could hear the sounds of the celebration continuing without her: the circled groups of husbands, their voices resounding from a few too many celebratory beers, their wives warning the children to keep away from the fire. If she held her breath, she could hear Jack Griffith whisper in his fiancée's ear. She exhaled loudly.

Viviane considered herself a rational woman. She was a Virgo. She was used to solving problems, even if it meant she spent far too much time mulling things over in the bathtub. But this. This didn't make any sense; when she tried to envision her life without Jack or his without her, all she could think of were platypuses. What was a platypus but a kind of duck with fur? The whole idea of it was ridiculous and wrong.

She delicately ran her finger over the place on the back of her neck where Jack had kissed her. The spot burned, like the pain in her chest that made it hurt to breathe. To move. To think. So instead, Viviane simply lay in her mother's dahlia bed watching the flames against the sky and exhaling whenever she heard Jack's furtive whisper.

Gabe watched as Viviane and that other guy—whoever the hell he was—rounded up the road leading to the reservoir, his heart skipping after them. Then he settled himself onto the curb outside the drugstore next to an old vagabond strumming a mandolin with long dirty fingernails. And there he remained, waiting for his heart to return and smiling politely at the vagabond's attempt at music.

Gabe marveled at the easy way the good Lutherans of Pinnacle Lane took to the pagan holiday, disguised as the birthday celebration of their little Portuguese matriarch, of course. In honor of Fatima Inês, neighbors danced together around the maypole with sunbeams painted on their limbs. For their daughters, they fashioned faerie wands out of wooden sticks and felt stars. The women who spent the rest of the year diligently cultivating roses for the church altar spent summer solstice eve gathering bunches of rosemary, thyme, and marjoram and nailing them to doors and entryways. For protection. Good luck. Wealth.

Eventually the sky grew dark, and the longest day of

the year finally ceded to the night. Seattle's mayor, wearing a pair of horns on his head, lit the bonfire. The crowd roared and the fire whooshed to life, but Gabe's attention was drawn to a fleeting Viviane. The young man Gabe didn't know was chasing after her. Gabe stood, preparing to join the race, but with his long legs he knew he'd catch up too soon. Then what would he do? Demand an explanation?

When he later made his way home to the house at the end of Pinnacle Lane, he passed the other guy stumbling down the hill, his clothes rumpled, his shirt buttoned wrong, his shoes untied. Gabe caught his eye and a look of self-loathing crossed his face before he hurried past.

It took Gabe a few minutes to find Viviane. He looked in the bathtub first. When he spied her lying in the dahlia bed, shivering and half-naked in the moonlight, it took every ounce of self-control he had not to run over and wrap her in his long arms. Or to go punch that other guy's teeth down his throat.

The next morning Viviane awoke with streaks of dirt on her sheets and her heartache over Jack Griffith slightly more tolerable than the day before.

Or so she told herself.

Chapter Eight

VIVIANE TOOK A JOB behind the soda fountain at the drugstore. She was banned again from the bakery after a batch of her éclairs made the customers cry so hard, the salt from their tears ruined a week's worth of bread. At the soda fountain, Viviane served sundaes with hot fudge and syrupy glasses of cherry Coke. When Constance Quakenbush smugly asked what she was going to do with her life, now that Jack Griffith was marrying that Laura Lovelorn girl, Viviane answered her with a soda fountain smile and a declaration: "I'm going to fly."

Air evacuation missions for wounded soldiers were begging for onboard nurses, and many stewardesses patriotically rallied to the call. It wasn't that Viviane hadn't thought about joining them. A few boys from the neighborhood had enlisted after high school. Two of them returned only a few months later in dark wood boxes, and the stars on the service flags in their parents' windows changed from blue to gold. Viviane had known them both—Wallace Zimmer was Delilah's brother, and Dinky Fields had sat behind Viviane in English class.

After the attack on Pearl Harbor, she'd earnestly prayed for the boys whose bodies remained trapped in the USS *Arizona* and knitted gloves for trigger fingers freezing in the trenches of European soil. Viviane indulged in daydreams in which she nursed wounded soldiers back to health, calling for *more bandages* as the skirts of her white uniform blew in the wind and bullets flew overhead. But Viviane hadn't any nurses' training, so when she envisioned her life in the skies, she was hardly flying over enemy territory. When it came down to it, Viviane just wasn't one for war; she didn't like loud noises and often jumped when the teakettle whistled. Plus, imagine the smells.

When she envisioned that life in the skies, she saw herself serving in-flight meals on pink trays. She'd keep her spectator shoes clean and white and her leg makeup dry. She'd smile at all the right people, flirt with all the right first-class passengers, and only occasionally go back to a pilot's hotel room after cocktails and dancing in the lounge. The next morning she'd ignore the wedding band on the edge of the bathroom sink as she repinned the pillbox hat over her tousled curls.

While waiting for customers one particularly slow day at the soda fountain, Viviane found an old newspaper stuffed behind the tubs of hot fudge under the counter. Next to an exposé on the discovery of the planet Pluto, there was an article about a plane that had run out of gas and landed in a wheat field near Cherokee, Wyoming. The stewardess on board said that people had come in wagons and on horseback from miles away to see the aircraft. She claimed they thought that she, the stewardess, was *an angel from the sky*. It was a story Viviane liked so much that she applied to be a stewardess for United Air Lines the very next day.

The man in charge of her interview had a clipboard and a bottom lip like a bicycle tire. He asked her to lift her skirt and walk up and down the hall so he could look at her legs. He looked at her hands and examined her nails, then her hair and teeth, with a critical eye. She was prepared for this and was surprised she didn't feel like a show horse. She'd pin-curled her hair the night before so that it floated in wispy waves at her shoulders, and she had made sure that her lipstick was just the right shade of red. At the end of the interview, the man smiled, his thick bottom lip jutting past his weak chin, and told my mother she was lucky to be so good-looking. She wondered if that was just something all homely men said.

While she waited to hear word, Viviane spent her days in the drugstore, imagining a life that looked nothing like the one she had once planned to share with Jack. Viviane often paused in her daily activities, while adding an extra serving of whipped cream to an already-dripping ice-cream sundae or dropping cherries into a full glass of cherry Coke, and thought, *If this is life without Jack, then life without Jack suits me just fine.* Soon, she told herself, her days would begin and end in the blue uniform of a United Air stewardess, the tiny gold wings pinned just below the lip of her Peter Pan collar.

But then in late August, while taking a bathroom break at the drugstore, something prompted Viviane to recall the day she had turned thirteen and awoken to a dull ache in the lower pit of her stomach; it was just strong enough, she'd thought at the time, for her mother to allow her to stay home from school. When she'd walked downstairs, however, planning to fake illness, she'd discovered that her mother already knew what was ailing her.

This was hardly a surprise. Emilienne was always getting strange messages from equally strange places. If she dreamed of keys, a change was on its way. Dreaming of tea implied an unforeseen visitor. A birdcall from the north meant tragedy; from the west, good luck; and from the east, it announced the arrival of good love. As a child, Viviane wondered if her mother's gifts stretched further into the supernatural realm — perhaps she could communicate with the dead. But Emilienne had dismissed Viviane's theory with a wave of her hand.

"Ghosts don't exist," she'd said, glancing furtively into the far corner of the room.

Emilienne had handed Viviane an elastic sanitary belt, which gave her a circle of red welts around her waist. Viviane was allowed to stay home from school that day and was even given a note that excused her from gym class for the rest of the week.

But in the two months between the night of the solstice celebration and now, Viviane realized, she hadn't felt that now-familiar ache in her abdomen.

While still in high school, Viviane had sat next to a girl whose cousin had gotten pregnant. The girl swore that the cousin had solved it by sneezing. At the time Viviane wondered why this girl had thought to tell this story to her. But now she went to the back of the store, ripped open a package of black pepper, grabbed a handful, and tossed it under her nose. After her eighth try, she realized that the only thing sprinkling pepper in her face was going to do was irritate a retina.

Next Viviane tried coughing particularly hard. That gave her a sore throat. At night she spent the hours willing that dull ache to reappear—in her stomach, in the small of her back, in the tops of her thighs—and praying for a miracle.

While at work, Viviane took trips to the bathroom six times every hour. It was after a particularly distressing break that Jack Griffith walked into the drugstore.

Perhaps it was out of decency, or maybe it was just out of shame, but Jack had made a point of keeping away from Viviane that summer. He'd taken a job at an army supply depot along the Seattle port, working alongside women twice his age who had sons and husbands overseas. On his days off, Jack drove to the coast with his fiancée, who was spending her summer in Seattle too, to be closer to him. To Jack, the air that summer always seemed to stink of fish.

Jack hadn't lied when he told Viviane that Laura Lovelorn was nice. She was. She was nice and good, and Jack knew he was supposed to love her. How could he not? Everyone loved Laura Lovelorn. She was everything everyone wanted her to be. But sometimes, on their trips to the coast, Jack would forget she was even there. He'd be thinking of that last night on Pinnacle Lane, and the sun would suddenly become the moon. Its reflection would beam up at him, not from the crashing waves of the ocean, but from the still water of the reservoir. Then he'd look up and there she'd be, Laura Lovelorn, smiling her perfect smile and twirling her hair around the engagement ring on her finger. He'd think, *Oh,* and life would go on.

Jack Griffith and Laura Lovelorn met at a Whitman football game in their freshman year. Not just any football game. The Whitman Missionaries were facing off against the Willamette Bearcats, the team to beat for almost nine years running. That game would turn out to be the last game for three seasons, with the war causing a league-wide cancellation of the football program. Jack had been writing a letter to Viviane—a letter that would remain forever unfinished in his top desk drawer—when he left for the stadium with his dorm-mates. They were all donning blue-and-gold sweaters and belting out the school's fight song. *Whitman, here's to you . . .*

In the stands Jack noticed a flash of copper-colored hair three rows below him. As the miserable game continued, with the Missionaries on their way to defeat, Jack watched the girl with the copper hair cheer after each Missionary score, her cheeks flushed pink from the cold.

Jack learned that Laura Lovelorn was a member of the Delta Gamma Society—noted by the tiny white shield she wore pinned to her sweater—and of the freshman Pep Club. She sold war stamps with the Minute Maids every Friday afternoon and was an accomplished ornamental swimmer—her routines could put famed synchronized swimmer Esther Williams herself to shame. Laura was also the daughter of a 1920 graduate whose donations to the college always surpassed even the most distinguished of other alumni. The Lovelorns lived in a large English Tudor-style mansion just outside of Spokane, where Laura's father smoked cigars with his business associates in the library while his wife entertained their wives in the tearoom. They had a herd of award-winning Arabians and a vacation house on the coast. Most important, Jack noted, none of the Lovelorns were strange or unusual. No one could ever dare to call any of them a witch.

Not even Jack's father.

When Jack walked into the drugstore that hot August day, he sat down on one of the metal stools in front of the soda fountain and ordered a cream soda. Viviane watched him sip the syrupy drink through a straw. Then Jack looked up at her and said, "I'll never forget you."

My poor mother ducked her head behind the counter and vomited.

Chapter Nine

SPRING—ALONG WITH THE ANTS, tulips, and hay fever—arrived early that next year. It was only late February, but the sun was warm on Viviane's back. She sat on the front porch eating from the bowl of cherries resting on her lap. Handfuls of cherry pits and stems covered the floor.

Viviane was waiting. It was hardly a rational thing to do, but it was the only option she had. For seven long months her body became something she didn't recognize anymore, and hope moved further and further away. She could barely see it anymore; as the months wore on, it had become a minuscule dot in the distance. But still she waited. Waited for Jack to come back for her.

The cherry tree along the side of the house had bloomed a season earlier than any other on the block. Throughout January, Viviane had watched the pink blooms scatter across the snow-covered lawn. Now the tree was bursting with cherries so red they were purple, and so large and ripe their skins were cracked, the juice leaking down the tree's branches and soaking into the ground. All the jars of cherry jam Emilienne made, all the cherry pie they sold at the bakery, barely made a dent in the amount of fruit falling from the tree. Fortunately, cherries were the only food Viviane could manage to keep down, although the doctor—a man who only a few years before had been her pediatrician—claimed that she should no longer be experiencing nausea.

Viviane stretched her swollen feet out in front of her; the bottoms had been perpetually lined with dirt since February, when her shoes no longer fit. Not that there'd been any reason to wear shoes. No one in the neighborhood had seen Viviane since she quit her job at the soda fountain when she could no longer pretend that her clothes still fit.

Emilienne inserted triangles of mismatched fabrics into Viviane's skirts and dresses. It was a fruitless attempt to get Viviane to change out of the white lace dress she'd worn for seven months straight, a dress that had turned brown and whose zipper could no longer be closed.

Viviane could barely look at herself in the hallway mirror, let alone dress herself. Or bathe. Grimy rings collected underneath her heavy breasts and around the areolas, which had grown strangely dark and foreign. Her hair hung in sullied sticks down her back, and her hands were constantly sticky with cherry juice.

She bathed only when her mother and Wilhelmina forced her to, when Emilienne added the day's milk delivery to warm water in the tub and pulled Viviane into the bathroom by her dirty feet. Wilhelmina doused Viviane's head with olive oil and lemon juice, scrubbed the grime from underneath those breasts with the strange nipples, and made sure she soaked long enough for the sticky gloss of cherry juice to come loose from the skin between her fingers.

Viviane watched a tribe of carpenter ants surround a glob of boric acid and honey, a toxic concoction Emilienne had put out underneath the porch swing. The ants resembled black petals around a golden circle. The ants drank their fill, then made their way back to their nest in the wall. There they unknowingly poisoned their babies before dying themselves. Viviane imagined the nests as tombs, the bodies piling up.

By this point Viviane Lavender had loved Jack Griffith for twelve years, which was far more than half of her life. If she thought of her love as a commodity and were, say, to eat it, it would fill 4,745 cherry pies. If she were to preserve it, she would need 23,725 glass jars and labels and a basement spanning the length of Pinnacle Lane.

If she were to drink it, she'd drown.

In the kitchen Emilienne feigned interest in the dish towel in her hand as Viviane slowly made her way back into the house, her steps awkward under her tremendous belly.

"Is it getting warm out there?" Emilienne asked, her tone more gruff than she intended. Did she always sound so cold? she wondered. So stern? So heartless?

"Hmm. A bit," Viviane replied.

The sound of hammer against nail could be heard coming from upstairs, where Gabe was converting one of the bedrooms into a nursery. The noise made Viviane wince.

"Viviane—" Emilienne started.

Viviane raised her head, and in that moment, when mother and daughter locked eyes, Emilienne felt a rush of cold fill her lungs. As her head flooded with images of last midsummer's night—a night of broken dahlias and broken promises—Emilienne recalled a time when love, and not longing, filled her, too, with its icy breath.

Before Emilienne could say what was on her mind, Viviane turned and walked out of the kitchen. "I'm going to take a nap."

"On your way, go take a look at the damn nursery!" Emilienne shouted after her. Emilienne threw the dish towel on the counter and ran her hands miserably over her face. "I'm going to the bakery," she murmured to no one.

Emilienne used the bakery to hide from the horrible mess that was her daughter's life. *Pregnant,* she thought disbelievingly, *and with Jack Griffith's child, no less.* That talent for avoidance was something that Wilhelmina never failed to mention when Emilienne came in on her days off.

The bakery's success had now lasted eighteen years thanks to Emilienne's skills as a French *pâtissier* and Wilhelmina Dovewolf's clever nose for business. It was her now-partner Wilhelmina's idea to hire local high-school boys to walk door to door through the neighborhood carrying baskets of fragrant loaves and morning buns. As business thrived, the routes became longer, and these boys—eventually known as Emilienne's Bakery Boys—began using bicycles to make deliveries, balancing their breadbaskets on either side of the back tire. Their shiny red bikes became a familiar sight not only on Pinnacle Lane, but also well into the Ballard neighborhood and up past Phinney Ridge.

The bakery survived the Depression by selling jams, jellies, cured meats, and eggs whenever Emilienne could get them. She kept her customers loyal by offering them store credit. Some attributed the very survival of the neighborhood to Emilienne during those tough times—if someone was hungry, they could always get bread from the bakery.

They added wedding cakes to their pastry repertoire after beloved high-school teacher Ignatius Lux married Estelle Margolis in a small ceremony at the Lutheran church. The celebration ended with a four-tiered cake baked by Emilienne just for the occasion. Happy smiles were shared between the bride and groom, but it was the cake their guests remembered—the vanilla custard filling, the buttercream finish, the slight taste of raspberries that had surely been added to the batter. No one brought home any slices of leftover cake to place under their pillow, hoping to dream of their future mate; instead, the guests of Ignatius Lux and Estelle Margolis ate the whole cake and then had dreams of eating it again. After this wedding unmarried women woke in the night with tears in their eyes, not because they were alone, but because there wasn't any cake left. Needless to say, the cake later became one of the bakery's most popular items, requested for every event, large or small.

Emilienne picked up the keys to the bakery from the counter and made her way to the front door. Emilienne kept the keys on a leather rope worn smooth from the hours it spent hanging around her neck. They never left her—she even kept them on her pillow as she slept.

Emilienne stepped onto the porch, blinking in the spring sun. As she closed the door, the sound of Gabe's diligent working quieted to a distant pounding. At the bakery Emilienne was always in charge. Not even Wilhelmina dared to make a decision without consulting Emilienne first. She sighed. If only that were the case at home.

What actually belonged in a nursery still remained a mystery to Gabe, but he'd managed to make a crib and placed it near the window. He was trying to decide the color for the walls when Viviane slipped into the room behind him.

"Green," Viviane said, glancing down at the buckets of white and blue between his feet.

Gabe looked up, startled to see her. "What kind of green?" he asked.

"Light, but not lime. More like apple green. Spring green."

Gabe nodded in agreement. "Spring green it is."

Gabe never needed very much sleep at all and instead spent most nights the way he spent his days — working on the house, the beat of his hammer and the raking of his saw making their way into my mother's dreams. Some nights he did no work at all and instead celebrated his renovations with creamy bottles of home-brewed beer. My mother spent those nights in a dreamless sleep.

Gabe watched as Viviane walked around the room. He was pleased to see her bathed. Gabe wasn't sure if it had been Emilienne's or Wilhelmina's doing, but he hoped Viviane herself had washed the cherry juice from her hands, tied the red ribbon in her hair. Perhaps it was a sign of something good to come.

She ran her fingertips across the newly sanded crib, paused to admire the curtains in the windows. Gabe held his breath when she noticed the tiny sculpture hanging above the crib.

"Feathers," she said, offering a vague smile.

"Well, I thought, maybe, it would be . . ." Gabe stammered, unsure how to explain what compelled him to collect discarded feathers from the neighborhood birds and hang them over the place where Viviane's child would sleep.

Once, after a particularly wet night of celebrating,

Gabe had found himself in Viviane's room, kneeling by her bed. Even though she was miserable, even though she was filthy—her feet were encrusted in dirt, and there were circles of red juice around her frowning mouth and on the palms of her hands—he still found her beautiful. He had lightly pressed a hand to the mound of her belly. In case she were to ask him, he had thought about names for the baby. Maybe Alexandria or Elise for a girl, and if a boy, Dmitry.

As he was about to pull his hand away, he felt it: a light fluttering from beneath his hand. And though Gabe knew the common term was *quickening*, he could hardly keep from laughing out loud: it had felt just like wings!

Viviane smiled again. "Feathers are fine, Gabe," she said, and walked out of the room, leaving Gabe to stumble over the fact that for the first time, Viviane Lavender had said his name. That fact filled Gabe with so much hope that he grew another two inches just to have enough room to hold it all.

Hardly a soul slept the night my mother was in labor. Nocturnal birds gathered in the lawns like pious parishioners to eat noisily, their doomed prey screaming wildly into the dark. Earlier in the day, the crows and sparrows had tormented the neighborhood with angry calls, flying into windows and after small children. Viviane, however, was unaware of the strange disturbance her upcoming delivery had brought to the neighborhood birds.

Gabe drove her to the hospital in the clunky Chevy

truck he'd bought for the odds-and-ends jobs he took around town. Emilienne was still at the bakery, and there was no time.

"No time!" Viviane screamed from the passenger side of the truck, her clenched fists as tight as the ball of her belly. She squeezed her eyes shut in pain, and a slick layer of sweat gathered above her upper lip.

Gabe reached across the old truck and grabbed her hand—slightly disgusted with himself for finding pleasure in being able to touch her at such a time.

"Hold on, there, Vivi," he said. "We'll be there soon."

Gabe was forced to remain in the waiting room as Viviane was whisked away by a pair of apron-clad nurses, who quickly set her up in a sterile white room before their squeaky shoes took them back down the hall.

Alone, my mother cried and screamed. Screamed for the nurses, for Jack, even for her mother—though Emilienne was hardly the type to hold her daughter's hand or wipe her forehead with a damp cloth. And when the pain felt too great, when it felt like the contractions would split her in half, the squeaky shoes finally returned, bringing with them a cold syringe of relief.

Just before slipping into a deep twilight sleep, Viviane swore she saw giant feathers falling from the ceiling, an image she attributed to the anesthetic.

When I was born, the on-call doctor examined the forceps in his hands in bewilderment before going in search of family in the waiting room.

According to the nurses in attendance, moments after I made my entrance, I opened my eyes and pointed a pinkie finger toward the light. This was an admirable feat considering I first had to unfold a pair of speckled wings sprouting from the edges of my shoulder blades.

My twin came as a surprise to them all—most especially the doctor, who had to be rushed back for his birth. It was later debated whether or not my wings had anything to do with how Henry turned out. But that wouldn't explain the many others like him—others who were born just as strange as Henry but without a feathery twin.

It took two hours for the press to catch wind of my strange birth. Soon there they were, crowding the hospital hallways, the nursing staff shooting them malicious looks. The head nurse was able to keep the cameras and journalists from the actual hospital room, but outside our window the devout gathered into the night, holding candles and singing hymns of praise and fear. The crowd was so dense, it took Gabe four hours to pick up Emilienne from the bakery and bring her back to the hospital. It took another four hours to take her back when Emilienne declared that, after an uncomfortable forty-five minutes, she had been away from the bakery too long.

It was the nurse's aide who attended to us during most of our stay, who emptied my mother's bedpan and enticed her with tiny cups of green Jell-O and bottles of chocolate milk. The nurse's aide was a feverish reader of the Bible and brought in pages of notebook paper on which she had jotted down all the feminine forms of Michael, Raphael, and Uriel she could find.

"She really does need a name," she said.

As a newborn, I was lovely in every sense of the word, or so I've been told.

I had dark eyes and a full head of black hair like my mother's on the day she was born — right down to the ringlet at the back of my head. Other than the fact that I had wings, I was perfect. And even the wings weren't that bad. Only a few days old and I was already able to wrap them around myself like a swaddling blanket.

"I like Michaela," the nurse's aide said, standing in the doorway. "Or maybe you could call her Raphaela."

It usually took Gabe a while to get from the elevator to the hospital room. He had to will his fingers to stop shaking and his chest to stop heaving first. When he did arrive, it was with a ceremonious bumping of his head on the door frame and a bouquet of flowers, wilted from his tight and sweaty grip.

"I was thinking you could call her Ava," he said, rubbing his head and handing the flowers to the nurse's aide. She gave him a quizzical look before adding the bouquet to the array of brown flowers from his other visits.

"What angel was ever named that?" she asked.

"It means bird," Viviane said softly. She tried not to look disappointed, but she and Gabe and Emilienne all knew that a very large part of her was still hoping Jack would walk through the door. She didn't care if he brought her flowers. Or even an apology. She just needed him to be there. She needed him because that was the only thing that made sense.

Then, for a moment, my mother caught a glimpse of Gabe's good heart and forgot that her own was in mourning. For a moment, she saw in him a common soul and smiled at the thought of spending the next fifty years sleeping in the crook of his long arm or walking together in stride — arms matching arms, step matching step. But then she remembered Jack and all those months she'd spent waiting for a love that never returned, and she wrapped her heart in its burial shroud once again.

"Well, fine," the young aide said, rolling her eyes. "Name her whatever you want, but what about the other one?"

To Viviane, one of the worst parts about all the attention — the reporters, the newspaper articles, the crowds of worshipful followers — was that it focused on one twin, as if I were a single entity. What were twins but a pair? They came together for a reason, after all. But maybe worse was that underneath her motherly indignation lay the underlying fear that Viviane wasn't so sure about the other one either. He was small and quiet, too quiet for an infant. He went limp when anyone tried to hold him. It seemed to Viviane that she'd given birth to not one oddity but two.

"Henry," Viviane decided. "I want to call him Henry."

Gabe smiled. "Ava and Henry."

Chapter Ten

IT WAS OBVIOUS Jack Griffith was the father of Viviane Lavender's children—anyone who knew Jack could recognize him in my brother's face—but no one in the neighborhood dared to mention it. Perhaps they took their cues from Jack's father, the disagreeable John Griffith, who furrowed his brow and clenched his jaw whenever he passed Emilienne's bakery. Some swore they'd seen him spit at Viviane the day she quit her job at the soda fountain, still pregnant and wearing that soiled white dress she refused to take off. His long, spindly drop of saliva had run down the back of her dress and landed on the pavement with a wet, milky splat.

Most preferred to give Jack the benefit of the doubt. They liked to assume that he simply didn't know about us. He'd returned to Whitman College the September before we were born. And hadn't come back since. It was two hundred seventy miles away, after all.

But then, on our second birthday, Beatrix Griffith came to visit us.

It was the first and only time.

My grandmother was the one who saw her come up the walk. The woman's tiny frail steps were so reminiscent of Emilienne's own delicate *maman* that she couldn't help but welcome Beatrix and usher her into the parlor. Later Emilienne would recall how remarkably overdressed Beatrix seemed for such a short visit. She was wearing a smart-looking gray suit with a wide belt cinched around her waist, a pair of white gloves, and a netted hat cupped around her short hair. On each paper-thin cheek, she'd carefully applied a pink oval of rouge.

When our mother introduced Henry and me to her, Beatrix clutched her tiny gloved hands together and murmured a soft *mmm* until her hands began to shake and tears slid into her smile lines.

She brought gifts—a spinning top for me, a set of blocks for Henry. And she held me in her lap until my wings tickled her chin.

Before she left, Beatrix seized Viviane's hand. "You shouldn't have to do this alone," she whispered.

Beatrix Griffith wasn't always such a quiet woman.

She used to be funny—spirited even—and was voted Most Outstanding Girl in her senior class. She was the one who distracted the rival football team with her wit while classmates stole the team mascot. She was the first girl in the neighborhood to cut her hair into a stylish new bob, then convinced her girlfriends to do the same once she felt the thrill of the fall air on her ears. When John Griffith came into her life, his blue eyes and firm jaw made her weak in the knees, and her friends saw a change in their fun-loving Beatrix. Before long, waiting at home for John to call was more important than attending the homecoming game. "What would I tell him if it ran late?" she'd worry, her fingers fidgeting with anxiety.

John—the son of an unsuccessful carpet salesman—worked as a laundry delivery truck driver. His illegal involvements were mere rumors, quiet whispers that followed him about like an elusive mosquito on a warm summer evening. People saw even less of Beatrix once she and John were married. When her girlfriends invited her over for tea, Beatrix always had an excuse not to come, a reason to hurry back out the door. She had to prepare dinner. John liked his promptly at six. She had to clean the house. John liked coming home to floors freshly waxed, the bathtub newly scoured. But, most important, she had to conceive a child, and John wanted a son.

Her friends stopped coming to call altogether shortly after Jack was born. What was the point? The sprightly Beatrix they once knew had long since faded away. Perhaps this was why, many years later, no one noticed when she did actually disappear. Not her neighbors or her old friends or even Emilienne, who was too busy trying to run a bakery to notice that Beatrix Griffith no longer stopped in for her weekly three loaves of bread.

Beatrix's own husband might not have realized she was gone if he hadn't arrived home at six and found his dinner wasn't waiting for him on the table.

"Goddammit, Beatrix!" he called. "What the hell is this about?"

That was when he noticed that all of his wife's belongings were gone—one side of their bedroom sat empty and bare. It looked as if she'd never lived there at all, as if John had spent the last twenty-three years merely living a half-life. He called out her name again and was surprised by how easily his big voice filled the room.

In all their years of marriage, Beatrix Griffith never once considered her husband a controlling man. Perhaps it had crossed her mind once or twice, but she'd always assumed that freedom was a sacrifice one made for love. Which was why she hadn't batted an eye when, on the night of their wedding, her new husband closely inspected their nuptial sheets for her virginal blood. Or when he'd thrown her carefully planned meals to the dogs when the meat wasn't prepared to his liking. No, Beatrix never considered her husband a controlling man until she heard him command their son, Jack, to break up with Viviane Lavender. Afterward, when they were alone, Beatrix took a deep breath and said, "You shouldn't be so hard on him, dear. He's fallen in love with her."

John looked at her in amazement, as if shocked to learn she still had a voice at all, and said, "What kind of man falls in love?"

After an unsatisfying meal of canned cocktail sausages and a jar of peach preserves he found in the basement, John Griffith went to sleep in that half-empty room. That night he dreamed he could fly. He dreamed of the whispery kiss of clouds, cold and wet on his cheek, as he soared into the night sky, the streets below fading into darkness.

But this wasn't his dream. It was his wife's.

The next morning John Griffith awoke feeling heavy and weak, as if in sleep he'd swallowed a handful of large rocks and no longer had the strength to carry his own weight. No one on Pinnacle Lane ever saw Beatrix Griffith again, not even John, but he knew she was still out there, that she had not simply faded into a small pile of blue ashes he would someday find between the sheets of their bed. He knew because every night after she left, he shared her dreams. Dreams of giant flocks of pelicans, mugs of hot chocolate, and foreign men's strong hands.

My mother didn't want to fall in love with her strange children. She was sure that she hadn't enough room in her heart for anyone but Jack.

She was wrong.

Lucky for us, Viviane found motherhood to be more

and more agreeable as time went by. She was amazed by how easy it all was: learning how Popsicles could be made with orange juice, toothpicks, and an ice tray; how to listen for noises from a child's bedroom even in the midst of a dead sleep; when a scraped elbow needed a kiss or a bandage. But more than that, she learned how to worry. She, who'd always thought love's only companion was sorrow, learned that worry came hand in hand with love.

By our third birthday, Henry still had yet to utter a sound. Not a peep, not a whimper, not a grunt, a moan, or a groan. He reached other developmental stages without any obvious difficulties. Just like me, he cut his first tooth at twelve weeks, could stand on his own by our first birthday, and was walking just a couple of months later. The fact that he was silent while doing so hardly bothered our mother, or so she told herself. And perhaps he just wasn't one for smiling. Or touching, for that matter. And when he stared into space in such a daze that Viviane couldn't get his attention, even when banging the kitchen kettle against a black iron pot, well, that didn't necessarily signify anything either.

The doctors, of course, had their theories, their special labels and terminology for Henry. They had their contradicting diagnoses, their remedies, their medical recommendations.

Our mother had her own ideas. She placed her good china bowls in the yard, and Henry was washed with the collected water every night for eight months because she'd heard that some babies who were bathed in rainwater spoke earlier than others. Though it hardly increased his verbal skills, after a while Viviane noticed that Henry's skin now permanently shared the crisp wet smell of Seattle rain.

Our grandmother was convinced that Henry had merely been born fluent in a language other than English. She spoke to him in French and in the Italian she still remembered from her life before. It was the most attention Emilienne ever paid to either of us, who, for our part, were much more Roux than Viviane ever was. Perhaps that was the problem. Perhaps my feathers reminded Emilienne of the days when canary feathers collected in the far corners of a Manhattan apartment. Perhaps Henry's lack of speech reminded Emilienne of the three silent translucent figures still lingering in the shadows.

When we reached the age at which most children typically begin to read, Viviane spent her nights secretly begging the sky to give Henry some form of language, some way to let her know she was doing a good job, some way to make it better. She read to him before bed and obsessed over the attentive way Henry listened to the story. She hired a specialist to come to the house and work with Henry. Still, Henry gave no sign that he knew his numbers or his letters, the word *hi* from *no*, or that he knew what the specialist meant when he held up a flash card and said, "This is a house. Can you point to the picture of the house? Henry?"

Everyone eventually gave up hoping. Our grandmother spoke to Henry less intentionally, using the partial-French, partial-English babble she used when she spoke to herself.

Our mother continued to read to us every night, usually from books that Gabe brought home from the library—books about carpentry or the wingspan of the southern brown kiwi and other flightless birds. And Henry was still bathed, of course, but in the water that flowed from the bathroom faucet and with charcoal soap to counter his fresh-rain smell. Viviane just came to accept that Henry was different from the rest. As was I.

Our mother decided that the best place for her strange children was within the confines of our house and the hill. My young childhood was spent among the familiar faces of my family: my mother, warm and smiling, a twinge of sadness hidden in the corner of her mouth; my grandmother, stern but beautiful, the grief of her past worn in lines around her eyes. There was Wilhelmina Dovewolf. Gabe, the gentle giant. And Henry, my mute, wingless half.

Some twins have their own language, their own "twin speak." There are reports of twins sharing the same dreams, of one feeling sympathetic pain when the other is injured. There was even a case of twins who died at the very same time, right down to the minute. I never experienced such a connection with Henry. My twin always lived in his own world—one that even I, in my holy, mutated form, was unable to visit. It felt as though Henry had been born my twin only to remind me of my own constant state of isolation. By the time we learned just how strong the connection between Henry and myself really was, it was almost too late.

There it was again. *Fate.* As a child, that word was often my only companion. It whispered to me from dark corners during lonely nights. It was the song of the birds in spring and the call of the wind through bare branches on a cold winter afternoon. *Fate.* Both my anguish and my solace. My escort and my cage.

Before I turned five, the religious stopped paying homage to me in clusters at the bottom of Pinnacle Lane. Eventually very few recalled the references in the local paper to the *Living Angel.* But what did that mean? Was my safety worth my isolation? It made my mother wonder if I was lonely. Or bored. Which may have been the reason Gabe decided to teach me how to fly.

Gabe spent his days off in a workshop he built behind the house, trying time and time again to build a set of wings with the same wingspan and contours as mine. He studied birds — the ones in our backyard and the ones in the books he borrowed from the elementary-school library. He measured my wings and my growth spurts, and he asked Viviane to collect my molted feathers so he could examine them more closely.

"Do you really think she needs to fly?" Viviane asked Gabe late one night. The two sat in the parlor, Viviane in the wing-backed chair across from the harpsichord, Gabe on the divan by the window. One of our cats sat in Viviane's lap. A fire crackled low in the cobblestone chimney, the soft light making the highlights in Viviane's hair glow red.

Now twenty-five, Viviane maintained her youthful appearance by keeping her hair long and applying cold cream to her cheeks with the same diligence she used to preen my feathers. She never got back into the habit of wearing shoes. Not that there was ever a reason to. My mother hadn't left the hill on Pinnacle Lane since the day she brought us home from the hospital. When she allowed herself to consider why, she realized that she was still waiting. Waiting for Jack to come back for her.

Viviane stole a glance at Gabe, whose own gaze was lost in the fire's flames. It wasn't that she didn't think Gabe was handsome. She did. Sometimes she'd catch herself studying him—the ease in his grasp as he reached for a bowl from the cupboard or the movement of the muscles in his forearms as he sanded the arched leg of a rocking chair—and she'd imagine how his hands would feel on her skin, the strength behind them as he lifted her hips to his. But before she got too far lost in her reverie, she'd remember Jack and the world would crash to the ground once again.

"It's not like she's shown any interest in it," Viviane said. This was true; once I'd learned how to tie the ribbons she sewed into the backs of all my clothes, and figured out that sleeping was most comfortable with the tip of one wing covering my nose, and how to pop open my wings with such force I could blow a candle out across the room, I figured I'd mastered everything that came with having wings. That I might fly never even crossed my mind.

"Maybe not yet. But when she does, I'll be ready," Gabe said. Gabe had decided a while ago that what Viviane's children needed was a father. He was afraid of letting us down. If the world that Gabe knew was unprepared for a Romanian beauty with royal blood, how would it treat a child with wings? Or another who preferred to be left alone, unable to stand a hug or a kiss? The problem was, he didn't know how to act like a father—it wasn't as if he'd had one himself. Instead, he improvised good parenting by strapping handmade wings to his back and taking unintentional nosedives off the roof of his woodshop. Gabe had yet to decide what to do for Henry.

"Besides," Gabe finished, "why would she have wings if she wasn't meant to fly?"

My mother didn't have an answer for that.

I acknowledged Gabe and his attempts at flight the way a legless child might view a hopeful but misguided parent buying a house full of stairs. After a while, when Gabe offered me a morning greeting, it didn't feel like he was greeting *me* but rather a giant pair of wings; no girl, just feathers.

By 1952 Pinnacle Lane, like the rest of the world, had undergone a few changes. Two years earlier the Cooper family built a house next door to ours. The father, Zeb Cooper, was a red-haired Irishman with a thick woolly beard, a large menacing stride, and a quiet demeanor. His wife,

Penelope, was a vivacious blonde quickly hired by my grandmother to help in the bakery. They had two children: a son, Rowe, who was quiet, but not quite as quiet as Henry, and a daughter, Cardigan, who had no problem declaring her age (eight) and the number of months (eleven) until her next birthday to anyone she met.

Cardigan Cooper was my first and only friend for many years.

We became such the day Cardigan peered over the fence at me where I was making mud pies in our yard and asked, "Are you a bird, an angel, or what?"

I shrugged. I wasn't sure how to answer such a question, not because I hadn't considered it, but because I didn't yet have the answer. I certainly wasn't a bird, as far as I could tell. But in the same breath, I couldn't say I was human. What did it mean to be human anyway? I knew I was different, but didn't that make me as human as anyone, or was I *something else*? I didn't know. And at only eight years old, I hadn't the time, the energy, or the mental capacity to form a more adequate response than "I think I'm just a girl." Which is what I said.

"Well, you're definitely not a bird," Cardigan answered. "Birds don't have noses, and they don't have hands or ears or nothing like that neither. So I guess you are just a girl. Do you want me to come over and play with you, or what?"

I nodded. Cardigan climbed over the fence and we shyly inspected one another.

"Lemme see you fly then," she demanded.

I shook my head.

"Why not? You ever try?"

I had not. Which was probably how my new friend quickly convinced me to climb up the cherry tree in the yard. Because, why hadn't I tried? I remember standing precariously on a branch, how the branch shook and arched beneath my weight. I remember looking down at Cardigan's blond head and her expectant face as she called, "Are you gonna jump?"

I closed my eyes, hoping both to fly and to fall, and equally terrified of both options. I jumped. And quickly landed, slightly bruised and bloody, on the ground.

Cardigan peered down at me. "Huh. Well, you definitely can't fly. I guess you really are just a girl."

I winced at the blood pooling on my scraped knee. "How d'ya know I'm not an angel?" I asked.

"Oh. That's easy, silly." Cardigan lightly touched one of my brown feathers. "Angels have white wings."

I considered my wings the way some might consider a clubfoot—a defect that had no apparent usefulness and made it impossible to walk down the street without being followed by small children's stares. Which was why I rarely fought my mother's decision to keep us cloistered in the house at the end of Pinnacle Lane. It was safer for us there. Dangers lurk around every corner for the strange. And with my feathered appendages, Henry's mute tongue, and my mother's broken heart, what else were we but strange? Sheltered beneath the shroud of my grandmother's reputation, my mother, my brother, and I remained on the hill, none of us eager to fling open the door and escape. Two of us didn't even try.

But I did.

The neighborhood kids often gathered after dinner to play a round of sardines, or some other wild game that left them all breathless—even me, my little face in the window, watching them play from the high vantage point of the hill at the end of Pinnacle Lane. There was Cardigan, of course, and her older brother, Rowe, and Jeremiah Flannery, son of Mart Flannery, who wasn't particularly nice but lived on Pinnacle Lane and so had all that was required of a playmate: availability.

It was while playing one such game that Cardigan came across an injured bird. It was sprawled on the ground along the stretch of yard that divided our house from that of our neighbor Marigold Pie. The bird was a starling. Its wings were fluttering and its head was red, most likely with blood, but how could she be sure? Did birds bleed red, like people did?

Jeremiah Flannery came up beside Cardigan. He looked down at the bird and raised his boot. We all heard the sickening snap of the bird's wing when he stomped. And we all heard Jeremiah groan from the swift blow of Cardigan's knee to his groin, a sharp leg punch that left young Jeremiah's left testicle deformed. Jerry—as he was later called—would subsequently ascribe his inability to impregnate his wife to this incident.

Hours later, after the other children returned home for dinner and their nightly baths, I snuck out my window and climbed down the old cherry tree that was planted too close to the house. With a shovel I took from the garden, I put the screeching bird out of its final misery and then dragged myself back up the hill, sobbing. It would not be the last time I would relate to flightless birds.

John Griffith shared his estranged wife's dreams for the rest of his life—nightly reveries of polar bears on black sand beaches, spiny pieces of exotic fruit, and tiny porcelain teacups. He feared sleep, dreaded nightfall like a child afraid of what might be lurking in the shadows. Sleep aids—those little white pills hidden in the medicine cabinets of so many good 1950s housewives—did nothing but make the polar bears move in slow motion.

This insomnia took a toll on the seemingly indestructible John Griffith. First he put on weight—a few pounds that made his belt a little harder to fasten. Then, just as suddenly, he lost that weight plus twenty pounds more. His complexion grew sallow. He awoke one morning to find all the hair on his head in a mound on his pillow. His sight and his hearing deteriorated. He couldn't concentrate on things the way he used to. Words seemed to melt from his lips in the middle of a conversation.

The tiny house behind the bakery fell to shambles, as

did John Griffith, who now spent all his days dressed in an old bathrobe and a pair of fluffy house shoes, no doubt once owned by his wife.

Then, one unusually sunny February morning—just a couple of weeks before Henry and I celebrated our tenth birthday—John Griffith made his way into the bakery.

My grandmother was busy writing the day's special—*mille-feuille*—on the blackboard behind the counter, and Penelope was putting the final touches on a box of chocolate éclairs for one of the Moss sisters. At the sound of the bells on the door, Penelope glanced up, ready to holler a cheerful *Be with you in a moment!* But when she saw John Griffith clutching the shabby bathrobe to his chest, the women's slippers on his feet, she could only tap Emilienne on the shoulder.

It took a minute for Emilienne to recognize the once-formidable John Griffith. When she did, she could only widen her eyes in alarm as he shuffled into the shop, pressed his nose to the countertop, and blew foggy halos against the glass. As he leaned back to admire his work, he looked up and saw Emilienne Lavender staring back at him.

"All I've ever wanted," he whispered.

Emilienne brought her hand to her throat. She glanced at Penelope and then back at the man standing before her.

"I'm sorry," she choked. "What was that?"

"All I've ever wanted in my whole damned waste of a life," he said, banging his fists against the countertop in front of him. Nervously, the Moss sister began eating one of her éclairs.

John pointed a shaking finger at Emilienne. "Is you," he said simply, then left.

For once my grandmother had nothing to say.

It was Penelope who muttered, "That poor man needs help." The Moss sister nodded in agreement.

It took a few weeks after the bakery incident for help to appear at John Griffith's door. That help brought with him a framed diploma from Whitman College; a slight twitch he'd developed in his right eye; his wife, Laura Lovelorn; and his wife's money — ready to prove just how useful he could be.

Some commented on how strange it was to see him, this grown version of Jack Griffith, taking over his father's affairs, turning the now run-down house into one far more impressive than it had ever been. The neighborhood watched, transfixed, as the kitchen was stocked with state-of-the-art appliances: a chrome toaster and coffee maker, a dishwasher, and a set of newly purchased Tupperware. There was a Formica dining set with vinyl and chrome chairs and a sunshine-yellow GE refrigerator. The living room had a Dunbar sofa and bamboo chairs, a sunburst clock, and a painting believed to be an original Jackson Pollock. The walls of the house were painted in popular shades of bubblegum pink, lime green, and pale blue; the rooms decorated with ceramic nodding dogs, pineapple ice buckets, and an ashtray in the shape of a pair of pink poodles. Jack had a sunken recreation room added to the back of the house, complete with wood paneling and wall-to-wall carpeting. A kidney-shaped swimming pool was dug into the backyard, overlooked by an angry-looking Tahitian statue; a thatched-roof bar was fully stocked with dark rum and brandy for mai tais and mojitos. There was a new washing machine and dryer, and a housemaid to use them. And in the attached garage was parked a brand-new Cadillac Eldorado, the largest on the market with its extravagant tailfins, twin bullet-tail lamps, and wide white-wall tires.

That isn't to say that Jack and his wife used her inheritance solely for selfish purposes. Far from it. After all, Laura Lovelorn was a good woman, and men are always influenced by good women. So, after the renovations on the house were paid for, Jack paid for several expensive electroshock therapies for his father. Jack then made several large donations to local charities. He and his wife threw extravagant parties at least three times a year for their neighbors and influential members of the community. And when Jack had his unstable father committed to the very psychiatric hospital they believed took in Fatima Inês, it was quite clear that Jack Griffith had finally slipped out from behind his father's shadow. It was Jack, not John, who now stood centered in the light of the frosted-pink glass ceiling lamp hanging in the center of the house's entryway.

When it was understood that Jack Griffith was back

to stay, many of his neighbors began to wonder when he would make his way over to Pinnacle Lane. But after a while, they stopped wondering. And my mother, who still hadn't left the house since our birth, had no idea that Jack had returned—after all, who would possibly tell her? Emilienne certainly wasn't going to. Emilienne started smoking cigars, perhaps hoping the heavy smell of tobacco could mask Jack's distinctive scent of soap and Turtle Wax—just in case it should find its way to Viviane's sensitive nose. And Gabe? Gabe was too busy suppressing the urge to walk up that impressive driveway and punch Jack in the face to even think about mentioning Jack's return to Viviane.

I, of course, had no idea of the personal implications of Jack Griffith's arrival, about whom I'd heard from Cardigan. But there was definitely a change in the air—and it wasn't caused by my grandmother's cigar smoke.

Cardigan and I often played the "Is that the rat fink?" game, where we rattled off the names of different men in the neighborhood we thought disreputable enough to leave my mother with two children to raise on her own. Our favorite was Amos Fields, who was actually my grandmother's age and a broken man since his son Dinky's death in the war.

"Maybe your mother was trying to comfort him," Cardigan offered.

I nodded. Maybe.

Secretly, I had always assumed Gabe was our father. After all, Gabe had been living in our house since before we were born, even after he'd made a good name for himself as a carpenter and could afford much more than a single room with a shared bathroom down the hall.

Why else would he have stayed so long?

Chapter Eleven

HENRY WAS FREED from our mother's protective rule on the hill just a few months after we turned thirteen. Thirteen years. I often wondered if my mother truly had our best interests or hers at heart when she imposed this way of life on us. Nonetheless, it was Gabe, our gentle giant, who convinced her to finally let Henry off the hill.

Gabe and Henry were quite the pair, driving around town in the old Chevy truck—Gabe with his long limbs folded uncomfortably inside the cab and Henry in the passenger seat, often patting his ears rhythmically with his hands.

On the way back from one particular outing, Gabe glanced over at Henry, who sat on the ripped upholstery drawing on a thick pad of paper with waxy crayons. Henry's drawings were hardly the scribbled circles and oblong squares typical of the creations he'd made just the day before. Gabe pulled into the driveway and leaned toward Henry. Being careful not to touch him, he asked, "What do you got there, Henry?"

Henry lifted his head and tossed the drawing pad and crayons to the side. Without a word, he jumped out of the truck and trotted up the stairs to the house.

Henry had drawn a detailed map of the neighborhood, complete with road signs and house numbers.

Later, after everyone was asleep, Gabe walked into Viviane's room and laid the drawing on her bed.

My mother pulled the cord to the lamp near her head, blinking in the light, and stared unseeing at the drawing on her bed. "What is this?"

Gabe was pacing the room. "It's Henry's."

Viviane picked up the drawing and looked at it: the house on the hill at the top of Pinnacle Lane, the bakery, the school, the accurate house numbers and road names, all ending at the newly constructed police station up on Phinney Ridge. Viviane shook her head.

"He drew it," Gabe explained.

"What? No. That's impossible." Viviane dropped the paper to the floor.

Gabe picked it up and looked at her until she exhaled, looking strange and defeated. "This is a good thing, Vivi.

Now we know there's something going on in there; we just need to find a way to reach it."

Viviane leaned toward the lamp again and pulled the cord, leaving Gabe in the dark but for the silvery light from the moon shining on Viviane's pillow. "Amazing handwriting, don't you agree?" she finally said.

"Yes. Amazing."

"Did you see that *L*? Impressive. I certainly don't make my *L*s anything like that."

"No, me neither."

Afterward, Gabe retreated downstairs to his room. He climbed into his own bed, and both he and Viviane imagined the other was asleep while they worried the night away on their own separate floors.

Gabe woke before dawn the next morning to the sound of the coffee machine percolating on the kitchen counter. Viviane was an awful insomniac. Gabe wondered if anyone else knew this about her, that while the rest of the house slept, she often spent her nights staring at the dark sky through the kitchen window. He often considered joining her. Maybe he'd finally say the right thing. Maybe he'd make her laugh. And then maybe they'd share a real conversation, something so much more than the kind of exchanges necessary between two people sharing the same living space: *Could you get more milk?* Or *No, go ahead—you can use the bathroom first.* Maybe, but Gabe was willing to admit this wouldn't be that day. Instead, he took a quick shower and made his way into the yard to watch the sun rise by himself.

At first Gabe thought he was looking at nothing more than one of the low white blooms of the peony bush. That is, until he saw a pink nose attached to it. Gabe walked across the yard, scooped the little thing up, and brought it inside. He washed the dirt from its paws in the kitchen sink and was petting it in puzzlement when Viviane walked up from the basement, carrying a basket of freshly laundered clothes.

"What is that?" Viviane asked, pausing at the kitchen sink.

"I believe it's a dog."

"Oh."

No more than seven inches long, the dog was nothing more than a pup with oversize paws and a growling belly. Viviane filled a bowl with the cream from the top of the milk bottle and placed it on the floor. They stood and watched as the dog lapped it up.

Viviane stayed in the kitchen with the dog long after Gabe left to attend to a broken gate in Marigold Pie's yard. The dog finished the cream and slid across the linoleum as it sniffed along the bottom edge of the refrigerator.

Years earlier Jack Griffith's final kiss had burned a strawberry-colored butterfly into the back of Viviane's neck. Only after applying multitudes of rose oil to the spot did it slowly fade to a dark beige mark that itched when she was nervous. She was scratching that spot when she heard the sound of shuffling feet coming from outside the kitchen.

Viviane set a piece of toast with orange marmalade on the table for Henry. It was his usual breakfast, the only thing he would eat for his morning meal. She resisted the urge to muss his hair when he sat down.

While he ate, Henry watched the puppy climb awkwardly into the laundry basket, rub its head against Viviane's clean white towels, sigh contentedly, and fall into a deep puppy sleep. Cautiously Henry got up from the table. Then, awkwardly folding his oversize teenage limbs beneath him, Henry sat down beside the puppy in the laundry basket. Henry reached over and ran a finger down the puppy's back and circled the goldenrod spot on its side. The puppy opened an eye. Henry closed one of his own. The puppy scratched its ear. Henry scratched his. Henry yawned. The puppy yawned, making a squeaky noise. That prompted Henry to fall over onto the floor, where he laughed silently. After he recovered, Henry took a deep breath and declared, *"Trouver!"*

At that, Viviane dropped the bowl she'd been holding to the floor. Amid the shattering porcelain, she said, "Well, yes." And whether it was a declaration meant for Henry, the dog, or perhaps a little of both, from then on the dog was known as Trouver, the French word meaning "to find."

Emilienne wasn't entirely correct in asserting that Henry solely understood one language over another; it was that he favored certain words from each. For example,

Henry preferred when someone offered to help him with his *moufles*, not his *mittens*; made him *petit pois*, not *peas*, for dinner; and served *pamplemousse* rather than *grapefruit* for lunch. He liked when Emilienne used the word *impeccable* instead of *clean* and was partial to a cup and spoon over a fork, knife, or plate. He liked *driftwood*, *trifle*, and *cavernous* and later would hate the word *pubic*, and prefer *mamelon* to *nipple*.

Henry went on to communicate in other unique ways. Good was *caramel*, and bad was *fumigate*. He called Gabe *cedar*, which we attributed to the way Gabe's hands smelled after a day in his woodshop. I was *pinna*, the Latin word for feather. Our mother, *étoile de mer*, which was French for starfish. No one could explain that one.

Chapter Twelve

THOSE BORN UNDER Pacific Northwest skies are like daffodils: they can achieve beauty only after a long, cold sulk in the rain. Henry, our mother, and I were Pacific Northwest babies. At the first patter of raindrops on the roof, a comfortable melancholy settled over the house. The three of us spent dark, wet days wrapped in old quilts, sitting and sighing at the watery sky.

Viviane, with her acute gift for smell, could close her eyes and know the season just by the smell of the rain. Summer rain smelled like newly clipped grass, like mouths stained red with berry juice—blueberries, raspberries, blackberries. It smelled like late nights spent pointing constellations out from their starry guises, freshly washed laundry drying outside on the line, like barbecues and stolen kisses in a 1932 Ford Coupe.

The first of the many autumn rains smelled smoky, like a doused campsite fire, as if the ground itself had been aflame during those hot summer months. It smelled like burnt piles of collected leaves, the cough of a newly revived chimney, roasted chestnuts, the scent of a man's hands after hours spent in a woodshop.

Fall rain was not Viviane's favorite.

Rain in the winter smelled simply like ice, the cold air burning the tips of ears, cheeks, and eyelashes. Winter rain was for hiding in quilts and blankets, for tying woolen scarves around noses and mouths—the moisture of rasping breaths stinging chapped lips.

The first bout of warm spring rain caused normally respectable women to pull off their stockings and run through muddy puddles alongside their children. Viviane was convinced it was due to the way the rain smelled: like the earth, tulip bulbs, and dahlia roots. It smelled like the mud along a riverbed, like if she opened her mouth wide enough, she could taste the minerals in the air. Viviane could feel the heat of the rain against her fingers when she pressed her hand to the ground after a storm.

But in 1959, the year Henry and I turned fifteen, those warm spring rains never arrived. March came and went without a single drop falling from the sky. The air that month smelled dry and flat. Viviane would wake up in the morning unsure of where she was or what she should be doing. Did the wash need to be hung on the line? Was there firewood to be brought in from the woodshed and stacked on the back porch? Even nature seemed confused. When the rains didn't appear, the daffodil bulbs dried to dust in their beds of mulch and soil. The trees remained leafless, and the squirrels, without acorns to feed on and with nests to build, ran in confused circles below the bare limbs. The only person who seemed unfazed by the disappearance of the rain was my grandmother. Emilienne was not a Pacific Northwest baby nor a daffodil. Emilienne was more like a petunia. She needed the water but could do without the puddles and wet feet. She didn't have any desire to ponder the gray skies. She found all the rain to be a bit of an inconvenience, to be honest.

On the last day it had rained—a seemingly normal day in February as it turned out—Emilienne got up, as she did every other morning, at exactly four o'clock. She looked out at the dark, wet sky and sighed. She pulled her boots from the mudroom and wrapped a rain bonnet around her hair, musing that it was something old ladies did. Because of the rain, it took Emilienne longer than usual to reach the bakery's door. Wilhelmina was already waiting for her when she arrived. Penelope too.

After the war, Emilienne had found herself competing with the growing availability of prepackaged treats—Jell-O instant pudding, Minute Tapioca, Reddi-Wip—not to mention the return of sliced bread. In desperation, she'd brought out her French *maman*'s recipes and replaced the jars of preserves and slabs of salted meat she'd sold during the Depression with *mousse au chocolat*, *feuilletage*, and *poire belle-Hélène*. In 1951 she purchased an old Divco truck once used to deliver milk and had Gabe paint *Emilienne's Bakery* in elaborate script across its side. She continued to use the old-fashioned brick oven, insisting that it was the brick that gave her bread its distinctive flavor. She ignored Wilhelmina's claim that a newer metal oven wouldn't make a lick of difference. The success of the bakery grew.

When Penelope Cooper was hired, she was just a young mother with very little baking experience, but the bakery needed the help and she needed the work. After so many years of working as a pair, it took a while for the two older women to get used to their new team of three. In time the three women could perform their morning schedule flawlessly; without words or even gestures, they knew what was needed. Hiring Penelope Cooper also proved to be a wise business decision. No man within walking distance could resist a daily dose of the blond woman's infectious laugh. When they bought a box of chocolate éclairs for their wives, they fantasized about licking a swipe of custard from the crease between Penelope's lovely breasts, of hand-feeding her every creamy morsel.

After stomping the water from her boots on that last rainy day of February 1959, Emilienne moved to the back to roll out the cheese rolls and knot the brioche, to shape the sourdough loaves and baguettes. Penelope mixed the dough for the scones and whole-grain breads. By seven AM, the specials of the day were written on the blackboard behind the counter, the smudges wiped clean from the windows, and the first loaves of the day rising in their bread pans. With a razor blade, Emilienne scored each one, listening for the audible sigh that came with each slice, as if the bread had been holding its breath. Emilienne slid the loaves into the oven, then sprayed the hot oven bricks with water to create the steam that helped form a perfect crust on each loaf.

Once the display cases were lined with paper doilies, and the breads and pastries put out for sale, Emilienne left Penelope to mind the front counter and joined Wilhelmina in the back, who was busily preparing *le dessert du jour.* Wilhelmina pulled out a flour sifter, a mixing bowl, and a baking pan. She quickly whipped up batter for a chocolate cake, poured it into the pan, and stuck it in the oven, where it would bake until perfect, the knife coming out clean on the first try.

The secret to a good chocolate cake had nothing to do with the actual cake. No, the secret was in the icing, and caramel frosting was Emilienne's specialty. It was the cream, the cream that could make it too heavy or too thin. With just the right amount of cream, she could make the frosting so enticing, so divinely rich and sweet, that it caused people to laugh out loud with just one lick of a finger.

On that last day of rain, while the chocolate cake was baking, Emilienne was pouring the cream for the caramel frosting with one hand and whisking with the other when she heard the jangle of the bells on the door. Marigold Pie had come into the shop for one of her regular penitential visits.

A devout member of the Lutheran church, Marigold Pie was always the first to dutifully welcome new neighbors. When the Lavenders moved onto Pinnacle Lane (before the whispers of *witch* followed my grandmother wherever she went), it was practical Marigold Pie who helped the baker's young wife get rid of the fire ants in the pantry and remove the hornet's nest from the porch eaves. In church Marigold read along from her red leather Bible with the weekly Scripture passages, and for longer than anyone could remember, she had been in charge of the confirmation classes. Helpful, capable, but hardly known for being personable, she objected to interfaith marriage, coffee stains on white gloves, and any form of appetite, food-related or otherwise. Fellow parishioners used to joke that Marigold slept in a position that vaguely emulated the Crucifixion. And they were right.

The night before her wedding night, a young Marigold painstakingly embroidered the nuptial sheets with tiny indecipherable doves and lambs, hoping to evoke Ines del Campo, Catholic saint of betrothed couples, bodily purity, and rape victims. She was intimate with her husband only while using that sheet, revealing to him only the parts of her body necessary for such an act. They never had any children.

After her husband's death, Marigold lived on a diet of oatmeal, which she ate raw, and tall glasses of skim milk. She never licked the spoon after making cookies or dipped her finger in the frosting of a child's birthday cake. She weighed a whopping seventy-five pounds. She shopped for her own clothing in the children's department at the Bon Marché downtown and weighed her shoes down with pebbles on windy days.

Emilienne considered her own shape. She'd always been tall and thought she'd grown quite nicely into her height with age. Her once-pointed chin had developed a slight roundness, and her arms had become nice and soft, which she easily maintained with the occasional cinnamon bun or sugar cookie. She wouldn't give up that ripeness for anything, especially not Marigold's teacake-size breasts.

My grandmother found the effect that desserts had on her neighbor highly amusing. The possibility of tempting Marigold Pie to lose control drove Emilienne to create evermore fantastic treats for the bakery's menu: caramelized *crème brûlée*, napoleons, apple *tartes tatins.* It was a twisted sort of habit—one she should have put an end to years ago.

On that last day it rained, Marigold came bustling into the store as usual to sniff at the trays of shell-shaped madeleines, glazed *palmiers*, and bite-size squares of cheesecake, testing her self-control. Emilienne, still mixing the bowl of frosting, watched from the back as her neighbor frowned at the gooey mounds of cinnamon rolls, defied the creamy waves atop the lemon meringue pie, and scowled at the plate of *petits fours glacés*. Always a customer favorite, each small cake was wrapped in soft green, pink, or yellow fondant and topped with a candy rose or other sugar embellishment, looking like a sweet, tasty birthday present.

Before her neighbor had a chance to object, Emilienne marched out to the front of the store and stuck the frosting-covered spoon into Marigold's mouth.

Few people know this feeling: what it is to give in to a long-denied desire, to finally have a taste of the forbidden. After swallowing that mouthful of frosting, Marigold stumbled backward out of the store. She forgot her umbrella, which she'd left in the corner, but arrived home completely dry just the same. In a daze, Marigold walked straight to her kitchen, tracking muddy footprints across her spotless linoleum floor. She pulled out her dusty cookbooks and began marking pages of the sweets she never allowed herself to eat. Then she tied an apron around her waist and set to making a coconut cake. Later, still wearing the apron—now covered in gratings of coconut and splashes of vanilla extract—Marigold ate the cake: the whole cake, including every lick of frosting left in the mixing bowl and on her fingertips.

Over the next few weeks, Marigold Pie became Emilienne's best customer. She was the first to arrive at the shop every morning, sometimes even before Emilienne or Wilhelmina, licking her lips in anxious anticipation for a gooey bite of *mille-feuille*. She rarely made it back home without delving into that white box, tied with string and holding so many mouthwatering treats. Her favorites were the multicolored *macarons*, so delicately crunchy on the outside, so moist and chewy on the inside. Marigold often had to buy three. The first she ate in the bakery, the round dome top still warm from the oven, the scent of rising bread in her nostrils. The second she kept for the walk back, licking the sweet filling from her fingers. The third she tried to save for later, though, more often than not, Marigold arrived home with an empty box and a very full belly.

It became clear to everyone that Marigold Pie was changing. Her cheeks were now plump and rosy. A soft roundness had developed around her middle and the backs of her arms. One morning she awoke to find that her wedding ring, which had circled the ring finger of her right hand for forty years, was too tight. She had to pull the embedded metal from her finger with a pair of pliers. Getting dressed became laborious, what with all that new weight attached to her bottom. The soft mounds of her breasts seemed to find their way out of even the highest-necked dress. Men around the neighborhood now took a second look at Marigold when she passed on the street, and several boys found they were thinking of Widow Pie when they satisfied themselves at night—not that any of them would ever have admitted to it.

Marigold, it seemed, did not intend to stop eating. By the end of April, she could no longer cross her legs or tie her shoes. Her eyes, nose, and mouth became tiny pinpricks in a mound of billowing flesh, and the tops of her arms resembled thick, red sausages. Sundays no longer found Marigold at church, perched in her usual pew with her white gloves and red leather Bible. She was quite content to spend her days in bed, balancing piles of *macarons* across her pillow, plucking them one by one from the stack, and plopping them into her insatiable mouth. Marigold's neighbors became concerned.

The day Marigold's sister, Iris Sorrows, came to find what had prompted the neighbors to raise the alarm, she took one look at this bloated version of her sister and stifled a short scream. Then she called her son and insisted he come stay with his aunt for a while.

"Don't worry, dear," she said, patting Marigold's puffy hand. "Nathaniel can surely fix this." Then she went to make a pot of tea, for no other reason than to keep from staring at Marigold.

Iris was quite confident that if anyone could do something about her sister, it was her son, a very pious young man. As a boy, Nathaniel's simple "hello" prompted neighbors to blurt out long-hidden sins or to donate new clothing to the local homeless shelter. Just the sight of him crossing the street with his mother led adulterous men to become celibate and avid hunters to develop appetites satisfied only by vegetarian recipes.

Iris Sorrows and her son lived in the broken part of Seattle, far from the magnificent Catholic church in Pioneer Square. So Iris would pack sandwiches every

Sunday morning and set out with her young son for the long trek to Saint James Cathedral. When they arrived, they sat on the steps outside and ate the sandwiches before venturing in for noonday Mass. Iris wasn't Catholic, nor could she understand the Latin recited throughout the service. She claimed she took comfort in the ambience of the holy place.

This was a lie.

Iris visited the Catholic cathedral not to light a candle for a beloved or to kneel in prayer, but to stand at the foot of the Holy Mother in a corner of the church. Iris associated deeply with the tragic beauty of the statue: the weeping eyes, the open palms, the blue folds of Mary's skirts. She searched the eyes of Mary, the Mother of God, for a recognition of the self she saw reflected in the mirror every day and ultimately convinced herself that *her* child, too, had been conceived by the seed of the Holy Spirit, and not by an evening of sinful and confusing passion with an older married friend of her parents.

Iris had Nathaniel baptized when he was five. At the time, Nathaniel mistook the baptism water for his mother's tears. As Nathaniel grew, so did Iris's belief that her son had been cut from the same cloth as Saint Anthony of Padua. So she made sure he received the finest Catholic education, and she kept a journal of the little miracles that occurred in his presence—for the eventuality of his nomination to sainthood.

By age twenty-nine, Nathaniel Sorrows had been rejected by three seminary schools. He continued to live with his mother and spent both his days and nights reading Scripture and preparing for the holy work his mother so firmly believed he was meant to do. He allowed himself an hour's break at the neighboring pub each evening for a bowl of soup and a handful of table crackers.

It should be noted that Nathaniel hadn't grown into a handsome man. Nevertheless, there was something decidedly attractive about him. Young coeds from the nearby college were drawn to his table not with the same intensity they might approach boys who were marriage material, but rather with the determination of a ranch hand about to break in their first horse. They never ended up staying at Nathaniel's table for long. If he had been any other man, they might have handed him their phone numbers. Instead, they went back to their rooms to throw away the contraceptives locked in their armoires and to call their grandmothers on the hallway community phone.

When Nathaniel arrived at his aunt's house on Pinnacle Lane, carrying all of his belongings in one tiny suitcase, he arrived as a man many believed had never used his hands to point his genitals toward the toilet bowl, had never glanced down the cashier's shirt as she made change, had never become angry at a traffic light, and never wanted more than what was given to him.

When Nathaniel Sorrows arrived at the house at the base of the hill on Pinnacle Lane, he exited the taxi and glanced around at the quiet neighborhood. And what did he see, this seemingly pious man? He spotted a pair of white and brown speckled wings behind the parched lilac bush in the next yard over.

And at that moment, an entirely new and unfamiliar feeling stirred inside him.

Chapter Thirteen

IF MY MOTHER KEPT a list of the reasons she confined me to the house on the hill, she'd have a length of paper that could stretch all the way down Pinnacle Lane and trail into the waters of the Puget Sound. It could choke passing sea life. It could flap in the wind like a giant white flag of surrender atop our house's widow's walk. To put it simply, my mother worried. She worried about our neighbors' reactions. Would they break me with their disparaging glances, their cruel intolerance? She worried I was just like every other teenage girl, all tender heart and fragile ego. She worried I was more myth and figment than flesh and blood. She worried about my calcium levels, my protein levels, even my reading levels. She worried she couldn't protect me from all of the things that had hurt her: loss and fear, pain and love.

Most especially from love.

During that spring when the rains had disappeared, Cardigan and I spent most afternoons sprawled in the browning grass in my yard, pretending to study as Cardigan beguiled me with tales of her latest beau.

By the tender age of fifteen, my best friend, Miss Cardigan Cooper, was already well versed in the complicated attributes of physical love. Jeremiah Flannery, the boy who'd once crushed a bird's wing under his boot, was her latest acquisition.

"The poor bastard follows me everywhere." Cardigan snorted. "And you should see the way he stares at me. I practically have to wipe the drool from his chin before I can kiss him. It's pathetic." She smiled wickedly. "I love it."

I laughed as I attempted to make sense of Cardigan's haphazard algebra notes.

That was another thing my mother worried about: my education. She modeled my daily home-schooling lessons off of Cardigan's messy composition books.

"Is this a five or a three?" I asked.

"No idea. Looks like an *R* to me." Cardigan arched her back like a cat and threw her arm over her eyes to shield them from the sun. I rolled my eyes. It was already late April, and though finals weren't far off, Cardigan seemed quite content to maintain her C-minus average.

On the other side of the house, my mother was on the front porch, washing the windows in soapy methodical circles, when Henry came flying around the corner and screamed, "Pinna hurt! Pinna hurt!" His eyes were wide with fear. Trouver was right behind him, barking madly.

In one fluid motion, Viviane dropped the soapy sponge, flew down the porch stairs and around to the backyard to find me, leaving Henry on the porch, pounding his ears with his open palms. As she ran, my mother thought, *This is it. This is the reason not to love. If I didn't love, then whatever I find, no matter how awful, wouldn't hurt.*

My mother found me lazing in the grass with Cardigan. She reached down, grabbed my arm, and yanked me upright. "What happened?" she asked, frantically looking me over for signs of injury.

"Nothing," I replied, blinking.

Viviane dropped her hands, suddenly aware of the wild beating of her heart, the labored pull of her lungs. "Are you sure?" she asked.

I exchanged a look with Cardigan. "Yeah. We're both fine. Are you?"

My mother looked me over closely before turning away. "Sorry. I thought—never mind." She sighed. "Do you girls need anything?" she asked as an afterthought. I shook my head.

Good, she must have thought, and slowly made her way back to Henry, who was frantically painting a map of our neighborhood across the front porch in soapy water.

It was just after that that Cardigan and I saw a taxicab pull up to Marigold Pie's house. A man got out and retrieved a raggedy-looking suitcase from the trunk, then gave a halfhearted wave to the cab as it pulled away. Though I didn't know it at the time, Marigold's visitor carried a well-used journal in his back pocket. He took the journal everywhere he went.

Curious and impulsive, I dashed down the hill and ducked behind a lilac bush near the road to spy. The man walked slowly up Marigold's front walk, taking in our quiet neighborhood. He paused for a moment, shielded his eyes from the sun, and stared up at my house at the top of the hill. Before he continued into Marigold's house, I swore he saw me hiding there in the lilacs.

The door closed behind him, and I ran back up the hill to Cardigan, who looked bemused.

"Who do you suppose that was?" I asked breathlessly.

Cardigan shrugged. "What a dreamboat, though, don't you think?"

I glanced back down the hill, my head reeling with the thought of this man having seen me. Could he have liked what he saw? "Oh," I murmured, blushing. "I don't know."

Years ago, when Emilienne's family was still whole and living in that tenement in Beauregard's Manhatine, Emilienne's *maman* spent a good deal of her time finding scraps of fabric to contribute to the quilts that were intended for her daughters' dowries. The quilts were meant to be enclosed in elaborately hand-carved *trousseaux*, along with lace pillowcases and heavy silver flatware. They were also meant to be split fairly between three daughters, not left as an inheritance for the lone survivor, but Emilienne had long ago learned that perfection was hardly something to expect in life.

Each quilt carried a telling name, and years later each would find its way onto an appropriate bed—"Bright Hopes" for Viviane before Jack, "Broken Path" for after, "Dove in the Window" for me, and the "Crazy Quilt" for Henry.

Emilienne herself slept under a pile of plain woolen blankets.

Emilienne straightened the quilt on Henry's bed, being careful not to disturb anything. Viviane all but ran the house those days, but occasionally Emilienne could find a menial task to fill her time and keep her mind off things she'd rather not think about. From out of the corner of her eye, she could see the faint outline of a man illuminated by the thin triangle of sun coming through the window. She'd learned over the thirty-six years since his death that the more she ignored him, the louder the ghost of René tried to speak. If Emilienne had looked at him, she would have seen the place where his mouth used to be. He seemed to be yelling right then and gesturing wildly out the window with his hands.

Instead, she gave a pillow one final thump and, with practiced immunity, stepped right through the apparition in the corner, never stopping to find out what he was trying to say this time. If she had . . . well, it's hardly worth fretting over *if*s and *when*s.

C'est la vie, as she might say.

Downstairs Emilienne found Henry at the dining-room table, licking frosting off a spoon. *They* were there as well. All three of them — René, who dogged her steps, along with Margaux and the canary, Pierette. And someone Emilienne had never seen before — a small, dark-haired child with thick eyebrows and chapped lips. The child ran her hand along the collection of antique teapots atop the oak hutch, her translucent fingers tracing the edges of the porcelain pots.

It wasn't just that they were *there.* That she'd gotten used to, along with Pierette's incessant chirping, René's mutilated face, the hole in Margaux's chest where her heart used to be. No, the truly awful part was that Henry was *talking with them.*

Well, he was talking with René, the only one who spoke. Even if Emilienne had allowed herself to hear him, René was hardly easy to understand, what with his not having an actual mouth and all. But Henry and René didn't seem to have any problem communicating with one another.

René would mutter something and Henry would nod, as if in agreement. "Bee in the bush and cat on the wall," Henry said seriously around the spoonful of frosting in his mouth.

Emilienne went into the kitchen and got out a plate

for a slice of the chocolate cake she'd left on the counter.

The ghost child followed her into the kitchen. With black, vacant eyes she watched Emilienne. And though Emilienne tried to block it out, she heard the child's quiet whisper clearly: "Ashes to ashes, dust to dust."

Very few in the neighborhood then knew or remembered the story of Fatima Inês de Dores and her ship captain brother — the way the child paced the widow's walk awaiting his return, the Communion wafer that burst into flame when it touched her tongue. Some mistook the story of the siblings for a fairy tale, even congratulating themselves for thinking up such a vivid bedtime story to tell their children. Emilienne knew better than to disparage something as powerful as a fairy tale, and she never forgot the tale of the ill-fated little girl who once roamed the hallways of the house on the hill. Or rather, it seemed, still did.

Emilienne coughed a mouthful of ashes into the air.

She wiped away the gray soot stuck to her teeth, left the cake in the kitchen, and joined Henry in the dining room, where he'd just finished his final spoonful of frosting. Henry went to his grandmother, took her face between his hands, and said, "The Sad Man needs you to know."

Startled, Emilienne looked to her siblings. The Sad Man? René? But they were gone. Only the young dark-haired specter stared back at her from the corner of the room.

"Yes?" Emilienne whispered, looking into Henry's wide eyes.

"There's red on the floor and feathers everywhere," he replied.

And with that, Fatima Inês faded away.

After Fatima's visit, Henry carried on an endlessly looping conversation that sounded a bit like this:

"Henry, what do you want on your toast this morning?"

"There's a bee in the bush!" he insisted.

"Jam? Butter? Honey?"

"And a cat on the wall!"

"What about cereal instead?"

"There's red on the floor and feathers everywhere!"

Then he would tear around the house calling, *"Pinna hurt! Pinna hurt!"* Trouver barking wildly behind him.

From the personal diary of Nathaniel Sorrows:

April 29, 1959

In the past, staying with my aunt Marigold meant sleeping on starched sheets, and it meant the musty stench of her potpourri seeping into the fabric of my clothes. It meant early morning services at the Lutheran church down the street and afternoon tea served on my aunt's finest china, but without the customary array of butter cookies or crumpets with marmalade. This time I arrived to a house in disarray—dust had gathered atop her decorative knickknacks, and the furniture had lost its usual pine-scented shine. And it seems my once-righteous aunt now has an appetite only for desserts: raspberry-jam-filled scones, maraschino cherry pudding, and butterscotch brownies fill the kitchen counters and the shelves of the refrigerator. It is rare to see her without her mouth full, without her swollen fingers brushing crumbs from her lips. She keeps tiny chocolates beneath the pillows on her bed. Her sheets are perpetually smeared with caramel and toffee and cherry liqueur. Once I even found a slice of chocolate cake, the frosting completely licked off, hidden under her bed.

Exactly how I am meant to help my now-fat aunt, I don't know. Of course, I admit to no one that I am at a loss. I've never had to work *at helping someone turn away from sin; for reasons known only to Him, my effect on people has always been somewhat spontaneous. Mother says it isn't for me to question* how *the Lord does His work through me; it is enough knowing that He does.*

Therefore, I know that He would not place something or someone so blatantly holy before me to disregard. An Angel, defined as I remember it, is an agent of God sent forth to execute His purposes. It is supremely fitting that this Angel should appear on the street where His most reverent follower is staying, where I have been struggling to hear His call and execute His purpose. It is true that I looked at her, perhaps much longer than appropriate, but on the day I arrived and caught my first glimpse of those wings and that beautiful angelic face, I thought I was going mad!

Chapter Fourteen

TROUVER HAD GROWN fast into his big paws. We had hoped he'd remain small and manageable, but once he passed one hundred pounds, we knew we weren't dealing with a Maltese or a shih tzu. Trouver was a Great Pyrenees—a purebred at that—which was quite remarkable considering he'd been found rifling through the peony bush in our backyard. His pelt resembled that of a white musk ox, and when he shed, tufts of fur the size of small rabbits blew like white tumbleweeds across the wood floors of our house.

Trouver and Henry were inseparable and often walked not dog following boy but side by side. They were walking in this way—a strange set of conjoined twins—when they strode into the woodshop where Gabe was nursing a bleeding lip after another failed attempt at flight.

Gabe had built the first set of wings out of lacquered cheesecloth stretched over a bamboo frame. When that didn't work, he tried wicker—a weave of willow bark and madrone twigs—but each of those creations proved too heavy. Another set he made out of aluminum wire and gauze, which sent Gabe spiraling into a panicky nosedive after he launched himself off the roof of the shed.

Gabe dragged himself back into the woodshop, bleeding from the mouth and glad that only Henry, and neither my mother nor I, had witnessed that test flight. "Failure number four," Gabe muttered, and he tossed the broken wings onto the growing trash pile in the corner of the shop. In doing so, he disturbed a bat living in the rafters of the woodshop. He followed the bat as it made its way outside, and when Gabe saw the bat's wings beat against the night sky, he realized he'd been looking for inspiration in the wrong place. He also decided he had to catch that bat.

"We need your mother's colander," Gabe said to Henry. "And a large supply of beetles, mosquitoes, flies, and—moths. Like that one!" Gabe reached out and grabbed a brown-winged insect in midflight. He carried it into the kitchen and placed it in an empty coffee can, the fluttery drum of its wings echoing against the tin sides. He dug through the cupboards until he found the colander. In the living room, he thumbed through the books on birds he received by mail order years before until he found what he was looking for: a short section on bats included in the back of one.

From a second-floor window, my mother watched Henry in the yard snatch moths out of the air.

Viviane suddenly recalled the day Jack left for college. She remembered the glass jar he presented her, and then watching as he made his way back down the hill, and the look of the taillights of his father's Coupe.

There was a dragonfly inside the jar. Viviane had never seen one so close before—its green iridescent wings looked far too fragile to be capable of flight.

Wilhelmina later told Viviane the superstition about dragonflies. "It's a saying so old I don't think anyone knows where it came from anymore," she said.

"How does it go?" Viviane asked.

Wilhelmina's eyes twinkled. "Catch a dragonfly, wed within the year."

Viviane's dragonfly had died within the week.

Downstairs she asked Gabe, "What's Henry doing?"

"Bats and birds share a similar wing-beat pattern," Gabe read from the book in his hands. He looked up at Viviane excitedly. "I'm going to catch a bat. Henry's catching bugs to feed it."

"Why not just catch a bird?" Viviane asked Gabe. "You can do that in the daylight."

Gabe glanced up from his book. "I can't replicate the feathers. I tried."

It took three nights to catch the bat. In the end, the little mammal made its own way into an ancient rusted birdcage Gabe had found in the basement crusted with old crow and dove feathers. Every night after dinner, Henry fed insects to the bat through the bars and Gabe worked on a new set of wings.

Chapter Fifteen

I HAD BEEN ASLEEP when I heard the tap of Cardigan's finger against the windowpane. She'd climbed up the cherry tree outside my bedroom window and breathlessly confirmed what we had both assumed since the day she had kneed Jeremiah in the groin.

"One of 'em looks like a fig—a pink shriveled-up fig," she said.

"Yuck." After letting her in, I climbed back into bed and wrapped my wings around me like a security blanket. "What's it supposed to look like?"

Cardigan shrugged. "Not like that."

My bedroom was typical of the late 1950s. There were stacks of fashion magazines on the floor and a vanity with a lace ruffle. A full-length mirror stood opposite my twin bed, which was covered in pillows and a quilt patterned with colored triangles. There was nothing about it that would indicate I was anything but a normal teenage girl. But there wasn't a pink princess phone for late-night conversations or a pair of saddle shoes, soles worn from doing the hand jive at high-school dances. I had little connection with the outside world; there wasn't any need for such things. Instead, there was a window where I spent my nights looking out at Salmon Bay and watching the ships drift by. And there were piles of feathers, which gathered mysteriously in my room's lonely corners.

"So, are you and Jeremiah still an item?" I asked.

"God, no." Cardigan pulled a tube of lipstick from her coat pocket. She slicked the gloss across her lips then tossed it to me. "Here, try it on. I snagged it from my mom." But I placed it on my bedside table. Cardigan smiled at her pretty blond reflection in my mirror and wiped the red stain from her teeth with the side of her finger.

I had long dark hair like my grandmother, but whereas Emilienne tied hers in a severe chignon at the base of her neck, I wore mine in a high ponytail tied with a black ribbon. According to Cardigan, the ribbon was the perfect accessory for me.

"You gotta accentuate what you got," Cardigan said. "And you, girl, have got *whimsical* beauty." She flicked my wingtips with her finger. "You gotta admit, it's definitely a strange kind of attractiveness."

A sharp *ping* reverberated on my window. Cardigan flung open the window and made a wild gesture with her hands.

"I told my brother to meet me here," Cardigan said.

Rowe Cooper was seventeen. He drove the delivery truck for my grandmother's bakery and had already received a full scholarship from Boston University for his unusual capacity for astronomical facts and figures. Most of his belongings were already packed and labeled in cardboard boxes. Rowe wasn't nearly as popular as his sister. He was tall and lanky, with a thick mop of curly black hair, and he always wore an old peacoat from his father's navy days, even during Seattle's summer months. He also stuttered. He was handsome, though, with deep-blue eyes and a quick smile.

Not that I'd noticed.

Cardigan threw her legs over the side of the open window. "A bunch of kids are going to the reservoir tonight," she said to me.

Like every other batch of teenagers, those who lived near Pinnacle Lane had a spot where ridiculous and foolhardy acts occurred. Instead of a drive-in movie theater or soda shop, the town reservoir—with its moonlit water and shadowy edges—was the perfect place for such imperative nonsense. By this time, the old caretaker and his wife had grown cantankerous but deaf, so the kids knew they only had to be quiet when they passed by the little white house. I, of course, had never been there. But I'd heard so many stories, I believed I could see the lights from the caretaker's house, could count the number of beer cans left on the reservoir's edge, could hear the kids' drunken laughter.

I found it ironic that I should be blessed with wings and yet feel so constrained, so trapped. It was because of my condition, I believe, that I noticed life's ironies a bit more often than the average person. I collected them: how love arrived when you least expected it, how someone who said he didn't want to hurt you eventually would.

When we were younger, my grandmother kept a small flock of chickens in a hutch Gabe built beside the workshop. I liked to watch them peck about the yard, flightless birds moving in nervous groups and scratching the ground with reptilian feet. I named them after places I would never visit: Pisa, Aiea, Nepal, Vermont.

Emilienne eventually complained that their eggs were hardly worth the mess they made of the yard and so decided to have the chickens slaughtered. Gabe caught them and took them, one by one, into the woodshop and snapped their necks with his large hands. Gabe had no reason to think that I might be hiding behind a pile of rubble in the woodshop, watching the end of each hen's life. What horrified me the most—what would haunt me for years to come — was how each bird flapped and flapped her wings, expecting them to carry her to freedom. I never could eat chicken after that. It seemed cannibalistic.

As Cardigan lowered herself onto the branches of the cherry tree outside my window, I got out of bed, shook out my wings, and said, "I'm coming with you."

Cardigan paused, stared at me, then pulled herself back into the room. "Cool."

It took us half an hour to concoct a harness strong enough to pin down my wings. We made it using an old leather bridle Rowe grabbed from the workshop behind my house and tossed up to us. He waited for us in the dark yard, the end of his lit cigarette glowing red.

The harness kept my wings folded flat to my back, but it was painful. I finally understood the phrase *seeing stars.* An old musty cloak we found in a forgotten hall closet hid them completely. The cloak was emerald-green wool with a satin lining and a giant hood that fell down my back.

We snuck off the hill and walked silently down Pinnacle Lane. We passed Marigold Pie's house, then the Fields' house. We passed the spot where the rough road turned to pavement and where a pair of worn sneakers hanging from an overhead power line danced in the wind. I was sure the other two could hear the quickening of my heart as I stepped farther and farther away from the only place I had ever known. We passed my grandmother's bakery and the house that stood behind it, the Lutheran church, the elementary school, and the spot where Rowe and Cardigan waited for the bus that took them to school. We passed the remodeled police station with its brick walls and clear, shiny windows, and the cluster of identical new homes that sprang up after the war. We passed the old deaf couple's little white house and the place where my mother once watched the moon disappear. Then we arrived at the reservoir, a dark spot guarded by maple trees and surly high-school students.

Much to my relief, no one seemed to notice me or that I was wearing a large and unfashionable cloak. Cardigan moved to join a group that was building pyramids out of empty beer cans on the reservoir's cement ledge.

"Maybe this wasn't such a good idea," I muttered, backing away until I bumped into someone behind me. Rowe.

He smiled down at me. "N-nah, it was a p-p-perfectly good idea. It t-takes a while to acclimate oneself to the d-deb-bauchery of wild t-t-teenage life. Come on," he said, and, taking me by the elbow, steered me to a secluded spot beneath the trees.

Years later the lights of the growing city would erase the stars from the sky, but back then they shone through the branches like jailed fireflies.

"Weird, isn't it?" Rowe sat next to me. "H-how it's sup-po-posed to be spring, but doesn't l-look l-l-like it?" I watched the bulge of his Adam's apple jump as he breathed and swallowed. He was right. Without the rain, it seemed spring would never come and the stars would remain forever imprisoned by the leafless branches.

"The only constellation I know is that one." I pointed to a cluster of stars that made the shape of a ladle.

Rowe swallowed hard. "A-actually, the B-Big Dipper is a p-p-part of Ursa Major — the Great Bear. It makes up his b-body and t-ta-ail. See his legs?"

"Oh, yeah," I murmured. "There it is." It did look like a bear, a big white bear, head down, rooting through the snow. "I wonder why I haven't seen that before."

"Maybe you just needed someone to help you see the parts that aren't so obvious."

I looked at him. "You didn't stutter."

Rowe ducked his head. "I don't always."

"Ava!" Cardigan commanded from the reservoir's edge. "Come over here!"

I pulled my knees to my chest, nervously tugged the cloak tighter around my shoulders. I shook my head. Not just yet.

"Are you afraid they won't like you?" Rowe asked.

"Oh." My eyes widened. "I hadn't even thought of that. What if they don't like me?"

"It's hard to imagine anyone not liking you," he said candidly, meeting my eyes. He cleared his throat. "Anyway, what's r-really bothering you?"

"It's . . . dangerous for someone like me to be out in the open."

As if in response, my wings started to flutter beneath their shroud. I gave the cloak a good yank.

"Someone like you? Someone different, you mean?"

I shrugged. "Yes," I answered quietly, suddenly shy.

"So, is it dangerous for us or for you?"

"What do you mean?"

"I mean, are you the threat, or are we?"

"You are! Well, *they* are." I motioned to the cluster of teenagers. Of course it was them.

Rowe peered at me thoughtfully. "Funny. I suspect they might say otherwise." He stood. "And that might just be the root of the problem: we're all afraid of each other, wings or no wings." Rowe smiled that quick smile of his. "Shall we join them?"

He offered his hand and pulled me up easily. I was surprised by how small my own hand looked wrapped in his. I blushed. I adjusted the cloak one last time and let him lead me toward the group, his hand gently pressed against the small of my back.

Cardigan sat on the edge of the reservoir with two boys and a girl. The boys were twins, identical in every way. The girl was small and bone-thin, her wrists like crane legs.

Cardigan stood and, with a flourish toward me, announced, "This is the Living Angel," resurrecting the name the newspapers had given me on the day I was born. On the day *Henry and I* were born.

The three stared at me, then the girl said, "Isn't she supposed to have wings?"

The twins laughed at her. I gaped at Cardigan, shocked that my best friend would give me away just like that. *Some friend,* I thought, glaring at Cardigan.

"She does!" Cardigan said. "They're just—hidden." Her face fell as she sat back down. "It is her, though."

Rowe moved slightly, shielding me from the group. He frowned at Cardigan. "You can't be s-serious," he said to her quietly. "You don't kn-now how they're g-going to r-react."

Still believing it was all a joke, one of the boys said, "I heard her wings are, like, six feet long."

"Twelve feet, five inches across actually," I murmured.

"Like an eagle?" he dared.

"Wandering albatross."

The other twin stood and crossed his arms. "So, if they're so big, how d'ya hide 'em?"

I sighed and moved out of Rowe's protective stance. I pulled the green cloak open just far enough to reveal the front straps of my harness.

One of them whistled. "Off the wall. That looks painful."

"It is," I admitted.

"Why do it, then?" the girl asked. She had a soft, wispy sort of voice that made me think of dandelion clocks. I shrugged.

"Take that thing off," the girl said. "We don't mind."

"Yeah, do your thing, baby," said one of the twins.

The other boy grinned. "And don't feel like you have to stop there either."

So I took them off. First the heavy cloak, then the harness. My wings popped free and opened, the tips stretching toward the sky. Suddenly everyone around the reservoir grew quiet. Conversations forgotten, they gathered around the mythical creature whose story they'd heard once as children but had mostly forgotten or never really believed.

"Let's see ya fly," a boy called out.

"I can't—" I began. I dropped my wings back to my sides. Flying had never felt like something I could do. But, then again, neither had leaving my house on the hill.

"Yes, she can!" Cardigan's excited voice echoed across the water.

I stared at her. "No," I muttered. "No, I can't."

"Of course you can!" she insisted, manic elation gleaming in her eyes. "Why would you be given wings if you weren't meant to fly?"

I didn't have an answer for that.

Cardigan grabbed my wrist in a tight grip. I clawed at her hand, begging her to let me go. I searched the faces around me for the one I could count on: Rowe's. But I couldn't find him.

"Oh, don't be such a baby," she said, laughing. "This will be fun."

Followed by a fervent and growing crowd, Cardigan gleefully dragged me to the end of the reservoir, where the ground fell away—a ravine.

I stood alone at the edge of the cliff. The kids crowded around, close enough that I could hear their enthusiastic calls, but distant enough that I couldn't grab and drag one of them with me if I should plunge to my death.

A body broke through the crowd and walked purposefully toward me. The next moment I was wrapped in Rowe's arms. I felt his twitching muscles in the quickening of my heart, his anger and indignation through my hands on his chest.

"Rowe!" Cardigan objected.

"Enough." His tone said it all.

Into my ear he murmured, "You don't have to do this." He gently moved his hand down my arm to steer me away. "I can take you home."

I let my head drop against the itchy wool of his jacket. The fabric felt coarse on my cheek. I found it comforting. Like his arms wrapped around me. And how perfectly I seemed to fit into the spaces of his body.

I breathed him in, wishing that I had my mother's gift and could smell him—the essence of him—the way that she would be able to. He made me feel safe. Protected.

But I'd been protected my whole life, forced to watch the world through the lonely window of my bedroom while the night called to me, like a siren luring forlorn sailors onto a rocky shoal. I didn't want to be protected from the world anymore.

I pulled away from Rowe and moved back to the edge of the cliff. I shuffled my feet. Dirt and pebbles gave way and bounced over the jagged rocks lining the side of the cliff.

I smiled back at Rowe, who looked at me quizzically.

"Watch this," I said.

I turned and spread my wings open, as wide as they would go, feeling the wind comb its cold fingers through my feathers. One feather came loose and danced its way down into the dark ravine below.

In my mind's eye, I could see myself arching upward. I could see the awe on the kids' faces. I could feel the ground fall away from me and a heavy ache in my shoulders as my wings lifted me up into the night. For a moment the act of flight seemed possible.

The sky suddenly looked so vast.

And I suddenly felt so small.

My wings opened and closed uselessly once or twice more before I stepped away from the ledge. "I can't," I said, my teeth chattering as much from the cold as from the adrenaline rushing through me.

Cardigan smiled. A real smile this time. She stepped toward me and rubbed my arms to warm them. "I know," she said kindly.

Rowe breathed an exasperated sigh of relief.

A girl in the crowd piped up. "What are they for, then?"

For? I didn't want to think about what my wings were *for*, so I showed off my one winged trick instead, knocking down a beer-can pyramid with a flap.

Not long after that, the small crowd dispersed, until it was just me, my wings, Cardigan, and Rowe.

"Wasn't that fun?" Cardigan exclaimed excitedly. "You should have seen their faces, Ava!" She laughed.

I glared. "How could you do that?"

Cardigan stopped laughing. She twisted her pretty hair around her finger nervously. "Well, I just thought . . ." Cardigan put her hands on her hips. "Look, you wanted to meet people, right? Now everyone knows you! You don't have to hide anymore."

"Are you kidding?" I was yelling now. "I'm lucky they didn't try to burn me at the stake!"

"Okay, I get it. Jeez, will you cool it already?"

"That was possibly the most selfish thing you've ever done, sis," Rowe offered.

"Selfish!" Cardigan spat. "I did it for her!"

"And how is it that you got to be the one to decide what she needed?" Rowe asked.

Cardigan opened her mouth, then closed it again. "Stay out of this, Rowe," she finally muttered.

I threw up my hands in disgust. "I'm going home," I said, and stormed off, leaving Rowe and Cardigan to run to catch up to me.

It was quiet on the way home—Rowe walked between me and Cardigan.

When we reached my house, Rowe said to us, "You two need to sort this out." To me, he said, "Ava, I'm glad you c-came. Truly, it was a spectacular night. T-terrifying, sure. But spectacular." Then he made a sharp right toward his house.

Cardigan and I watched Rowe walk away before turning to face each other. Cardigan sighed. "Listen, I thought I was doing you a favor, getting your wings out into the open, so to speak. Cross my heart I did. I wanted them to see that you're nothing to be afraid of."

I looked out at the quiet neighborhood around us. It all seemed so simple, so harmless under the night sky. "I would've liked just one night. One night to be . . . normal. To just be a girl."

"But you're more than that. When are you gonna realize that that's pretty swell, too?" She threw her arms around me in a tight hug. "Will you come out with us again? Please say yes."

I shrugged. "I'll think about it."

Cardigan smiled. "Okay, but you know you don't have to wear the harness or anything now, right? Unless you want to, that is."

"I think—I think I do, honestly. Well, at least I want to keep wearing the cloak."

"But why?"

I shrugged. "I like pretending to be normal."

Cardigan cocked her head and studied me thoughtfully. "I never thought about how hard it must be for you. Guess I am pretty selfish." She snorted. "Just don't tell Rowe he's right. He'll never let me forget it." She smiled. "Hey, where is that cloak anyway?"

I groaned. "I forgot it at the reservoir."

"Well, let's go get it." Cardigan looped her arm through mine.

I thought for a moment. "You know what? Go home. I'll go get it myself."

Cardigan hesitated. "Are you sure?"

"Absolutely."

Cardigan hugged me again before running home.

Now that I was alone, I felt more afraid than free; the dark seemed more formidable. I took a deep breath and reminded myself of all the times I'd wished I were out here instead of in my room. Still, I quickened my pace and pretended that my mother was standing on our front porch, watching over me.

By the time I reached the reservoir, the deep blue of the night sky had lightened—the color now diluted with specks of white clouds. Still, the shadows of the leafless trees danced eerily on the water. A birdcall became a woman's scream. A dog's howl became a cry of warning, the wind in my feathers, the hand of a ghost.

I found the cloak and harness—just where I'd dropped them—grabbed them, and ran, keeping my wings folded tightly against my back to keep them from slowing me down. It wasn't until I passed the drugstore where my mother once worked that I slowed to a walk. At my grandmother's bakery, I paused briefly and ran my fingers over the script on the window.

Wisps of orange and red were making their way across the blue sky, and I realized with a happy start that I had been out all night and hadn't gotten caught. I let out a giddy little laugh and skipped toward home, feeling miraculously like a normal teenager.

From the personal diary of Nathaniel Sorrows:

May 11, 1959

I've begun attending services at the Lutheran church. I had hoped to entice Aunt Marigold to return to her virtuous ways. My plan didn't work. I, the baptized Catholic, have been well received by the parishioners and by Pastor Trace Graves, but Marigold remains snug beneath the crumb-covered blankets on her bed. The other old women find me charming. The Altar Guild elected me as their new head—it is my responsibility to put away the Communion wafers and wine after the service. In the Catholic church, not even the altar boys are trusted to do that.

I like to set up for worship and make it a point to get up early on Sunday mornings just to be sure I can set up the altar, just to make sure nothing is forgotten by a more neglectful parishioner.

There are parts about the Lutheran service I will never get used to. For one, there is too much singing. For another, these Lutherans have little reverence for sacred space. Once the service is done, they leave their Bibles and hymnals discarded in the pews, laugh, and slap each other on the back.

The worst part, however, is that midnight services are reserved for Christmas, Easter, and Pentecost. My

Saturday nights feel empty and Godless without my usual midnight Mass. I try to spend that time on my knees in prayer, which is how I remain awake until she walks by, returning home in those early morning hours from her nightly escapes to the reservoir, accompanied as always by the other two. As she passes my window, her feathers ruffle in the wind, and I am seized by a memory of the Nativity set my mother unpacks at Christmastime — I remember how the angel's robes reveal a long white neck and how her lips seem stuck in a perpetual holy pout.

I didn't plan on speaking to her that first night, but as she skipped by the place where I stood, hidden behind the dense rhododendron bushes that line Aunt Marigold's property, I couldn't help myself. I called hello.

She froze and her wings instinctively sprang open, as if for flight. "Who's there?" she called, her voice like church bells.

I stepped out into the road. "I'm sorry. I didn't mean to frighten you," I said.

Her wings fluttered closed. "You didn't," she replied defensively. "I just wasn't expecting to see anyone — that's all."

I admit I wasn't anticipating her to be so very human, as much a young girl as she is a holy creature. It was quiet for the next few moments as I awaited my grand message from Him through her: a point of the *moral compass, perhaps even a* The Lord is with you. *But it seemed that was not her purpose. Not this time, at least.*

"I should go," the Angel said, turning to continue up the hill.

"Wait," I called after her.

She stopped and turned an awkward circle. "Yes?"

I smiled and took a few steps toward her. "I was wondering if I could touch them."

She hesitated at first. Perhaps she didn't know what I meant. But then she nodded. I ran my hand across her wings, felt the softness of the feathers course through the tips of my fingers to settle magnificently in my groin. When she broke away from me, she did so with a curt "Good night." I watched her make her way up the hill. I raised my hands in exaltation to the Lord for granting me a visit of supreme ecstasy as only ever experienced by Saint Teresa of Ávila herself, I'm sure.

Chapter Sixteen

"WHAT'S HIS NAME?" I asked. Cardigan and I sat in my bedroom, awaiting the arrival of night and my freedom. In the days following my first escape, my trips to the reservoir continued, and I began to catch on to the things other teenagers took for granted. I learned, for example, how to smoke with a cigarette holder balanced between my fingers and how to paint in my eyebrows using black eyeliner. Through Cardigan, I learned which of the high-school boys knew what to do once they got a girl alone (answer: none), how many of the girls were sincere in their kindness (answer: very few), and what sort of stir the arrival of Marigold Pie's nephew had caused in the neighborhood.

Cardigan thought for a moment as she studied the deep-red polish she'd just applied to her nails. "Nathaniel Sorrows."

I repeated his name, softly, under my breath. I liked the way it felt in my mouth. I saved it on the tip of my tongue to use later, when I wanted to hear my voice wrap itself around the syllables. Na-than-iel Sor-rows. In the middle of the night—when the neighborhood cats mated in the yard or when Trouver ran in his dreams—I would awake, calling out his name.

"What do you think about him?" I asked, hoping my voice didn't give me away. I stole a peek at Cardigan, still busy admiring her nails, and was grateful that her self-absorption made her deaf to the increased beat of my heart. I never told Cardigan about my encounter with him. I wasn't sure why, but every time I thought of telling her, some impulse held me back. Maybe I felt that I'd finally earned the right to a secret, something to keep from even my best friend. Just like any other normal girl.

Cardigan blew on her nails. "He seems kinda square. Cute, though."

I nodded, lost in thought. I found it odd that this stranger affected me so. He was attractive, sure. But was that it? When he'd asked to touch my wings, I wanted to say yes. So I did. And afterward, as I lay in bed, I could still feel the warmth of his fingers on the tips of my wings.

My mother often suffered extended bouts of melancholy, times when her thoughts of Jack Griffith would not dissolve with a sigh or a shake of the head. In bed she would think of that solstice night beneath the dahlias and Jack's chest, white in the moonlight, until her skin tingled. She flushed thinking of his mouth moving across her collarbone, his hand pressed hotly against hers, their palms slick with mingled sweat. Like warm wax, the memory of his touch melted on her thighs, dripped down her leg.

For several nights' running, she would dream of him: his smile revealing the gap between his incisors, his hands clasping a bouquet of flowers—all wilted but for the daffodil, the symbol for unrequited love. She would awake with tears in her hair. Before bed, she drank cups of tea made from the crushed dried leaves of California poppies, which Wilhelmina swore could cure any type of insomnia. Only then could she sleep, a dark sleep of empty hallways and locked doors.

When that didn't work, Viviane did the laundry. On those nights when sleep proved impossible, she sat deep in the basement, lulled by the lazy dance of the towels in the dryer. She loved the smell of the detergent, the rumble of the machine, and the warmth of the sheets when they emerged. But more than anything else, she loved the satisfaction of removing a stain: she loved how, with a little hand soap or a drop of bleach, she could remove a pen leak from a shirt pocket, a lipstick mark from a sleeve, or a rust stain from a lace curtain. Blood was the best; how satisfying it was to remove a drop of blood from a white shirt, a glove, or a pair of women's underwear. How satisfying to watch the red slowly fade from the fabric, leaving it clean once again with no sign of having ever been anything but white.

There remains only one photograph of my mother in her youth. My grandmother was hardly one for capturing childhood memories. Gabe found the photo pressed between the pages of an old book on dragonflies. He kept it hidden in a box he'd carved from a block of cedar. I recall seeing it once when snooping through the woodshop when I was a child.

The photograph, yellow and cracking sharply along the edges, was taken when Viviane was still Jack's girl and Gabe had yet to arrive at our front door. The picture was, in fact, of Viviane and Jack. Viviane's mouth was open wide in laughter, and Jack was looking at her in such a way that made it obvious: Jack had truly loved Viviane.

Gabe often compared the laughing Viviane in the picture to the Viviane who found solace in the laundry room and with cups of tea and busy housework, the Viviane who'd spent the last fifteen years waiting for Jack to come back for her. How the pain she carried didn't knock her to the ground, he never knew; that it didn't only made him love her more fiercely.

It took several visits to the elementary-school librarian and one trek to the zoo on the hill for Gabe to figure out what kind of bat he'd caught. It was a little brown *Myotis*. And a spirited one at that. Every time Gabe reached into the cage to try to get a look at its wings, the bat bit the tips of his fingers. The bat had no such problem trusting Henry; it ate tiny grasshoppers and mosquitoes straight out of his hands. Eventually, Henry had even coaxed the bat to climb onto his outstretched finger. There the bat slept upside down, permitting Gabe to finally pull its wings open to locate the humerus and the metacarpal.

This new set of wings took several weeks to build. Basing the structure on the bat's skeletal system, he made the wings' frames out of oak — not a lightweight wood but with good bending qualities. Then he stretched an old piece of canvas across the frames. Again, the sounds of Gabe's hammer and saw filled my mother's dreams.

When the wings were finished, Gabe carried them to the roof of the woodshop. He peered down at Henry, who sat with his back against Trouver's front legs; the bat hung upside down from Henry's left thumb. It looked to Gabe like Henry was giving him a very large thumbs-down.

Gabe slipped his arms into long pockets he'd sewn into the fabric of each wing. He stepped to the edge of the roof. It was dark, but Gabe could see most of the neighborhood from where he stood — the lights in his neighbors' homes shone like lighthouse beacons. His initial impulse was to jump, but after some careful thinking, Gabe stretched out his winged arms and dropped over the edge in a perfect swan dive. He'd practiced flapping many times before, perfectly emulating the wing beats of the duck, the seagull, the California brown pelican. This time he only had to flap once before the wind caught under his wings and he was flying.

He was flying!

He wasn't actually flying. He was gliding, and only gliding until he came to a rather disappointing stop via the lilac bush at the bottom of the hill.

It was a harsh landing—the lilac bush was never the same. The wings, unfortunately, were ruined. There was a slash through one side of the canvas, and the frame was snapped. Gabe was, remarkably, unharmed.

Henry shook the bat from his thumb, waving to it as it disappeared into the night.

Gabe trudged into the house, dragging the jumble of canvas and oak behind him.

Viviane raised her eyebrows at the mess he dropped on the kitchen floor. "How many failed attempts does this make?" she asked.

"Four," he admitted. "It's the feathers, Vivi. I can't imitate the feathers."

"Yes. *That* is the problem," she said, her tone unkind.

Gabe ignored it.

Viviane sighed. "I don't know what's worse—thinking yours will work or hoping hers will."

Gabe stared at her. "Why won't you let me help her?"

This was too much for my mother. "Because it's stupid, Gabe!" she snapped. "It's stupid and mean to tell a young girl that she can fly, only to have her heart, not to mention her bones, broken when she realizes she can't."

"So, you think it's better she doesn't even try?"

"I do."

"What about what I think? I should have a say, Vivi."

"What gives you a right to have a say in the lives of my children?" she spat.

"Are you kidding me?" Gabe's booming steps rattled the house as he stormed around the kitchen. "I've been here from the very beginning. I've fed them, I've changed them. I take care of them when they're sick. I hold them when they're sad. I've done more than their own father has or ever will!"

"Is that why you're still here? For my kids? Because it's pathetic," she said meanly. "It's pathetic that, after all this time, *you're still here*."

Gabe grabbed Viviane's shoulders. Neither seemed to know whether he was going to shake her or kiss her.

"Why have you stayed?" she asked softly.

Gabe dropped his hands and shook his head. "Vivi, if you don't know that by now, then I'm not the only stupid one around here."

He looked at her one last time before storming out the back door.

From my bedroom upstairs, I had heard the entire argument. My hands were pressed against my mouth in disbelief. No one ever yelled in our house. Still vibrating from the shock of the slammed door, I ran downstairs. “You’re not going after him?” I asked my mother with alarm.

When she spoke, it was just a whisper. “Let him go, Ava,” she said. “It’s for the best.”

But I couldn’t. I raced out after Gabe. At the bottom of the hill, I stood helplessly as his truck took him away.

“Please,” I called softly, “don’t leave us here alone.”

From the personal diary of Nathaniel Sorrows:

May 15, 1959

My days spent studying Scripture are finished; I've learned all I can from their musty pages. I let Aunt Marigold sit unattended for hours as I look through her personal library instead, searching for the words my heart craves, words written out of love: the letters Abelard wrote for his Héloïse, Napoleon for the empress Josephine, Robert Browning for the budding poetess Elizabeth Barrett. I scrawl my thoughts of her in the margins of the pages—mimicking their words of love. I imagine folding the pages into elaborate creatures to leave on her window's ledge or transcribing my feverish devotions onto the glass with a finger and my own hot breath. I imagine the wet words greeting her when she awakes. How she might tremble when she reads them again and again, until the sun rises and dries up my message of unwavering adoration and fidelity.

She is the glorious reincarnation of every woman ever loved. It was her face that launched the Trojan War, her untimely demise that inspired the building of India's Taj Mahal. She is every angel in Michelangelo's Sistine Chapel.

In my mind, her voice is tinged with an Italian accent or the dialect of Provence. In my mind, she is dressed as a lady of the Renaissance. I imagine peeling the many layers of dress from her body, worshipping her wings. In my dreams I watch our children—all birds—fly from her womb. I name each after one of the apostles: Simon Peter a crane, Thomas an owl, Judas a big black crow.

When a stray feather fell from the sky and brushed against my face, I had my first true experience of spiritual ecstasy. Once I awoke in such a state of excitement that I took a knife to one of my bed pillows and pleasured myself with the feathers inside. Because that's what I believe an angel will feel like: like slipping into a pillow of downy feathers. So soft, so light. Nightly I watch as she preens her feathers in front of her open window. Light illuminates her from behind, making her glow like the holy being that only I know her to be.

Chapter Seventeen

THAT MAY I SPENT MY EVENINGS waiting for the house to fall silent with sleep so that I could make my escape to the reservoir. As I waited, I preened in my bedroom, practicing coquettish smiles in my window's reflection and pretending to smoke cigarettes with the same careless air that Cardigan did. I imagined the boys in the neighborhood, the very ones who vehemently avoided me at the reservoir, climbing the rickety limbs of the cherry tree outside my window, whereupon I would pluck their fingers from the branches, then howl with laughter as they fell.

I imagined Widow Pie's nephew watching me, his eyes, like fingers, leaving hot prints on my skin. I tried to leave for the reservoir around the same time each night and would feel jittery and wound up until I passed Marigold's house. I imagined him standing faithfully in the dark behind a rhododendron bush as I passed by and cast furtive glances his way.

One night, I left one of my feathers on Marigold Pie's front step, intending for him to find it. From behind the broken lilac bush in my yard, I watched, blushing wildly, as he opened the door. The wind lifted the feather into the air, then let it float back down gently against his face. I ran up the hill, feeling giddy and bold.

I imagined myself his bride; I pictured the white dress and the flower I'd tuck behind my right ear as the Hawaiian maidens do. I pictured a little house somewhere far from the hill at the end of Pinnacle Lane: dinners with neighbors, the husbands drinking Tom Collins in the parlor, the wives swapping recipes in the kitchen; the dog we'd have — a spaniel named Noodle. From these daydreams I always omitted my wings, mentally erased them from my shoulder blades.

In my daydreams I was always just a girl.

The more my infatuation grew, the more deeply I mourned the potential loss of the life I dreamed of. It was all too precious, too thoroughly imagined and yearned for to lose. I stopped sleeping. I stopped eating. My wings lost feathers.

My nightly escapes were put on hold in the middle of May when my infatuation got the best of me and I fell ill with a fever. I emerged from my bed only to go to the bathroom and with help at that. My mother spent the week piling quilts on my shivering body and heating batches of chicken noodle soup so hot her face flushed red when she leaned over the pot.

I'd never been so deliriously sick; even my waking moments were spent in dreams—nightmares in which infants turned into bloody animal bits, hallucinations in which the night sky fell into a burning ocean.

Then late one night, on the night of Pentecost, I sat up suddenly in bed, my hair plastered to my forehead, my feathers damp with sweat.

A young girl stood at my window, her back to the room. The lace on the old-fashioned white dress she wore trailed behind her, ripped and dirty. Her black hair, a matted mass of tangles, cascaded down her back. She turned to face me, and I could see the stars shining brightly through the back of her head.

She motioned for me to follow her, then stepped through the wall.

I threw back the piles of quilts and stumbled to the window. Peering outside, I could see her waiting for me in the grass below, her ghostly form shimmering silver in the moonlight. Without another thought, I grabbed my green cloak and climbed through the window and down the bare branches of the cherry tree into the yard.

The rains still hadn't arrived. The grass was brown and dried. It crunched underfoot. The water of the bay had crept so low that the local teens could walk straight across it without the girls getting the hems of their skirts wet.

I followed my ghostly guide to the Lutheran church and through the church's heavy double doors. The church was decorated for Pentecost with red linens and baskets of red silk chrysanthemums. There hadn't been any fresh flowers in months. It was the first midnight service of Pentecostal Sunday that anyone could remember when deadly puddles hadn't formed in the doorways, waiting to break a hip or fracture a pelvis. Even the little old ladies left their rain bonnets at home. Red banners waved gently from the ceiling. Someone had prepared a batch of sugar cookies dyed with food coloring that looked more orange than red. The parishioners were mingling in the narthex of the church, holding their plates of orange cookies, when I entered. I dropped my cloak to the ground and all conversation stopped at the sight of my uncovered wings.

The black-eyed ghost led me to the sanctuary, where the head of the Altar Guild, Nathaniel Sorrows, was gathering the unblessed wafers and leftover wine to store in the sacristy near the altar.

He turned and saw me, my wings exposed. He paled. For reasons even I remain unsure of, I dropped to my knees, raised my chin, and opened my mouth. For a moment he stood unmoving, possibly awestruck by the close proximity of the blooms of my lips. Then he held up a paper-thin wafer and brought it to my mouth. I reached up and touched it with my tongue.

A strange pink fire sparked and jumped from my parted lips. A sharp gasp came from the doorway of the nave where the rest of the parishioners now stood.

The fire was still dancing on my tongue when Nathaniel, regaining his senses, dropped the flaming host from his singed fingers. He stamped the flames out with his foot, instantly immortalizing the incident with a black mark on the carpet. I blinked as though emerging from a trance, then scrambled to my feet and stumbled from the church.

Cardigan Cooper remembered the next moment more vividly than any other in her life. She had been walking past the church alone, meaning to meet Jeremiah Flannery at the reservoir, when she saw me in my green cloak stumbling up the stone pathway of the church. She knew I'd been sick. Curious, she followed me inside and watched the entire scene play out from the back of the church. I ran by her as I was fleeing the nave. She grabbed the cloak I'd dropped earlier inside the church doors and joined me in my escape. We ran all the way back to my house on the hill on Pinnacle Lane, where we both dropped to the ground and lay with our pink faces turned toward the sky. Our breath made tiny clouds of condensation against the stars.

Cardigan turned to me. "Damn, girl. What was that about?"

But the dark-haired specter in the tattered white dress was there, too. She raised a transparent finger to her lips, then smiled eerily at me before fading away into the night.

I turned my feverish cheek to the grass and sighed. "I don't know."

By June I was a familiar face among the nightly crowd that gathered at the reservoir. Though I always wore the cloak, my initial visit and exposure had left its impression. So had my fevered visit to the church. Many still stared. Some even pointed, saying, "Look! There she is!"

I scowled and tried, unsuccessfully, to ignore all the furtive whispers.

"F-forget them," Rowe said. "What they th-think isn't important."

"Maybe not to you," I muttered.

He held my gaze for a moment. I blushed a deep pink remembering the feel of his wool coat against my cheek on that first night at the reservoir. And for a brief moment, I compared how I was feeling to how I felt when I thought about Nathaniel Sorrows. I thought of the life I'd created for us in my head: the cocktail parties, the dog named Noodle. But it was an illusion, a prefabricated dream, while Rowe was real. I could touch him. And he could touch me. A shiver rolled up my spine when I thought of how much I would like the warmth of my palm pressed against Rowe's, our fingers intertwined. Was this the difference between infatuation and . . . ?

"What do you mean?" Rowe asked.

"People don't look at you like you're—"

"A monster?" Rowe suggested.

"Yeah."

"See my sister?" Rowe motioned to Cardigan, who stood laughing with a group of people. "The moment she o-opens her mouth, everyone im-m-mediately loves her. The m-moment I open mine, everyone immediately p-p-pities me."

I winced. "I'm sorry."

Rowe shrugged. "The point is, if I cared what everyone else th-thought, I'd see myself as p-pitiful, but I don't." He smiled. "I think I'm pretty cool."

I laughed.

"I just don't think you should let other people d-define you," Rowe said quickly. "I think you could be anything you wanted."

There were very few people who made me feel as if they saw me as *me*, and not as some winged aberration. My mother was one of them. Henry was another (not that being regarded as "normal" by Henry was anything to brag about). Rowe, I was coming to realize, was another.

"Thanks," I said softly.

We walked slowly around the edge of the reservoir. I balanced on the ledge, occasionally dipping a foot into the water as I walked. I could feel Rowe's eyes on me. I turned to him and made a face. "What?" I asked.

Rowe shrugged. "You. Just—you."

When I passed Widow Pie's house that night, I forgot to imagine Nathaniel waiting for me behind the rhododendron bushes. I tried saying his name aloud to myself and was surprised by how foreign it felt on my tongue. And with that, the love I thought I had for Marigold Pie's nephew ran off me like water from melting ice. Like so many others, Nathaniel Sorrows was interested only in my wings. *Unlike Rowe,* I considered thoughtfully.

I reached over and closed my curtains with a determined snap and went to bed.

That night I dreamed I could fly.

Every once in a while, Emilienne allowed herself to contemplate what she might have done with her life if she'd never married and had instead grown old in Beauregard's Manhatine apartment; if she hadn't fallen in love with the way prospective suitors praised the half-moons of her fingernails; if she had instead allowed them to climb the rickety rungs of the fire escape to her floor whereupon she would pluck their fingers from the bars, then howl with laughter as they fell.

She reached up and touched the belled lip of her old cloche hat—the one painted with red poppies—and the house on Pinnacle Lane fell away, replaced by the crumbling plaster walls of that derelict apartment: the kitchen sink, with its cracked porcelain and lines of rust circling the drain; the old-fashioned icebox, with its metal hinges and the square block of ice that made them feel rich even when the cupboards were bare; the bureau with the drawer where Pierette slept and the corners where her feathers gathered; the sofa René balanced on his forearms.

And though she still wouldn't converse with her ghostly siblings, Emilienne could, in a fashion, communicate with them as they might have been.

She started with an inquiry after Margaux's child. When Margaux showed off her infant, Emilienne at first smiled, then turned away when she saw his eyes—one green, the other blue. Margaux held her son protectively against the hole where her heart used to be. She was exceedingly proud of her offspring; he was the greatest thing she'd accomplished in her life. And in her death.

Where was Maman? Beauregard? They didn't know. There was only ever the three of them and the baby—and sometimes a young black-eyed girl. What was death like? she wondered. They did not seem able to answer, nor could they tell her why, in the afterlife, they would continue to carry the evidence of their sins in such a gruesome way.

"Maybe you are in purgatory," Emilienne offered.

René shrugged. Maybe.

Sometimes Margaux would motion to the harpsichord in the corner of the parlor, a request for Emilienne to play. That's when the walls of the Manhatine apartment would melt away—along with the warbling voices of her siblings—and the walls of the house at the end of Pinnacle Lane would spring back up around her, the harpsichord unused, yellowing in the corner.

From the personal diary of Nathaniel Sorrows:

May 26, 1959

It seems that the Angel has passed her fire into me—from her mouth through the burning host and into my fingers. At first the fever showed itself as a pink flush across my cheeks and down my neck. Beads of sweat sizzled on my forehead. I woke up in the night covered in a prickly heat rash and sat in a tub filled with ice cubes until the melted water steamed off my body. I tried suppressing the rash through starvation and lashes and desperate prayer, through a week spent kneeling on a hairbrush, a board of nails, a pincushion. I tried pushing the heat away with a glass of wine or a mouthful of food, but the only things edible in Marigold's kitchen made me choke.

Perhaps this heat is punishment for my impure thoughts. Despite this, I still watch for her every night. I stand in Aunt Marigold's dark yard, wiping the sweat from my face and from under my arms with a red handkerchief, and wait. I carefully prepare conversations to share, but every time she passes, flanked by the other two—the girl wearing a revealing crop top, the boy in a navy-issue wool peacoat—I become transfixed by the way the wind ruffles her feathers, and all my planned words slip down my throat.

I am unable to concentrate. One moment I am changing the reader board in the church's yard—making sure each letter is properly aligned and positioned, that I am spelling each word correctly—and the next I am lying in an imaginary bed of feathers.

When it comes to Aunt Marigold, I admit that I am failing quite spectacularly. She has grown—it should be recorded—to roughly the size and shape of the mattress on her bed. I now believe that the reason for my being here on Pinnacle Lane has nothing to do with my aunt, and everything to do with the Angel. I've started slipping tranquilizers into the éclairs she eats by the pound. It is the only way I can maintain the number of visions the Lord sends me of the Angel. The hours I used to spend in prayer I now use on the memory of her wet mouth. This is now how I pray.

Perhaps this heat isn't a penance I am meant to suffer. Perhaps it is a gift, each drop of sweat the Angel's kiss, sweetly progressing down the length of my spine.

Chapter Eighteen

THREE WEEKS INTO JUNE, the meteorologists brought out their fancy rain gauges and showed the public what we already knew—it still hadn't rained. The rich Seattle soil dried up in the garden beds, and the winds blew great gusts of it into the eyes of those along Pinnacle Lane. Even the rose gardens down in Portland were suffering. It had been three months since any fresh flowers had graced the altar at the Lutheran church. There would be no flowers for the women to wear in their hair at the summer solstice celebration, which made them weep. Well, either that or the wind had blown specks of dirt in their eyes.

Ever since the night of Gabe's attempted flight with bat-inspired wings—an attempt that ended up being his last—the farther away from the house at the end of Pinnacle Lane Gabe was, the better it seemed he felt. Before then he'd been disinclined to accept jobs that took him away from the neighborhood. Now he was spending as much of his time outside of it as he could: Mercer Island, Silverdale, Belltown. He left the house before dawn and returned after dark, seeing Henry, my mother, and me only when he peeked in on us as we slept. Henry slept on his back, his fingers clasped around the satiny edge of the quilt and Trouver curled in a large furry ball at the foot of the bed. I always slept with the tip of one wing covering my nose. On the nights when Viviane did sleep, she did so curled on her side, her arms wrapped protectively around her chest, as though holding her heart in place.

Watching Viviane sleep, Gabe's heart leaped the way it did when he saw her hanging the sheets in the yard or walking down the stairs. But then he'd remind himself how foolish it was to love someone who didn't love you back. He'd go to his room, climb into bed, and count the black spots against his closed eyelids until he fell into a fitful sleep, waking hourly to stop himself from dreaming of Viviane Lavender's hair.

Falling out of love was much harder than Gabe would have liked. Normally led through life by the heart attached to his sleeve, finding logic in love proved to be a bit like getting vaccinated for some dread disease: a good idea in the end, but the initial pain certainly wasn't any fun. He came to appreciate that there were worse ways to live than to live without love. For instance, if he didn't have arms, Gabe wouldn't be able to hide in his work. Yes, a life without arms would be quite tragic, indeed.

In Gabe's view, the whole world had given up on love anyway and clung instead to its malformed cousins: lust, narcissism, self-interest. Only his own stupid heart sent up flares when he thought of any woman besides Viviane Lavender.

When June came around, he forced himself to ask out a waitress from Bremen, Maine, who lived alone in a Craftsman bungalow behind the elementary school. On Friday nights he and the waitress sat around the fire, sharing platters of Ritz crackers with lobster Newburg spread, bacon wraparounds, and hot cheese puffs. Gabe watched her knees—bare because of her fashionably short skirt—turn red from the heat of the flames.

Eventually, Gabe was sure his heart would get used to the idea and allow him to finally touch her. After all, that was what people generally did when they couldn't be with the one they loved.

Wasn't it?

Henry had continued making maps of the neighborhood. He drew them on the backs of old letters, in the front pages of books, in the dirt using a stick or the sharp edge of a trowel. Much like his muteness and then his nonsensical speech, Henry's compulsive mapmaking was considered another idiosyncrasy not meant to be understood. We never considered there might be a reason or a purpose for the maps. No matter — Henry knew what they were for. And that was enough, for a while anyway.

Until Trouver arrived, we thought that Henry couldn't talk. Turned out, he could; he just didn't like to. He made himself a rule to say only things that were important. No one — not even his own family — knew about this rule. No one needed to.

On the morning of midsummer's eve, Henry awoke and stretched his toes toward the spot on the bed where Trouver was still curled in sleep. Henry liked the feel of the fur on his feet and wiggled them in pleasure until the dog sighed and moved to the floor. Trouver's fur was one of the few things Henry liked to touch. He liked the feel of my feathers and the soft worn edge of the quilt on his bed. He liked the warm hood of the truck, the engine going *tick-tick-tick* long after Gabe drove back from town. He liked that too, the engine going *tick-tick-tick*. He liked that some tree trunks were rough, like the cherry tree in our yard, that others were smooth, and that some were in-between, like the birch trees in front of our grandmother's bakery. There might have been more things he would like to touch, but he wasn't sure. He didn't touch many things.

Henry got out of bed and pulled on his red-and-blue-striped T-shirt — the stripes faded from so many washes — over his head. Trouver stretched and licked himself in *inappropriate* places. Henry didn't like that word. When Henry heard a word he didn't like, he had to lie facedown on the floor until the bad feeling stopped. Humming sometimes worked too.

Henry and Trouver shared a piece of toast with orange marmalade for breakfast. If that day were any other day, he might have gone out in the yard to count bugs afterward. He no longer needed to catch them to feed the bat, but Henry liked counting things and he still liked knowing how many there were out there. He liked knowing that there were sixteen stairs to his bedroom and eight bowls in the kitchen cupboards above the sink. He liked clapping his hands five times in a row, even nine times if he needed to, and knew that if he clapped his hands ten times, our mother would ask him to stop in her loud mother voice. If that day were any other day, Henry might have gone back upstairs to his room to find the notebook in which he wrote his favorite words, struggling to keep each letter between the blue lines. But that day wasn't any other day.

Henry did go back upstairs to his room, but instead of getting his notebook, he emptied his toy chest. He lined up all his stuffed animals along the wall in order of size, and then placed his building blocks and toy cars on the cracks of the floorboards.

When the toy chest was empty, Henry climbed in. Though the toy chest was fairly large and Henry was a fairly small fifteen-year-old boy, he could fit only by hanging his legs over the side. Being in the chest made him feel safe. And safe was how he needed to feel right then. With his knees pointed at his chin Henry could talk to the

Sad Man about the maps and the cat on the wall and the bee in the bush.

There were good people and bad people, this Henry knew for sure. His mother was good. And me, of course. Gabe. Trouver wasn't a person, but he was good all the same. Policemen were *good* people too. He had learned that a few days earlier when a policeman came into the bakery. The pretty blond woman who worked behind the counter handed the policeman a cup of coffee and a croissant fresh from the oven. When the policeman tried to pay, Penelope said, "On the house." When he left, the woman turned to Henry and said, "That's honorable work there. He's a good man for doing it."

As for bad people, Henry knew only one. Henry knew he was a bad person because the Sad Man told him so. He also knew that no matter how hard he had tried to tell them, no one else understood this. Not his grandmother, not his mother, not me, not Gabe. Trouver probably did, but he wasn't a person. Trouver was a dog, and, even if he did understand, what good would that do?

Somehow he had to find a way to leave the house on the hill before the rain came. Because the rain was coming and it all happened after the rain. That's what the Sad Man said.

From the personal diary of Nathaniel Sorrows:

June 21, 1959

I haven't left my aunt's living room since June 18. Three days. I haven't eaten or slept; instead, I stand in front of the window and watch and wait. Sometimes I write. Sometimes I pace. When I need to relieve myself, I just open the window and piss onto the dried-up flower bed below.

I started this vigil on the day the postman delivered a letter from Pastor Graves. The letter, typed by the church secretary onto reverent-looking parchment paper, stated that my assistance was no longer needed. It also asked me to refrain from crossing onto church grounds. The pastor's reprimand barely made a bruise on my fevered skin.

The change came four days ago in the midst of the homily. I realized that the church, the holy doctrines, the religious ramblings I'd once tried so hard to follow were all just parts of a lie created by humans so blind and so flawed they'd mistake a divine being for one of their wretched own.

My neighbors are content to sing useless hymns about rivers, fountains, and rocks, but their devotions are empty.

None of them know anything about devotion! I pushed through the parishioners and made my way to the front of the church. From the wooden pulpit, I told them as much, pounding my fist in anger. Behind closed eyes, they prayed for promotions and the newest kitchen gadget. What could they give with their flawed, human love? I had known what she was from the very beginning. An Angel — one of God's true messengers — lived at the end of my road. I had touched her feathers with my outstretched fingers, had caught a fever from the mere touch of her rosebud tongue.

I know what they saw: my wrinkled clothes; the dark circles under my eyes, weak and red from so many sleepless nights; hair matted with unwash. Pastor Graves approached me. He covered my hand with his own. I could read the fear in his eyes, saw how the irises bled black into the brown.

"Of whom do you speak?" he asked quietly.

I began to laugh.

I pulled my hand out from under Pastor Graves's light grip. How sorry I felt for the reverend, his life wasted on such a monstrous bunch of tricks! I left the church then, knowing, even before receiving the letter, that I would never return.

Chapter Nineteen

FOR FOURTEEN YEARS, I could only watch from my window each time Pinnacle Lane was transformed for the solstice celebration. From a distance, I watched the neighborhood men set up booths where chocolate truffles, plates of *krumkake*, and husks of yellow corn would be sold for a nickel; I watched gaggles of girls from the high school's Key Club arrive with their mothers in tow, toting pies to sell for the benefit of the Veterans Hospital downtown; I watched the musicians gather, bringing mandolins, accordions, creaky violins, xylophones, clarinets, and sitars; I watched the giant bonfire in the school parking lot blaze against the night sky; and I cursed every living thing with feathers.

But that year was going to be different.

Cardigan had been secretly preparing for solstice for weeks. She didn't even let Rowe or me in on her plan until the day before, when she told Rowe to meet us not at the bottom of the hill as usual, but at the festival itself.

"You'll see why soon enough!" Cardigan told him, laughing.

I stood in front of my bedroom window, watching the sunset paint glorious shades of orange and purple across the sky while Cardigan brushed my hair. The festivities were already well under way, but I'd insisted on waiting until the sun had set to make my escape. It would already be far earlier than I'd ever been out before — it was risky.

But what a risk to take, I thought, smiling to myself.

It took Cardigan a few hours of persistent nagging to convince me to cut and dye my hair.

"Just think," Cardigan said, "no one will recognize you."

"I think the wings will probably give me away," I said dryly.

"That's what *those* are for." Cardigan pointed to a set of wings in the corner, the very ones Gabe had made when he had hoped to teach me to fly. Seeing those wings made my chest ache. I looked away. I didn't want to be sad. Not that day.

Cardigan and I suspected Gabe had a new sweetheart. He'd rarely been home in weeks. When I did see him, it seemed he was always on his way out, his hands scrubbed clean, the collar on his shirt freshly pressed, his woodsy smell replaced with the sharp tang of cologne that my mother always pretended to be offended by. He left his dilapidated pickup truck in the driveway. Perhaps his sweetheart was too delicate for those tattered, threadbare seats. Whoever she was.

I wrinkled my nose. "How are those supposed to help?"

"If I wear them, there will be two angels, not one," Cardigan said defensively. "It'll throw people off your scent." She held up the mangled mess with her fingers. "I glued a bunch of feathers to 'em. So, see? No one will think your wings are real. They'll just assume we're both wearing costumes. Plus, a lot of people still think the Angel never leaves the house. *And* that she only wears white. *And* that she has talons—"

"I don't have . . . what?"

"Talons," Cardigan made her finger into a hook. "You know, like an eagle."

I folded my arms across my chest. "I do not have . . . those."

Cardigan shrugged. "I know, but there've been speculations. Which," she quickly added, "only further supports what I've been saying: no one will know it's you because you won't be what they're expecting."

I watched nervously as dark strands of my hair fell and gathered at my feet.

"It keeps sticking to your feathers," Cardigan said, checking to be sure she'd cut each side evenly.

The bleach took the longest, and for a moment we both feared I would end up with orange hair. But when the smell of bleach finally stopped burning my eyes, Cardigan took a step back and whistled. "Jeez, Ava. You are one hot blonde!"

In ancient Gaul the midsummer celebration was called the Feast of Epona, named after the goddess of abundance, sovereignty, and the harvest. She was portrayed as a woman riding a mare. The pagans celebrated solstice with bonfires believed to possess a form of earthly magic, granting maidens insight on their future husbands and banishing spirits and demons. The men of the Hopi tribe dressed in traditional masks to honor the kachinas, the dancing spirits of rain and fertility who were believed to leave the villages at midsummer to visit the dead underground and hold ceremonies on their behalf. In Russia young girls floated their flower garlands down rivers, reading one another's fortunes by the movement of the flowers on the water. In Sweden neighbors gathered to raise and dance around a huge maypole draped in greenery and flowers. They call it Litha or Vestalia in Rome, Gathering Day in Wales, All Couples' Day in Greece. It's Sonnwend, Feill-Sheathain, Thing-Tide, the feast day of John the Baptist.

For the people of Pinnacle Lane, the solstice celebration was a chance to shed their cloaks of modesty and decorum, and replace them with wildflowers woven in their hair. Only during the summer solstice did the old

Moss sisters remove their crosses from between their low-hanging breasts and drink themselves silly on great pints of malt liquor. Only during solstice could Pastor Graves forgive himself for his favorite sweet, the Nipples of Venus, feasting on white chocolate from the truffle's teat. And only during solstice could Rowe Cooper arrive at the festival to find two identical winged girls waiting for him.

"How d-did you . . . ?" Rowe flicked his fingers at the feathers sprouting from his sister's shoulder blades.

Cardigan hit his hand away. "Don't. They're not dry yet. Pretty neato, huh?"

Rowe turned toward me. "I like your hair."

I smiled.

Rowe glanced from girl to girl. "So, why do you look the same?"

Cardigan put an arm around me. "We're blending in."

As we wandered through the festivities, I saw something new or strange at every turn: an ambush of tiny tigers and panda bears, their face paint smeared, their fingers clasping giant sticks of cotton candy; men and women in medieval garb; a small girl in a wheelchair, her legs encased by a shiny fabric mermaid tail. There were Norwegian *mormor*s dressed in their woolen *bunad*s, and Shakespeare's mule-headed Bottom stumbling from tents of sheer turquoise and white. The crowds of solstice revelers were so strange that, for perhaps the first time ever, I fit in. I grabbed Cardigan and swung her around right there in front of a booth selling wind chimes. Then I laughed out loud because no one even glanced at the angels dancing to the chimes ringing in the growing breeze. Cardigan was right. We blended in beautifully.

I'd spent so many years imagining the event, placing myself in the crowd, that I wondered if maybe, in the end, it wouldn't matter if I actually felt the flames of the bonfire on my face. I often wondered the same thing about being kissed. Or falling in love. Did I need to experience them if I could imagine them? A part of me feared that Pinnacle Lane's solstice celebration couldn't possibly live up to *la fête* in my head.

I was thrilled to discover I was wrong. From my window for the past fourteen years, I hadn't been able to hear the crowds sing along when the street-corner musicians played rowdy drinking songs on their mandolins and sitars. I couldn't observe lovers finding shadows perfect for private trysts. I hadn't known how easy it would be to avoid getting caught by my grandmother, the heat from the ovens clouding the bakery's windows all night. Or how hard I would laugh when Rowe let the Kiwanis Key Club girls paint a tri-colored rainbow across his left cheek. And I hadn't known how my heart would pound when Rowe pulled me aside, gently took my face in his hands, and pressed his lips to mine.

When the celebration came to an end, the fire was doused with buckets filled with water from the bay. Mothers gathered their children and husbands. Panda bears and tigers became sticky little boys and girls once again.

And two angels and one boy with a rainbow painted on his cheek made their way back to Pinnacle Lane.

My mother insisted she had smelled the rain before it came. It had been a beautiful day, all clear blue skies and warm sunshine. There had been no indication that it would be anything but a picturesque midsummer night, except for the smell. The coming rain smelled different from any other she'd ever known. It didn't smell like a summer rain, or even like a spring rain that had been waiting to escape water-heavy clouds since February. It didn't smell murky, like the rain from last winter's floods that poured into basements and left the neighborhood dogs stranded on the roofs of their doghouses. This rain smelled eerily to her like nothing at all. Or, if anything, it smelled the way she suspected an omen might smell: a lunar eclipse, the evil eye, the number 13. It smelled, also, like fear.

When Viviane sensed its approach, she had to suppress an instinct to hide. Fear had that effect. Instead, she washed the dishes in the sink. She made a casserole, not that there was anyone around to eat it. Her mother was still at the bakery—had been since early that morning—preparing for that night's festival. Viviane hadn't seen Gabe in a while, days even, though his truck sat parked in the driveway. She tried not to think about where he might be. Cardigan and I had insisted we weren't hungry, and my mother assumed we were holed up in my room for the night. Then there was Henry.

Henry had been particularly agitated lately. Viviane had caught him sneaking off the hill—by himself!—at least three separate times that day. It seemed whenever she looked outside, there he was, marching down the hill with that big white dog traipsing beside him. At least right now she knew both he and Trouver were in Henry's room, fast asleep. Just in case, she peeked in on him one more time, relieved to see his sleeping head resting on his pillow.

The barren smell of the coming rain drove her to plug her nose with a clothespin. Viviane tried to remember what her mother had said about counteracting bad omens: a robin flying into the house was considered lucky. As was meeting three sheep or an itch on the top of your head. None seemed a very relevant (*or practical,* Viviane thought) solution until Viviane remembered the one about salt. Returning to the kitchen, Viviane hesitantly reached for the saltshaker, slowly spilled a bit of salt into her hand, then tossed it over her left shoulder. Tentatively, Viviane pulled the clothespin from her nose and breathed deeply, but, alas, the stench of impending disaster was still there.

Within that same hour, Viviane picked up a pin, dropped a glove, and turned her dress inside out and wore it with the pockets exposed and flapping at her sides. She knocked on wood until her knuckles ached and went searching through the house on her knees until she found a penny, since, apparently, picking them up was supposed to ensure some kind of daylong good luck. She turned around seven times clockwise. Crossed her fingers. Hopped backward over a broom. After all of these, she unclasped the clothespin from her nose and took a deep breath, waiting to be filled with a sense of relief. But it never came.

Finally, she surrendered and retreated to hide in the basement with the tumbling towels and the warm dryer and one of her mother's cigars.

Tossing the clothespin aside, Viviane took a few puffs on the cigar. She felt calmer and was relieved to discover that the only thing she could smell then was the crude odor of the cigar. She rubbed her eyes. *Imagine, getting this unsettled over a smell,* she thought. Feeling somewhat embarrassed and silly, Viviane stubbed out the cigar and made her way back upstairs.

And that's when the rain began to fall.

The rain increased steadily over the next hour, beating a staccato rhythm against the rooftops. People in the same houses had to yell over the noise to ask if there was a bucket to place under the leaks that were appearing in hallways, kitchens, bedrooms.

In the Lavender house, water leaked in around the poorly sealed windows, flooded the entryway with puddles, and filled the rooms with an unpleasant stink of fear.

Viviane made a mental checklist for Gabe—water damage to carpets, wood floors, and walls; leaking roof and windows—then climbed up the rickety stairs to check on the second floor.

Viviane knocked softly on my bedroom door. "Ava?" she called. "Cardigan?" Receiving no answer, she opened the door. Tufts of my long dark hair blew across the floor. The redolence of bleach stung her nose. The room, Viviane realized with stark dread, was empty. She stuck her head out the open window and peered into the rain. The bark of the cherry tree outside my room was spattered with wet brown and white feathers.

She closed the window and left. As she made her way back down the hall toward the stairs, her feet sinking into the waterlogged carpet, she paused outside Henry's bedroom. On impulse, she pushed the door. His room was empty too.

She ran her hands through her wet hair. "Well, shit," she said.

From the personal diary of Nathaniel Sorrows:

June 22, 1959

My pacing has worn the rug bare. My clothes have begun to smell. It doesn't matter. Today marks the summer solstice. That they would put such effort into celebrating a pagan holiday seems only appropriate! Monsters.

She passed by once already, walking hand in hand with the other girl, who had a pair of ridiculous home-made wings attached to her back. I've decided to wait until they return. The most I have to wait is a few hours; that I can manage.

As I write this, I peer out at the darkening sky, distracted by . . . Is that rain?

Though I usually keep the front porch light off, I flicked it on. In the beam of light spilling across the sidewalk, I saw one, then two dark spots appear on the cement. Maybe I will ask her inside. And if she won't come . . . No, she'll come. She'll have to.

Chapter Twenty

FOR THE FIRST TIME, my mother understood how parents lost control. Through it all — the lonely pregnancy, fifteen years of sleepless nights — she'd managed to keep her bearings. She'd learned to adapt to whatever came along: Henry's untouchable world, my wings. If she devised a plan and the plan proved impossible, she just created a new one. She'd never understood how other parents just *lost it.* Now she did; children betrayed their parents by becoming their own people. She'd never thought that could happen to her, whose children were so . . . strange. Could the strange survive on their own? Viviane hadn't considered it possible until that moment.

The only telephone in our house sat atop on old forgotten bureau in the hallway along the stairs. The phone had been installed sometime in the early forties. It was heavy and awkward and rang so infrequently that when it did, Viviane hardly recognized the noise at all. It was out of sheer wonder at the sound that she stopped to answer it.

She was greeted by an old familiar voice—funny how, after all this time, he still sounded exactly the same—telling her he'd found her son walking along the side of the road.

"He must have walked nearly two miles in this rain. I've got him down here at the house. The dog, too. Tried to dry the boy off, but he'd have none of that."

Viviane nodded at the phone. "Is he okay? Henry, I mean."

"Ahh, well, you might wanna hurry over here. He's acting a bit odd."

"I'll be right there," she assured him, and hung up. She hadn't the courage to tell him right then that his son was probably acting perfectly normally. For Henry at least.

Viviane threw open the hall closet and grabbed the first thing she saw—a red wool jacket from what seemed like a lifetime ago. Viviane fastened it with shaking hands, grateful it was long enough to cover the dress she was still wearing inside out for luck. By the time she reached the truck, the rain had already soaked right through the wool. *Who doesn't have a rain jacket?* she thought.

The truck sputtered and began its slow ascent to life. As she waited, Viviane reached into her purse and pulled out her compact and a tube of lipstick. Holding the mirror close to her face, she slowly slid the red gloss across her lips. It was too dark to see about her hair.

Viviane attempted to back the truck down the hill but stopped when she felt the tires slip in the mud. Instead, she shifted the sliding truck into first gear and veered around the back of the house, driving right through the flower bed that once held the most glorious dahlias in the neighborhood.

As the truck slammed onto the road, Viviane pushed the clutch to the floor, threw it into second gear, and soared into the deluge.

When we left the solstice celebration, Cardigan, Rowe, and I noticed a change in the air. All three of us tipped our faces to the sky, puzzled.

"I think it might r-rain," Rowe said.

By the time we got as far as the bakery, it was pouring and most people had escaped to their warm houses and cars, leaving the streets empty.

We ducked underneath the awning in front of the drugstore. Cardigan reached her hand behind her back and made a face. "I've ruined my shirt. It's all gooey." Cardigan's wings had dissolved into a wet, sticky mess of feathers and glue. We all had puddles in our shoes.

The wind picked up considerably. It peeled the bark from the three birches in front of the store. The strips hung from the branches, whipping and twisting in the angry air.

Though Rowe's navy peacoat was wrapped around my shoulders, I shivered at the sight of the naked trees.

"It's getting worse. You should probably get going." Rowe squeezed my hand before letting it go. Rowe had to drive his mother home from work that night, and we all agreed it was too risky for me to hide in the back of the delivery truck. The chance of getting caught was too high, although I did find the thought of it a bit thrilling.

"Are you sure you're okay to make it home by yourself?" Even standing right next to me, Rowe had to yell over the pounding beat of the torrent.

I put my hands on my hips and feigned annoyance. "Listen. I may be a bit strange, but that doesn't mean I'm afraid of the dark."

He grinned. "Just trying to be p-polite."

Cardigan smiled knowingly and ran into the rain. She disappeared into the cascade of falling water. I turned to follow.

"Hey. Where do you think you're going?" Rowe teased. I smiled as he put his hands on my hips and pulled me to him. He tenderly brushed the hair behind my ears and ran his fingertips over my face, as if trying to memorize every detail. I closed my eyes, and he kissed me again.

Then, with my lips still tingling, I ran into the rain after Cardigan.

Throughout the city, the rain was proving to be a disaster. Large puddles formed at blocked storm drains and took over yards, street corners, parking lots, playgrounds, empty flowerpots, and raised garden beds. Tree limbs broke and fell to the ground with sharp snaps. Cardigan and I raced toward Pinnacle Lane. Water coursed down my arms and legs, fused my newly cut bangs to my forehead. Cardigan's makeup ran down her face. As we passed below the worn sneakers hanging from the overhead power line, we both watched with open mouths as the shoes twisted free and flew away into the night.

At the end of the Coopers' driveway, Cardigan grabbed me and gave me a tight squeeze. "We're going to be sisters-in-law!" she yelled over the rain, then ran to her house.

If not for a dim glow in the first-floor windows, my house would have looked like just another dark part of the sky. I glanced up at the black second-story windows. I smiled at the thought of sleeping Henry, his fingers curled around the edge of his quilt. I checked my pocket for the chocolate I'd gotten him, making sure it hadn't melted. The woman at the booth had told me that chocolate came from the Mayans, an ancient people who believed that drinking hot chocolate could bring them wisdom and power. They considered it the food of their gods. I had laughed at the thought of the Mayan gods ripping open little bags of powdered cocoa to stir into warm mugs of milk, but the woman had said the Mayans made their hot chocolate from cacao beans and that they called it *xocoatl.* I didn't know if Henry would actually like the sweet, but I knew he would appreciate the new word I'd learned.

The sound of a car door made me jump. At the side of the house, I saw the taillights of Gabe's truck lit up, glowing red in the dark and the rain. Gabe hadn't been home for a few days. I tried not to think about where he might be. *Whom* he might be with.

The truck disappeared around the back of the house. I ran to hide as it careened down the hill and into the road. I stayed hidden until it had driven away.

"Your mother seems frantic to find you."

I whirled around.

Nathaniel Sorrows stood behind me, holding a black umbrella over his head.

"It can't be my mother," I shouted through the rain. My mother hadn't left the house in fifteen years. She didn't even know how to drive, did she?

"She'd probably say the same thing about you if she saw you out here right now."

I blushed. He had a point.

"It is her, nonetheless," he said. "I saw her leave the house and get into the truck."

"But what makes you think she's gone out looking for me?" I asked quietly.

Nathaniel shrugged. "Why else would she leave?"

As I thought of the few things that could motivate my mother to venture out from the security of the house on the hill, like discovering that her daughter had snuck out without permission, dread slashed through my chest like a knife. I wasn't sure what to do. Should I go home and wait for her to come back? Go to Cardigan's? But then I thought about how angry my mother would be, the injured look on her face when she realized what I'd done. I wanted to avoid seeing that look for as long as possible.

As if reading my mind, Nathaniel said, "Why don't you come inside? I have a fire going. You can dry off here while you wait for her to get back." He smiled.

I chewed my lip and thought. I could always go over to the Coopers' house, but as lenient as Cardigan's father was, he probably wouldn't be pleased I'd snuck out. I might even get Cardigan in trouble.

Nathaniel was watching me patiently. He seemed different, I noted. Less pious. More normal. Not nearly as attractive as I thought he was. With a twinge of shame, I remembered my infatuation of only a few weeks ago. What had I been thinking?

"There's little point to getting reprimanded for sneaking out *and* the dangers of pneumonia. I know how mothers can be. I could be of some assistance," he said, "determine some way you could explain your momentary disappearance."

I nodded. "Okay," I said finally.

Chapter Twenty-One

MY GRANDMOTHER was in the back of the bakery, trying to keep up with the demand brought on by the solstice celebration. It seemed no matter how many trays Penelope slipped into the display case, there were still hungry mouths to feed. So feed them they did. *Éclairs au chocolat, mille-feuille, pâté sucrée.* They'd even designed a special solstice cookie shaped like the sun and topped with yellow frosting. While taking a moment's break, Emilienne watched with pride as the girls carefully folded boxes around purchases, rang up orders, made change, smiled at impatient customers—all with efficient grace. Emilienne chuckled to herself. It was hardly appropriate to refer to them as girls. Wilhelmina had helped her run the bakery for more than thirty years now, and Penelope's children were both teenagers. While her own reflection constantly shocked her — the delicate wrinkles around her eyes and mouth, the coarse white wisps of hair threading through the black — Emilienne didn't notice how time had changed the women with whom she'd spent every day for so many years.

In the front of the store, Ignatius Lux flirted with Penelope as she tied the string around his purchase with a flourish. *That poor husband of hers,* Emilienne thought with a smile. Penelope's marriage to Zeb Cooper could have been a rocky one, considering Penelope's flirtatious manner, but Zeb was a trusting fellow and adored his playful wife. From what Emilienne had been able to tell, they'd also done a good job raising their children. *Both Cardigan and Rowe have proven to be good friends to Ava,* she thought. Rowe would turn eighteen in a couple of months. He'd leave for college soon after. *How time flies,* Emilienne mused. Though it meant losing her delivery driver, she was glad to see that Rowe wanted to do something with his life beyond driving a truck full of baked goods. He was smart, that one.

Wilhelmina, toting another empty tray over her head, brushed by Emilienne. "That Ignatius Lux just bought the last *congolais*," she said. The coconut biscuit was a customer favorite.

Wilhelmina's long braid was dusted with white, whether from flour or age Emilienne was no longer sure. Wilhelmina tossed the tray on top of an already-wobbling stack waiting by the sink to be washed. Emilienne meant to move then, to get a start on those dishes she knew would take all night to clean, but her feet seemed unwilling to move. She leaned heavily on the wooden table in the middle of the room. Nostalgically, she smoothed her hands across the top, feeling the little cracks and nicks that covered it. Over the years this table had been used to pound out the dough for baguettes, croissants, morning rolls, and cinnamon buns. When Viviane was a baby, this was the table upon which Emilienne set her bassinet while she made all those loaves of bread no one would buy.

"Lord knows that man could stand to miss a few sweets now and then," Wilhelmina added, puffing out her cheeks and making a big arch over her own flat abdomen to indicate the girth that hung over Ignatius Lux's belt.

Wilhelmina's hands were quick as she arranged a tray of *tartes tatins* for display.

She glanced over at Emilienne. "You sure are quiet tonight, boss-lady."

Emilienne rubbed her eyes. "Just a long, strange day. That's all." It seemed to Emilienne that more than her three deceased siblings were haunting her today. Earlier she could have sworn she'd seen Levi Blythe, the first love of her life, ordering a solstice cookie. The boy she knew only as Dublin had winked at her through the window. Satin Lush watched her from one of the wrought-iron chairs in the middle of the bakery. And each step she took was echoed by the hollow thump of her husband Connor's cane. All the loves of her life.

Wilhelmina whistled. "Has the solstice gotten to you? Made ya all nostalgic and weepy?" She threw Emilienne the dish towel she had slung through her apron strings. Emilienne hadn't known she was crying. She quickly wiped her eyes with the damp towel. Emilienne hated to admit it, but the busy day had been especially hard on her. The backs of her knees throbbed with fatigue, her feet and wrists ached, and she could feel a headache coming on. The pain was so sharp, it glowed behind the lids of her eyes. Maybe it was the rain.

"Did you know I was raised by my grandmother?" Wilhelmina asked.

Emilienne shook her head.

"I surely was. I was five years old when they took me from her—both of us screaming and hollering. They took me from my home and put me in that school where I was beaten for just thinking in my own language." Wilhelmina gave a sad chuckle. "And sometimes when I'm feeling extra down, when I'm missing my grandmother, I have to remind myself that love comes in all sorts of packages." She motioned to the bakery. "I got this place. Hell, Emilienne, I got you."

Wilhelmina went over to place a hand on Emilienne's

cheek. "Just because love don't look the way you think it should don't mean you don't have it."

Emilienne could barely see him when he appeared, his flickering form translucent under the glare of the overhead lights. Despite this, Emilienne could still make out the mangled mess of René's once-beautiful face.

The last customer bid them good night and walked out into the rain. Penelope locked the door behind him and flipped the sign in the window to read CLOSED.

"How'd we do?" she asked, slipping off one of her shoes and wincing as she rubbed her red feet.

Wilhelmina's hands flew as she counted the till, nodding to Penelope that they'd done well.

"Do we have anything left for tomorrow?" Penelope asked, fluffing her youthful blond ponytail. Even after a full day's work, Penelope managed to look fresh—her skin dewy, her nose lightly kissed by a splash of freckles. Emilienne couldn't help but envy the woman for her youth, though many people would argue that—in terms of beauty—Emilienne far surpassed Penelope.

"We've got a couple of batches of *pain au chocolat*," Emilienne told them absentmindedly, distracted by the way René glided around the bakery, passing through the cast-iron tables and chairs. She was fairly certain that the majority of tomorrow's customers would consist of the neighborhood housewives donning dark glasses and toting cranky children. The chocolate croissants would keep the children quiet; for the parents' hangovers,

Emilienne brewed a special tea she kept hidden behind the counter. It was only peppermint, but Emilienne believed self-induced illnesses were all in the head; that is, if someone believed Emilienne's "special tea" would cure them, it usually did.

"What will we serve once we run out?" Penelope asked, drawing her pretty eyebrows together in concern. "People are going to want more than a couple of batches of croissants." Emilienne sighed, suddenly feeling as though she hadn't slept since moving to the house at the end of Pinnacle Lane, as if she'd been forced to spend the last thirty-four years without the comfort of a single night's rest.

"We'll close," she answered.

Both women turned to stare at Emilienne; Wilhelmina lost count of the till money. "We've never done that before," she said, shuffling the wrinkled bills into a single pile and starting the tally again.

"Well, here's something else we've never done." Emilienne pulled the leather rope of keys from her wrist and placed it on the counter before Wilhelmina. "You open."

Wilhelmina looked up in surprise, but this time she didn't lose count. Emilienne could see the number balanced on the tip of her tongue. She patted Wilhelmina on the shoulder. "I'm going home," she announced, and pulled her apron off in one grand gesture, slapping it onto the counter next to the keys.

"Well, you won't be walking home in this rain. Rowe will take you," Penelope said, motioning to the back door, where Rowe now stood quietly waiting.

"No. I'll be fine," Emilienne insisted. The cloth awning above the door made sharp cracking noises as the wind whipped at the fabric.

"We have to get ready for tomorrow, anyway," Wilhelmina said. "You go with Rowe. One of the fellas from the festival can drive me an' Penelope home later."

Emilienne slipped her arm through Rowe's. Together they walked to the truck. René followed silently behind them.

Emilienne felt each step in her aching joints. She hoped Rowe didn't notice how much she needed his help. If he did, he didn't let on. She admired him for this.

"Your ch-ch-chariot awaits," he said, opening the truck's passenger door with a flourish.

He was funny, too.

"I hope my granddaughter falls in love with you," she said, and when his face flushed red, she immediately regretted having said such a thing. "I'm sorry," she apologized. "I don't know what's gotten into me." She tried to ignore René's eerie shadow in the back of the truck.

"Wilhelmina says the solstice can have that effect on people," Rowe said.

Emilienne smiled.

They were quiet during the drive, listening to the rain

beat across the top of the old Divco truck. Rowe drove all the way up to the end of the Lavenders' driveway and then walked Emilienne up to the front door of her house. From the foyer, Emilienne watched Rowe navigate the truck back down the slippery hill. She turned and looked directly at René. "I hope he falls in love with my granddaughter," she confided.

Chapter Twenty-Two

THE GRIFFITH HOUSE was nothing like Viviane remembered, reminding her of how fast the world changed and of how insignificant she was in the grand scheme of things. She thought it unfair that her life should be both irrelevant and difficult. One or the other seemed quite enough.

As Viviane made her way up the front walk, a gust of cold, rain-soaked wind rushed up the bottom of her coat. It took the strength of both Viviane and the housemaid to keep the door open enough for Viviane to slip in.

"Quite the full-blown storm out there, isn't it?" the housemaid said, taking Viviane's coat.

Viviane nodded and watched as her sodden red coat was hung carefully in the entryway closet alongside several mink stoles and a chinchilla fur muff. The maid offered Viviane a box of tissues. She obligingly took a few, wiped them over her face and hair. If her hair wasn't already a mess, it surely was now.

When she was finished, the housemaid gave her a complaisant nod. "Come this way, please."

Viviane followed the housemaid through the house. Gone were the cramped rooms, the rotted floorboards, the crumbling fireplace. Everything was so *chic*—the sunken living room, the wet bar, the big television set. Gone were the details that made it a *home*—the tiny bowls of potpourri, the lace curtains Beatrix Griffith hand-washed each spring with furze-blossom ashes. There weren't even any family photos. The house looked like it belonged in a catalog.

The maid left Viviane to wait in the kitchen—a room full of shiny appliances, some of which Viviane had never before seen. The countertops were a ridiculous shade of green. A large windowed door led out to the backyard. Looking outside, Viviane saw a pool in the spot that once led to the mysteries of King Tut's remains. Rain bounced angrily off the surface.

On one side of the kitchen stood an oblong chrome table. In a teal-colored vinyl chair at the end of the table sat Henry, furiously finishing a detailed map of the neighborhood. Eight other such maps were spread across the table.

Trouver lay at Henry's feet, and the big dog raised his head when Viviane entered. He thumped his wet tail against the floor, splattering mud on the wall.

She heard him walk into the kitchen behind her. "He's pretty good with those maps, isn't he?" he asked.

Viviane turned. Though his tie was undone, in every other way his suit was immaculate: clean and sharply creased, not one missing button or loose-hanging thread. Who was this unfamiliar man?

"Did you know that one of the most distinguished American mapmakers of the early nineteenth century was named Henry as well? Henry Schenck Tanner."

"Did you read that somewhere?" she asked quietly.

He smirked, suddenly cocky. "Must have."

He shrugged off his suit jacket and slung it coolly over one of the chairs. Viviane wondered if he sat on his bed every night polishing his shoes and expensive cuff links, or if he had someone to do that for him.

"I picked him up on Phinney Ridge. I have no idea where he might have been going. And in this weather." He shrugged. "I figured I should collect him and call you."

The last fifteen years had taken their toll on Jack Griffith—there were flecks of gray near his temples, but that wasn't what threw her. It wasn't even the impersonal house or the ridiculous red-and-white-striped suspenders he wore under his jacket. It was that he seemed unable to look her in the eye.

"It's good to see you, Viviane," he said, in what Viviane heard as an attempt to sound casual.

She had imagined this moment many times. She'd prayed and wished for the chance to see him again, yet now that it was here, she couldn't think of anything to say. It was strange. He was strange. Different.

My mother nodded, cleared her throat. "Yes. Well, thank you for finding him," she murmured. She turned and began collecting the scattered maps from the table. "We'll be out of your way in just a minute."

From out of the corner of her eye, she saw Jack's face fall.

"You don't have to go right away," he said in a rush. "I could get Rita to make up something to eat. It's really no trouble." He walked up behind her, stopping so close that the toes of his shoes lightly touched the backs of her heels. "It's just so good to see you," he said, his voice cracking.

Viviane turned around. He smiled, revealing the gap between his teeth that haunted Viviane's dreams.

"Listen, I—" He paused. He pointed to Henry. "He's mine, isn't he?"

Viviane froze, then nodded. Yes. He was his. So was she, come to think of it. For fifteen years, in fact, she had been his.

"God, Viviane!" Jack exclaimed. "I have a son. You have no idea how exciting this is!" He reached over to ruffle Henry's hair. Henry cringed and pulled away. "He looks exactly like me, doesn't he?"

"He doesn't like to be touched," Viviane explained softly.

Jack seemed not to hear her. He turned suddenly and took her face in his hands. "I think about you all the time. You have to believe that. I think about you every day." Viviane's face turned a glorious pink at his touch. She closed her eyes and breathed in deeply, delighted to find that he still smelled of soap and Turtle Wax.

"No one has ever loved me the way you did, Vivi. And the thought of you having to raise our son all alone . . ."

Vivi? Viviane looked up sharply. There was only one person who called her Vivi, and that was Gabe. Hearing Gabe's nickname for her—*just* for her—in Jack's voice was unsettling. She could feel coils of doubt creep over her. She tried to ignore them. "I wasn't exactly on my own," Viviane replied softly, irritated that she was suddenly thinking of Gabe when she finally had Jack standing right in front of her. Gabe with his kind eyes, his strong hands, his unfaltering . . .

"But I wasn't there." Jack touched his forehead to Viviane's.

Why haven't I seen it before? she thought. *Gabe loves me.*

"I can help you now," Jack boasted. "Look around. I can give you anything you could ever need!"

She glanced at Henry. It was funny. Henry resembled Jack so much, but when she looked at her son, the other person who came to mind was Gabe: Gabe helping Henry climb into the truck before taking off on another one of their adventures; Gabe and Henry chasing down that ridiculous bat; Gabe looking at her shyly when he cradled Henry in his arms for the first time fifteen years ago.

"Can you ever forgive me?"

Viviane sighed, closed her eyes. Of course she could forgive him, and then surely be happy for the rest of her life.

"In a way, we could even be a family," he added.

Viviane opened her eyes. "What do you mean, *in a way*?"

Jack motioned to the room around them. "Look what I've done with my life! I'm finally someone important in this town. You can't expect me to forfeit all of this?"

Viviane narrowed her eyes. "Don't tell me you're still searching for your father's approval? He's been gone for years, Jack!"

"That's irrelevant," Jack spat. "People who never respected my father respect *me* now," he said. "They look up to *me*; they ask *my* opinion. I'm not going to just give all of that up to take up with—"

Viviane flinched in anticipation of the old and ugly phrase.

Jack ran his hands over his face, sweaty with aggravation. "Look, I'm sorry to be so blunt. But, Jesus Christ, Viviane, I thought you of all people would understand."

Viviane helped Henry into his coat, and the two quietly left the impressive house, followed closely by Trouver. She forgot her red coat hanging in the hall closet.

Back in the truck, she wrapped Henry in two old, scratchy blankets she found under the seat. She used a third one to dry off Trouver. The blankets smelled a bit musty, but neither Henry nor Trouver seemed to mind. She turned the key and the truck sputtered and gasped and died.

Then it hit her. She *did* understand. At last, when it came to Jack, she could say that she understood completely. The house was renovated. There was a pool in the backyard. And there were his ridiculous, expensive clothes. A lot of things had changed. In spite of all that, Jack hadn't changed at all. And with that realization, my mother began to laugh. And she laughed.

And she laughed.

And she laughed.

She laughed until Henry covered his ears with his hands and Trouver began to howl. She laughed until her cheeks were sore and her throat hurt and her eyes watered. She laughed for her wasted, difficult life that never had to be wasted or difficult in the first place. She laughed for her two gloriously beautiful but strange children and for a carpenter she should have loved from the moment her mother heard the birdsong announcing good love's arrival.

But more important, she laughed because finally, after all these years, she didn't love Jack Griffith anymore. It was the laugh of relief.

Viviane turned to Henry. "Are you okay?" she asked.

"There's a bee in the bush and a cat on the wall," he

said miserably, pushing one of his hand-drawn maps into Viviane's lap. It was remarkable, she noted, how accurate the drawing was. Even the street signs were posted on the correct side of the road. Then she noticed that this particular map was different from every other map Henry had made in one way. On the door of one house appeared to be a smear of blood.

"What is this? Are you bleeding?" Viviane did a quick check of Henry's fingers and arms, his nose, ears, stomach, tongue.

Henry shook his head and slapped her hands away. "There's red on the floor and feathers everywhere!" he shouted, stabbing the map with angry fingers.

"Henry, listen to me . . ." Viviane spoke slowly. She hated when other people did that, spoke to Henry as if he were still a small child, but sometimes it was hard to tell if he was listening.

She took a long look at her son, wrapped in blankets and a rain jacket, his worried face sticking out from the hood.

"You were certainly smart to wear a coat," she mused. The day had not implied that such a fierce storm was on its way.

"It happens after the rain," Henry said.

After the rain?

"You knew," she whispered. "You knew it was going to rain." And if he knew that, what *else* did he know? *What happens after the rain?*

Henry pushed his map at her again. "Pinna is hurt," he pleaded. "The Sad Man says listen."

The engine of the old truck finally turned over and roared to life.

Chapter Twenty-Three

NATHANIEL LED ME to the back of the house, where a fire blazed. The fireplace was made of stacked stone and ran from the ceiling down to the floor, where it yawned into an opening large enough that I could feel the heat of the fire from the hallway. A pile of newly cut wood was stacked beside the fireplace, the ax delicately tipped into the top log.

I'd never actually been in anyone else's house before—not even Cardigan's. It was strange, doing things that other people—*normal* people—did. But the thing was, being in that house didn't make me feel like everyone else. Instead, I felt as if I were acting out a part in a play, a fictional character playing a role that someone else had written for me. When it was over, I would take my place at curtain call, and then I would go home to where I was real again.

Marigold Pie's living-room floor was covered with a soft brown carpet. There was an olive-green couch and a glass-topped coffee table in the room. A tall table in a corner held glass bottles of different shapes and sizes, each containing a fluid of some color or another. An impressive ship in a bottle was displayed on the mantel. The only thing that I wasn't sure about was the huge needlepoint kitten staring at me from over the mantel. I figured that was just an isolated lapse in taste.

Nathaniel leaned his umbrella against the metal screen in front of the hearth and walked over to the table of bottles. "How about something to drink? Might help with the cold," he said.

I hesitated for a second. "Okay."

I stood quietly in front of the fire, the warmth of the flames wicking through my calves and my outstretched hands until I stopped shivering. I pulled off my socks and shoes, hung the socks on the fire screen, and stretched the tongues out from my shoes before setting them in front of the fire. I pulled Rowe's coat from my shoulders and draped it, lovingly, next to my socks. I shook out my wings, scattering little droplets of water across the room, sprinkling pictures and furniture.

"Some brandy should warm you right up," Nathaniel said, handing me a glass. He sat down on the floor in front of the fire.

I sat down next to him, watched the way he swirled his drink and placed his nose at the edge of the glass before drinking the gold liquid. When I tried to do the same, I inhaled too deeply. My nostrils burned and I could already taste the brandy in the back of my throat. Determinedly, I took a sip. It stung my lips. When I swallowed, my tongue wanted to spring from my mouth. But then a warmth, like slow-burning honey, ran through me. It was not entirely unpleasant, but I didn't drink any more.

The fire crackled; the flames faded to short purple triangles. Nathaniel added another log to the blaze, and I watched the fire grow with a sharp hiss. He settled next to me and tipped the last of his drink into his mouth, then got up and set the empty glass on the fireplace before sitting down next to me again. "I'm so glad you're here," he said.

I could smell the tang of the alcohol on his breath, the stink of unwash on his skin. I was suddenly very aware that I was alone in a strange house with a strange man I hardly knew.

"Where's your aunt?" I asked.

"She's around," he said noncommittally.

"I should go," I said, pulling away. "I need to find my mom."

"You can't go yet," he commanded, and grabbed at one of my wings, making me yelp. A dark look crossed his face. But when he looked down at the handful of feathers in his hand, he laughed a little and let go. "I have something to show you," he said, his voice amicable once again. "Just wait for a minute."

I swallowed hard. "Okay," I lied.

I jumped up as soon as he left the room, knocking over my glass of brandy. As quietly as I could, I wandered up the hall. I took a wrong turn and found myself in a room where I could just make out the shapes of furniture in the dark — a couch, a lamp, a chair. I stepped in farther and felt the floor under my feet dip and change. I crouched down to peer at the carpet. A path that ran the length of a large center window had been worn into the carpet, like a trail cut through a forest grove.

I stood back and looked up. The window provided a clear view of my house, of my bedroom window. Then something on the windowsill caught my eye. It was a feather — not brown and white like my own — but jet black and as long as my arm. The feather was beautiful, shiny and gleaming. I reached for the floor lamp standing next to me and switched it on. Then I saw them.

Birds. Littering the floor, covering the chair and the couch, piled around the room in stacks of ten or twenty. Some had been pinned to the wall with wings outstretched, as if in flight; others hung upside down from the ceiling by tiny bits of string wrapped tightly around their curled feet, as if being punished for a terrible crime. Some had been stripped of their feathers, some stripped of their wings. Others were missing their eyes.

The once-warm brandy turned cold in my stomach. I gagged, then swallowed fast to keep from vomiting.

"I didn't intend for you to see them." Nathaniel had come up behind me. He gently plucked the long black feather from my hand. He sighed.

"What do you mean?" With growing dread, I noted that he was between me and the door.

He picked up one of the dead birds and shook it in my face. "Masquerading as a holy creature," Nathaniel said with disgust. Then he dropped it back onto the floor, where it landed with a sickening thud. It was a spotted towhee—a male—with black-and-white wings and a patch of red on each side. The bird's insides dribbled from a wound in its belly.

"Blessed with wings like God's messengers, and what do they do with them? Soil them in birdbaths and mud puddles. Eat garbage." He kicked at a pile of carcasses near his foot. "These monstrosities are the reason no one sees you for what you are."

He reached out and stroked my wings.

"But I've never been fooled," he said, gently now. "I've always known."

I made a move to step around him.

What I remember most vividly is that he told me he loved me before he grabbed me.

"Please!" I begged, struggling against him. "Let me go!"

I kicked at him wildly. When my foot made contact with his shin, he tightened his grip. I threw my arm back and cracked his rib with my elbow. He dropped to the ground with a shout, and his grip loosened enough for me to break free. I ran for the door, but he caught me and wrenched me back.

He pulled me by my hair back to the room with the fireplace. He seemed surprised to find me so strong; to be honest, so was I. He wrestled me to the ground, shoved me flat on my back, and pressed his knee against my sternum. The pressure against my lungs made it hard to breathe. Or maybe it was the fear choking me. I tried to scream. He gagged me with one of his handkerchiefs. Hot tears streamed from my eyes.

"I wish you didn't make me do that. You have such a pretty mouth," he said, stroking my cheek.

He flipped me on my stomach then, my face pressed against the carpet and my arms trapped beneath me. Keeping a firm grasp on my wings, he undid his belt. My wings shuddered. I felt as much as heard my own screams, so wretched and desperate that they sounded inhuman.

"I can't tell you how many times I've imagined this,"

he whispered. “How many times I’ve been aroused by the thought of downy pillows and cotton balls and rain-heavy clouds.”

He rubbed my feathers between his fingers, then dipped his face to my shoulder blades. I could feel his breath on my skin. “Because that’s what I imagine an angel will feel like.”

I remember pain. White-hot searing pain. And shame.

Then, clutching my feathers in his fists, he began to cry. “You’re just a girl!” he wailed. “Jesus Christ. You’re just a girl after all.” Huge racking sobs rattled his chest.

“You stupid bitch!” he screamed, his voice hoarse with rage. He ripped feathers from my wings as he pushed into me deeper. Fiercer.

The ax blade was little—no larger than his fist—but it was sharp and when he yanked it from the woodpile, maybe he thought it would slice through my wings easily. But mine were nothing like the tiny bird wings he’d amputated before. My wings were strong and virile and had no intention of giving up without a fight. They thrashed and flailed so much that in the end he had to lunge and hack away at them like a crazed butcher.

When it was over, he tossed the ax to the floor next to my amputated wings.

“You tricked me,” he sneered. I moaned while he wiped the blood from his face.

Then he ran.

Emilienne made her way through a puddle in the hallway of her house with slow, cautious steps. In the kitchen she took a glass from the cupboard and placed it under the faucet. With a weary glance at the rain seeping in through the cracks around the windows, she realized that more water was the last thing she needed. One of the cats — the needy orange tabby — rubbed against her legs and mewed. What did Viviane call this one? Underfoot? *Well,* she thought, reaching down and lifting him into her arms, *that seems fitting.*

"Are the kids upstairs?" she asked the cat. He blinked once with his cerebral green eyes, which she took as a reassuring yes. As she was carrying him past the living room, the cat made a low moaning sound and jumped out of her arms, skidding on his hind legs as he fled down the hallway. In the living room, René sat on the harpsichord bench, his fingers tapping various keys in a silent song; he was alone.

Emilienne could still see the damage William Peyton had done to René's face so many years ago. One eye stared blindly over her shoulder, the color muted by a white film; the other eye hung from its socket and rested on the sharp edge of his exposed cheekbone. Of his nose there was only a sliver of cartilage left. There was no mouth, no chin; his jaw hung at a crude and broken angle, which explained why his voice sounded so thick-tongued. As far as Emilienne could tell, he hadn't a tongue at all. Or any teeth.

"Oh, René." Emilienne sank down beside him.

Later, when remembering this moment, Emilienne

would recall how morbidly suitable she found his deformed face, how apt it seemed to hear such horror related by such a gruesome source. Because it was horrific, what he was telling her. Indescribably, unimaginably horrific. She thought it strange that she felt nothing at all when he tried to hold her hand; his transparent fingers slipped through hers. When he finished telling her the terrible truth, she rose from the bench, smoothed the wrinkles from her skirt. She walked out of the room and through the water in the hallway to the phone, dialed the number to the police station, and in a clear voice gave the operator the address on Pinnacle Lane where Marigold Pie lived with her nephew.

Before she left the house herself, she turned back to René. "Don't you dare take her with you," she pleaded.

"I don't want to," he croaked.

Chapter Twenty-Four

WHEN MY GRANDMOTHER reached Marigold Pie's front yard, a crisp lightning bolt cracked overhead, quickly followed by a thunderous *boom!* In the moment when the lightning lit up the sky, Emilienne noted that the letter *P* in Marigold Pie's name was missing from the mailbox. It lay under the giant rhododendron bush that blocked the house from the road. The letter must have fallen off, landing upside down and backward so that it resembled not a *P* but a lowercase *b*. With ironic despair, Emilienne thought, *Henry, I've finally found your* b *in the bush.*

The front door was open, the house dark and quiet. Emilienne shivered, partly from the cold, partly from fear. But then she entered and resignation settled over her. She found a light switch and flicked it on. The floor and walls of the hallway were splattered with what looked like paint, so bright was the red. The air was thick with brown-and white-speckled feathers. She choked as if they were going into her mouth, up her nose, into her lungs. Frantically, Emilienne brushed them away from her face.

There's blood on the floor and feathers everywhere.

When Emilienne first entered the back room, her heart galloped with some relief: her granddaughter didn't have blond hair. But then she saw the bloody stumps on my back. And saw my wings—a bloody mess of torn sinews and feathers and broken bones cast aside on the carpet. The bile rose in her throat, and her heart sank. It was me after all.

Emilienne knelt down and pressed her face close to mine, refusing to breathe until she felt my breath on her cheek. There it was. Quickly she pulled off her wet coat and pushed it against the wounds. There was so much blood. The carpet was sticky with it. Red rings leaked through both sides of the coat, and Emilienne's hands were soon covered with blood too. And though she didn't need to see it to know it was there, she looked up anyway. There it was, hanging over the mantel.

The cat on the wall.

"Heart in my mouth" was a phrase my mother had never understood. As she sped toward Pinnacle Lane, Henry and Trouver trying to stay upright in the seat beside her,

Viviane's heart was not in her mouth. What good could it do in her mouth? Her heart had leaped out of her chest and was racing two feet in front of the truck. She could see it in the headlights, its arteries pumping like arms at its side. Viviane wished she could send it farther ahead. She wished that it had already rounded the curve onto Pinnacle Lane. She wished that it was sitting beside me, wherever I was.

Henry whimpered with worry.

"We'll be there soon," Viviane crooned, creating a little song with the words, something she used to do to soothe him when he was little. Even now, as Henry began to hum the song to himself, she could see the tension wash away from his face.

The truck sped past the elementary school, the church, and the post office in a wet blur. The rain surged; the wipers barely kept pace. Viviane leaned forward, knuckles white on the steering wheel, and peered into the dark.

When she saw him — the man running straight toward her — she slammed on the brakes. The tires ripped hard through the clattering rain with a squeal, and she threw her arm out to stop Trouver and Henry from crashing into the windshield. The man stopped in front of the truck and stared at Viviane with wild black eyes, his face streaked with red. *Blood,* she realized with horror.

Before Viviane had time to react, two figures appeared behind him. Translucent and pale, they shimmered in the truck's headlights. Their eyes were opaque and blind;

water poured over their monstrous gray skin. One figure cradled a baby over the place where her heart should have been. The other flashed from canary to girl, reaching out an arm in rage to grab at the man.

And then they were upon him.

Viviane watched in terror as the translucent figures engulfed him. His screams, hoarse and inhuman, filled the night.

With a sudden flash, the street burst into flames. The heat scorched the glass of the windshield. The man tried to flee—wildly thrashing his arms—but his movements only seemed to feed the fire.

And then, just as suddenly, the fire and its victim were gone, leaving only the heavy stench of singed skin.

Trouver turned a nervous half-circle on the truck seat, whining and stepping on Henry.

"You stay here. Don't move," Viviane told Henry. She threw the truck into park and flung open the door. The dog leaped out after her and circled the truck in hurried steps, his body tucked low to the ground. In front of the truck, a black mark scarred the pavement where the wretched man had stood. She recalled the man's eyes—black, feral, and unblinking. Viviane dropped to her knees, sinking into the puddle of water around the truck, and ran her fingers over the mark. It was still hot to the touch.

She looked up in time to see the specters fade into the darkness.

The ambulance arrived at Marigold Pie's house, soon followed by the local police. The flashing lights had drawn all of Pinnacle Lane to the scene. There were the old Moss sisters in their matching house shoes and coats and a single umbrella protecting their curlers from the rain. There was a sleepy and bed-clothed Mart Flannery and his son, Jeremiah. Zeb Cooper had jumped out of bed at the sound of the ambulance's wail. Wearing nothing but red long johns and a pair of galoshes, he was trying to persuade his curious neighbors to move to the sidewalk. His son, Rowe, was there and his crying daughter, Cardigan — both of their faces white with shock. Next to them was his wife, Penelope, who'd wept upon learning that her own family was all right, and then again when she learned Emilienne's family was not. There was Wilhelmina Dovewolf, guiding my mother inside Marigold's house, both quiet in stoic despair.

There was Constance Quakenbush and Delilah Zimmer, best friends and first-grade teachers at the elementary school. There was Ignatius Lux, the high-school principal, and his wife, Estelle Margolis, and, next to them, Amos Fields, who'd never been much good to anyone since his son died in the Second Great War but always seemed to have money for a morning croissant at Emilienne's bakery. There was Pastor Trace Graves and some of the high-school kids who'd wandered down from the reservoir. One of the boys thought to grab the big white dog standing in the street and loop his belt around the dog's neck to keep him out of trouble. A girl wiped the dog's muddy paws with her jacket. Eventually there were several teams of ambulance attendants and more police officers in stiff blue uniforms, their vehicles crowding the street in a chaotic jumble of flashing lights. When they carried me out — my wingless body prone on a stretcher, my mother and grandmother walking beside me in blood-covered clothes — it was said that the entire block fell silent in reverence.

The lead attendant was a big surly man who led Emilienne and Viviane into the ambulance behind me, telling his partner to watch them both for shock. Unintentionally, this left Henry to his own devices.

Though his sister, his mother, and his grandmother were on the way to the nearest hospital, Henry was happy. He was happy because the whole thing was over and he no longer had the responsibility of trying to make the Sad Man's warning heard. Because once things turned out, good or bad, there's nothing you can do about it. It just is. And Henry liked *just is.* Anything else was too complicated.

Our mother had told him to *Stay here. Don't move.* So that was what Henry did. He stayed in the truck. But after a while, Henry realized that though he didn't see anyone he knew, he did see lots of people he didn't know, and that made him feel a little sick. Then he saw Trouver. Henry got out of the truck and walked toward the big dog, counting things as he went. Henry counted the flashing lights, the number of people gathered in the street, the umbrellas, the raindrops. He counted because counting always felt good, and it felt bad not being able to see anyone he knew. It also felt bad that Trouver was sitting with another boy, one Henry didn't know. So Henry stayed focused on counting—counting the number of steps it took to get across the street to Trouver—until someone put a hand on his shoulder.

Henry screamed. The woman with her hand on his shoulder jumped and pulled her hand away.

"I'm sorry!" she gasped. "I just thought—you looked lost." The woman twirled a strand of her copper-colored hair around one of her fingers. She looked around frantically. "I didn't mean anything by it!" she insisted.

Wilhelmina rushed over, Penelope right behind her. Wilhelmina spoke to Henry in a soothing voice, all the while motioning for the boy with his belt looped around Trouver's neck to bring the dog over. Penelope turned to the woman. "What'd you touch him for?" she scolded. "Don't you think he's had a rough enough night as it is?"

The woman released her hair from her finger. "Well, I certainly didn't mean to upset him. I didn't know he—I just thought I could help."

"And what made you think you could do that?"

"He looked . . . He needed . . ." she stuttered nonsensically.

When Laura Lovelorn moved to the neighborhood five years ago, she hadn't known about Viviane Lavender. Hadn't even remembered meeting her that night at the summer solstice so many years ago. And during her many trips to the bakery for a loaf of the thick-crusted *pain au levain* or a dinner baguette, she'd never noticed how much Emilienne Lavender's grandson resembled her husband. Now she was embarrassed by how blind she'd been.

After Beatrix Griffith disappeared, Laura moved away from her beloved eastern Washington—with its hot summers and snowy winters—to live with her husband in Seattle, a town known for its year-round rains. She was quickly welcomed into the neighborhood, due mainly to her themed cocktail parties and sweet disposition. She could always be counted on to buy at least one box of shortbread cookies from the local Girl Scout troop, never left the house without her white gloves, never served her husband a meal of leftover casserole, always did everything she was supposed to do. When Jack didn't want any children, she told the girls at the hospital where she volunteered that she and Jack needed to take care of his father before they started a family of their own. After John Griffith died, she told them she and Jack wanted to travel the world instead, visit the pyramids in Egypt, walk the boot-shaped coastline of Italy. Then when Jack moved to the separate bedroom on the other side of the house, she stopped telling them anything at all.

It might have been clear to anyone else that Jack was unhappy—that, perhaps, he had never even loved her at all—but Laura refused to see it. She didn't see the way he avoided the bakery, didn't see how his eyes squinted shut whenever they passed Pinnacle Lane. She didn't notice that he rarely spoke to anyone during their infamous parties, that while she served guests from trays of cheese balls and deviled eggs, Jack spent most of the night standing in the corner, smiling blandly while the ice melted in his highball glass. She didn't see it because when it came to love, she saw what she wanted to see. Laura had always been a good wife. The years she'd been married to Jack Griffith, she'd spent in a love-induced fog, believing that Jack was happy with the life they'd created together and, more significant, that he loved her.

On this summer solstice, Laura Lovelorn returned home late in the evening to find her husband sitting in the dark, an empty bottle clutched in his hands, his breath reeking of bourbon.

"I'm a fool, Laura," he blubbered. "I lost the love of my life tonight."

Laura leaned down to stroke her husband's hair. "What are you talking about, sweetie? I'm right here." She kissed his forehead.

Jack looked up at her, blinking. "I wasn't talking about you."

Laura smiled sweetly. "Who, then?"

"Viviane. Viviane Lavender."

And as Jack continued to blubber on about a secret life, a life of love and betrayal, the fog finally lifted from Laura's eyes.

"Oh," Laura had whispered. "Oh my."

When he was finished, she walked into the bedroom where she'd slept alone now for so many years. She pulled her suitcase from the closet and packed her belongings, carefully choosing the items she'd take with her and deciding which ones would have to stay until later. She dragged her suitcase out into the hall and told Jack she was leaving him. He only waved at her halfheartedly with his bottle, which told Laura how very wrong she'd been. Jack Griffith had never loved her, not as she thought he had and never as he loved Viviane Lavender.

Laura threw the heavy suitcase into the back of the car and backed out of the driveway. Turning out onto the street, she saw the flashing lights and swarms of people filling the end of Pinnacle Lane. She pulled the car to the side of the road and got out, shielding her eyes from the heavy current of rain pouring from the sky.

She saw Viviane Lavender's son before she'd even had time to find out what had happened. Looking at him, she could only shake her head. Henry was a mirror image of Jack Griffith in his former years. Yet there was a look behind the boy's eyes that was much different from anything Laura ever saw in Jack's. It was as if Henry carried the world, misshapen and imperfect, in his lovely wide pupils.

How could she not have seen it?

Laura grabbed Wilhelmina's hand in her own. "I just

want to help," she said. Wilhelmina peered over Laura's shoulder at the crowd. "Help, huh? Well, we might need a bit of that."

In the bakery Wilhelmina flipped the switch on the coffee pot. She pulled the porcelain cups and saucers from the cupboard, lining them up on the front counter, each cup balanced on its particular plate. The coffee would have to do until she got the oven started. Penelope sent Zeb off for supplies as Wilhelmina began feeding the brick oven with logs of dried eucalyptus, dismissing any ideas for pastries or other desserts. What everybody needed was bread. Hearty, sustainable bread warm from the oven, with thick crusts on the outside and soft on the inside, topped with butter, honey, or hazelnut spread.

When Zeb returned, Wilhelmina pointed him to the hand mill and set him to work grinding the fresh spelt, rye, and red wheat they would use to make *pain de campagne.* She gave Rowe and Cardigan the job of pounding the dough for the baguettes and showed Laura Lovelorn how to tend the fire.

It took all night for the bakery to fill with the aroma of freshly baked bread, but, no matter, no one had any intention of leaving. Besides, where would they go? Every once in a while, they would look up from their particular tasks, their faces smudged with flour, and catch in one another's eyes the look of despair. Then Trouver would shift in his sleep or Henry would start to hum, and the bakers would return to their work.

Outside, the crowd around Pinnacle Lane grew larger, the wet street bulging with neighbors who'd heard of the attack. For reasons they themselves couldn't fully explain, each felt compelled to pay their respects. They battled the pelting rain in their Oldsmobile Sedans, their Studebaker Starliners, their Ford Model B pickups with the family dog sniffing the wet air in the bed of the truck. They gathered around Pinnacle Lane, spilling down the street and into the neighboring yards. They kept clear the place in the street stained by the black mark that was once Nathaniel Sorrows. They came with their children, their wives and husbands, their parents. They came dressed as if coming to church or to a funeral, or as if coming straight from bed, which most of them did. They came with tents and umbrellas, hats and gloves; they came with nothing at all, not even a jacket to protect them from the rain. By dawn a donation box had been set on the counter at the bakery, and people solemnly offered their spare change in exchange for a slice of bread, a warm croissant. The rain continued to fall. And still, the people kept coming.

Some brought with them their Bibles—the passages they thought most poignant underlined in red. Some sat in silent circles and walked their fingers around strands of beads in unplanned unison. Others brought along mats to kneel on as soothing chants rose from their throats. As water poured over their upturned faces, their prayers were sent to the sky. They weren't prayers for forgiveness or salvation. They weren't sent in gratitude for the angel walking among the wretched human race. They weren't for the soul of a deformed and cursed half-human creature who lived at the end of Pinnacle Lane. They were, quite simply, prayers said for a girl.

For me.

Viviane opened her eyes to a white hospital room. The morning sun peeked mildly through the bare window. She stretched out her legs, cramped from spending the night tucked beneath the metal folding chair, and glanced up at the nurse quietly entering the room. I moaned softly from my hospital bed. Thick, large bandages covered the gaping wounds on my back; a needle dripped cold liquid into my arm. A thick strip of gauze had been wrapped around my head. Emilienne was asleep in another chair next to the bed, her head leaning against the wall, her open mouth tipped toward the ceiling.

"There's coffee in the waiting room," the nurse offered. "Just made a fresh pot."

My mother closed her eyes as the nurse pulled back the bandages, revealing the gruesome, haphazard gashes across my shoulder blades. She swallowed a sudden wave of nausea. "No. I'm fine."

The nurse raised her eyebrows. "Honey, after the night you've had, nobody would blame you for not being fine. Go get some fresh air. We'll still be here when you come back."

In the waiting room, Viviane found the pot of coffee, as well as Gabe asleep in a chair, his chin resting against his chest. With his long legs stretched out in front of him, his feet nearly reached the windows across the room.

Viviane dropped into the seat beside him, noting the days' worth of stubble across his cheek, the lines of worry newly formed around his mouth. One hand rested in his lap; the other on the chair's armrest, the fingers curled away from the palm as if waiting for Viviane to lace her fingers with his. Viviane looked at the hand, the jagged fingernails, the white calluses, the cuticles permanently lined in black. She found his life line, the long crevice pointing away from his thumb, a nod to the years Gabe had spent traveling before coming to Seattle. The arc in the head line meant a creative mind, the star at the base of the fate line meant success. His heart line was long and curved, and she traced it with her eyes over and over again. A person with a curved heart line was a person capable of great warmth and kindness, a person willing to give their whole selves to love, no matter the cost.

Viviane reached over and threaded her fingers through Gabe's. *If I'd only looked down sooner,* she thought, *I would have seen that everything I ever needed was here, in this hand.*

Gabe's eyes fluttered open at Viviane's touch. He smiled wearily, wrapping his fingers around hers. "How's our girl?" he asked.

"Alive."

"Well, that's something."

"Is it? I thought I was protecting her. It never dawned on me that she could live like everyone else. Now that I know she can, it feels like it's too late."

Gabe pulled Viviane to him. "Henry?" she asked.

"With Wilhelmina," he replied. "Emilienne?"

"With Ava. Hasn't left her side since last night."

"Stranger things have happened."

Viviane nodded. A moment passed. "That man. The one I almost hit with the truck? It was him, wasn't it?" With a shudder, she remembered the monstrous ghosts in the road.

Gabe shook his head. "I can't be sure. But nobody's seen him. They found poor Marigold Pie up in one of the bedrooms. She'd been drugged. For how long, no one seems sure. Months maybe."

Viviane sighed. "I feel like the whole world's been tipped on its axis. Just walking upright feels like too much today."

Gabe pulled her closer. "You just lean on me, Vivi. I'll keep us both upright for a while."

Many would have typically preferred the rains to appear more gradually—say, as a warm spring shower typical of April or in the shape of a dense fog, the air clinging wet to eyelashes and nostrils. But when the rain persisted throughout the summer months and well into September, they hardly complained and instead wrapped cellophane around their good shoes to protect them from the mud along the sidewalks. They knew that rain meant green lawns, fall foliage, and chrysanthemums for the church altar on Sunday mornings. Wistful thoughts of that spring without rain came and went on occasion, when, for example, the mail carrier grew tired of sorting sodden letters, or Penelope Cooper became listless at the sight of the bakery floor streaked with mud yet again. But then that weariness would pass, and they would join their neighbors in a collected sigh of relief at the piles of wet fall leaves gathering in the street.

My mother remained at the hospital for the length of my stay. She refused to leave even for a change of clothes. After that first night, she coaxed the nurse to bring in a cot so that she could stay in the room with me. She was surprised when the nurse brought in not one, but two. She was even more surprised when she found out the other cot was for Emilienne.

Emilienne sat down on the cot before glancing up at her daughter. "What? Did you want this one?"

"No," Viviane said, shaking her head. "I'm a little confused as to what you're doing."

"I'm staying as well."

Viviane raised her eyebrows. "Why?"

"Because—" Emilienne's voice broke. "Because I'm your mother, that's why."

And so it was.

Chapter Twenty-Five

WE RETURNED TO THE HOUSE at the end of Pinnacle Lane barely three months after the summer solstice. Gabe carefully placed me on my bed, and my grandmother covered me with a quilt her *maman* made many years before. Emilienne willed herself not to weep, but I saw it in her face. The gauze hid my sutures well enough, so she didn't have to stare at the stitchery holding my frail body together. But the bruises would not be hidden. They seeped down my sides, across my arms and hips, down the backs of my legs. And the color—so dark they weren't purple, but red. The very color of violence.

Those deep-red bruises called to mind the faint brown mark Jack's kiss had left on her daughter Viviane's neck so many years ago. They also made her think of René's lovely face after William Peyton shot it off, of the hole in Margaux's chest where her heart once beat, and of all the scars love's victims carry. Then she would have to leave the room.

My grandmother felt no rush to return to the bakery. She could hardly will herself to cook enough to keep her own family fed, not that anyone cared. The appetite of my whole family had dwindled enough so that each ate only when the gnawing pains of hunger fired in their bellies. And even then, they did so without gusto, taking a fork to a neighbor's cold pan of macaroni and cheese left in the fridge. No one paid any attention to where the food came from, just that it was there.

Something had happened to Emilienne. She could not summon the strength she once had, no matter how hard she tried. While she waited for some sign of life to return to my eyes, it was my mother who held the family together.

Wilhelmina and Penelope were more than capable of running the bakery on their own. They added a popular pastry to the menu; in honor of me, they sold the *feuilletage* on Sundays. They even hired another baker to replace Emilienne. They hired my mother.

The bakery was exactly as Viviane remembered it:

the walls the same golden shade of yellow, the black-and-white-tiled floor still impeccably shined. When Wilhelmina handed her an apron and pointed her toward the oven, Viviane was hardly stunned by how quickly she recalled the trick to a good pear *tarte tatin* or how to make *crème brûlée.* Soon her chocolate éclairs were deemed just as good as Emilienne's.

It shamed her to admit it, but Viviane relished her hours in the bakery, away from the awful odor of misery and despair that wafted through the hallways of our house. It was so strong that my mother often covered her nose with a handkerchief just to walk by my room. They had to hire a nurse to change my bandages. What happened to me was so horrible, Viviane tried not to think about it, often tried not to think at all. Instead, she filled her time with menial tasks, like baking bread and pastries, which she always brought home to serve after my lunch.

Back in our kitchen, my mother folded a paper napkin in half and placed it under a plate of warm bread pudding drizzled with chocolate sauce and topped with a scoop of vanilla ice cream. She watched the ice cream melt into a plate-size puddle. Viviane heard the soft tread of footsteps behind her as Cardigan made her way down the stairs from my room and into the kitchen.

"Is she hungry?" Viviane asked halfheartedly.

Cardigan shook her head. Out of all of us, Cardigan had changed the most since my attack. She'd let her hair grow out from its stylish bob so that it hung at her shoulders in natural waves; occasionally she threw it in a haphazard ponytail just to get it out of her face. She rarely wore makeup anymore. The first time Viviane saw Cardigan without it, Viviane hadn't recognized her. The makeup had made her glamorous, untouchable even; without it, Cardigan was pretty but in a less obvious way. Her lashes, blond like her hair, were barely visible around her blue eyes, and her lips were a pale shade of pink and much thinner without the usual swipe of rich red lipstick. She dressed differently, often coming to the house in her brother's old work boots and a pair of oversize jeans. She was enrolled in honors classes and was secretly planning on taking over Rowe's old delivery job in October once she passed her driver's test.

"Heard anything from my brother?" Cardigan asked Viviane. Rowe had left for school a month ago, and not a day had gone by without the mail bringing a letter addressed to me. My mother gathered he wrote to me more often than to his own family. He'd tried calling on the phone a few times, but I had barely spoken four words in the past few months. So Rowe stuck to the post. At first Viviane wasn't sure what to do with the letters, so she just piled them up on my bedside table.

Viviane pointed to the brown envelope on the kitchen table. Cardigan swooped it up and pressed it to her nose. "I told him I'd whale on him if he ever sent her a perfumed love letter."

Viviane laughed. She was glad Cardigan hadn't lost her sense of humor completely.

"What's the assignment this week?" Viviane asked, nodding to the book in Cardigan's hand.

"*The Scarlet Letter.* I'm reading it to Ava so she won't fall behind." Cardigan turned toward the stairs. "Don't you think that's a good idea?" she added quietly.

Viviane nodded. She'd spoken about my enrollment in the high school with her old teacher Ignatius Lux, now the high-school principal, earlier that summer. Ignatius was a large, barrel-chested man with the tangled mop of red hair that went well with his name. Due to his size, his students considered him a fearsome force. Some even feared the Lux more than they feared their own parents. But Ignatius Lux was actually very soft-hearted, so much so it often embarrassed his wife, and the big man had wept—literally wept!—when he'd heard what had happened to me. So when Viviane stopped by to set up an appointment, the principal immediately ushered her into his office, offering her a cup of coffee and instructing his secretary to clear the rest of the day's meetings. Ignatius had always liked Viviane—years ago, when she was just a spunky student in his class, he had thought, *Now, there's someone who could probably do just about anything.*

Ignatius was impressed, but not surprised, by how closely Viviane's curriculum matched that of the school. He assured her they would save a spot for me in the fall enrollment.

Viviane placed her coffee cup on the principal's desk. "Considering the severity of her . . . *condition*, I don't think any of us are expecting her to fully recover before the spring term."

Ignatius stammered an apology and gave his word that I could register for classes whenever I was ready. After the meeting Viviane had gone back to her truck and cried, not knowing that only thirty feet away, with his head resting on his big principal's desk, Ignatius Lux was doing the same thing.

Viviane walked outside to where Gabe sat on the porch swing watching Henry collect insects in the yard. She handed Gabe the two glasses of lemonade in her hands before lowering herself into the crook of his arm, then took the second glass and wrapped his now-free hand around her shoulder.

"Any change?" Gabe asked.

Viviane shook her head wearily. "No. No change."

Gabe kneaded the sore muscles in Viviane's neck with his long fingers until the tension she held there began to fade. Viviane had been surprised by how quickly her body responded to his, how the lines of where she ended and he began seemed to melt whenever they touched. It felt natural for him to share her bed, to spend his nights asleep on her pillow. But the best part was that after twenty-seven years, Viviane was finally free of Jack Griffith—a feat so miraculous that sometimes Viviane wanted to call it out from the rooftops just to hear the echo.

"Where's Emilienne?" Gabe asked suddenly. "Asleep again?"

"Yes."

Since the night of the solstice, the hours my grandmother spent awake had dwindled to only a few a day. Even when I was still in the hospital, it was common for Viviane to walk in on her sleeping daughter *and* mother, me in the bed and Emilienne in the chair next to it, her graying hair spilling from the chignon twisted against the paper-thin skin at the nape of her neck.

Henry looked up from the grass, proudly holding up some multi-legged or winged insect trapped in between the mesh sides of the bug catcher. "See?" he called.

Since the night of the solstice, Henry spoke less and less. They tried not to let it discourage them—there was enough of that to go around already. Viviane assumed it had to do with my condition, but the truth was that Henry now found very little worth talking about. And he only talked when what he had to say was really important. That was the rule.

The day they brought me home from the hospital, Viviane had found a large unmarked envelope leaning up against the front door. Inside were two sizable checks—one made out to me, the other to Henry. Trapped in the envelope glue was a strand of copper-colored hair. As far as

Viviane knew, Laura Lovelorn had returned to her beloved eastern Washington as soon as her separation from Jack Griffith was official.

"The world is definitely changing," Viviane murmured. Gabe gave her shoulder a squeeze.

Gabe often teased Viviane about the bare ring finger on her left hand, implying, in his own gentle way, how much he wanted to marry her. She knew she would spend the rest of her nights dreaming beside the gentle giant, his chest pressed against her back, his palm lightly cupping her hip. But she also knew that she would never marry. Not Gabe or anyone else. *What use did the heart have for jewelry anyway?* To use her words.

Through the fall, I lay in bed with my stomach pressed against the mattress as I had since the day I was brought home from the hospital. The days and nights meshed together, forming a heavy black shroud that covered my eyes, my nose, my mouth, until I could no longer remember what it was like to feel the sun on my face. When the leaves began to change, my mother asked Gabe to move the bed so that, by turning my head to the side, I could look out the window. But when the leaves turned from green to brown, and I watched them fall to the ground to rot, I found they only reminded me of death.

By December the rains had calmed; the gray storm clouds that some suspected would never pass did, and winter arrived, carrying with it mornings of icy roads and icy car windows, and only a few scattered showers. Snow would come later, in January and February, catching them all by surprise when they awoke to a city draped in white.

December 21 marked the winter solstice. It also marked the six-month anniversary of my attack and the auspicious death of Nathaniel Sorrows. For the first time ever, Pinnacle Lane recognized the winter pagan holiday, though it was in somber, solemn tones.

Those days I often thought about death, often wondered what it might be like to die with such intensity that I could feel the edges of my body melt away, as if I were already a decomposing corpse. I imagined that being dead would feel a lot like those days when the nurse gave me a chalky white pill that left me so numb, the hours melted away like morning ice on a window. Like I was nothing at all but an insignificant shadow, a whisper, a drop of rain left to dry on the pavement.

But while the thought of being dead seemed appealing, the actual act of dying did not. Dying required too much action. And if recent events proved anything, my body wasn't going to give over to death without a fierce fight; so if I were to kill myself, I'd have to make sure I could do it. That I'd be good and dead once it was all over and not mutilated or half deranged but still dreadfully alive. I thought of collecting handfuls of those chalky white pills, of hiding them in my cheek and stuffing them under the mattress, later washing them down in one gulp with a glass of cold tap water. I thought of sneaking into the kitchen for a steak knife sharp enough that a single slice to just one wrist would suffice—I wasn't sure I could try to kill myself twice. I thought often of jumping from the rickety widow's walk on the roof of the house. If it weren't for my constant visitors, those thoughts might very well have led to some dark and dreadful act. Perhaps this was the very reason those constant visitors were there.

Gabe was in charge of breakfast, and each morning prepared simple culinary comforts: plate-size pancakes with gobs of butter and maple syrup licking down the sides; browned links of sausages; slices of smoked bacon; hard-boiled eggs—all served using Emilienne's good china and linen napkins and the heavy silver knives and spoons. Gabe put everything on a tray and brought it upstairs to my room, bringing Henry along with him. In his own silent way, Henry was best at getting me to eat, and on the days when I wouldn't, well, there was always Trouver.

Lunch was brought up by Cardigan, who dutifully arrived at our front door every afternoon, first just as the sun moved to its one o'clock spot, and then a little later in the day once school began. She brought her schoolwork with her, reading aloud from the books whose pages she'd been assigned and whispering secret plans she'd made for us when I was better.

"When you're better . . ." she'd begin.

Most of the time Cardigan spent the hours of her visit

lying next to me, holding my hand as we stared at the wall in silence. Once I turned my unfocused eyes to my best friend and said, "This suits you," meaning Cardigan's new, simplified look.

To which Cardigan replied, "This doesn't suit you," meaning everything else.

Dinner always varied. Sometimes it was brought by my mother. Sometimes it was Penelope or her husband, Zeb, who did card tricks with his calloused hands as I took a few meager bites from my meal. On the days Wilhelmina would come, she'd bring with her tiny satchels of dried herbs, which she'd hand to Viviane with specific instructions for water temperature and seeping time before heading upstairs. When it was ready, Viviane brought the bitter tea with my dinner. We watched and listened as Wilhelmina stood by the open window and sang in a low, melodious voice, tapping out the rhythm of her healing chant on the elk-skin drum she held in her hand. When Wilhelmina sang, my heart slowly became the beating of the drum. My breathing steadied, and I fell into a semi-hypnotic state not unlike that brought on by the chalky white pills, but a much more pleasant one.

I often thought I was going crazy—or maybe not going but already there. As if my future was only a locked room with white painted walls and white painted floors, with no windows or doors or any means to escape. A place where I opened my mouth to scream but no sound came out.

Instead of dying, instead of slowly disappearing until

only a broken body remained, what happened was quite the opposite — my body began to repair itself.

I was grateful to the nurse who came every day to change my bulky bandages, even when it was quite clear that I no longer needed them. The nurse never said a word to either my mother or grandmother. I appreciated this; it gave me time to think, and I needed that time, what with all these images of death muddying my thoughts.

Then one night I awoke to find a man sitting by my bed, one hand covering the place where his face had been shot off.

"Don't be afraid," the man said. His words were thick and warped, as if his voice were leaking out of parts of his body other than his mouth.

"I'm not," I replied, my own voice strange with disuse. "I know who you are."

If the man could have smiled, he would have. "And who am I, then?"

"You're death, of course." I sighed. "To be honest, I find it comforting that you've been looking for me as much as I've been looking for you. Will it be long now?"

"Not long."

I shivered. "What is it like? Being dead?"

"What do you think it is like?"

I pondered this question, noticing only then that I was still clutching one of Rowe's letters. "I think death is something like being drugged or having a fever," I whispered.

"Like being a step away from everyone else. A step so large and wide that catching up quickly becomes impossible, and all I can do is watch as everyone I love slowly disappears."

"Is that what you want?"

"Do I have a choice?"

"We all have a choice."

I laughed cruelly, but I didn't care. "Do we? What about you? Did you choose to come here? To spend your afterlife as a misshapen monster?"

"Ah, *ma petite-nièce*, I volunteered."

"Why?"

The man stood. "Love makes us such fools," he said, his transparent form shimmering slightly before disappearing completely.

For the first time in six months, I pulled myself up into a sitting position. I lowered my weak legs to the floor and tried to walk across the room in shaky steps to the window. The maple tree outside stood against the dark sky, its bare limbs shivering in the cold. I looked down at the road knowing that in only a matter of hours it would bring Rowe home on break for the holidays. I had read every one of his letters so many times it was as if each word had been permanently inscribed on the inside of my eyelids. I knew that in the second letter he misspelled the word *existence*, replacing the second *e* with an *a*; in the fourth he forgot to dot the *i* in *believe*. I slept with them not under my pillow but clutched in my hand, with the sweat from my dreams leaking from my palms and smudging the ink. And I'd read the last line of the letter I received only a few days before—the final Rowe would send before coming home—until the words had lost all meaning to my head and only my heart still understood.

I loved you before, Ava. Let me love you still.

Chapter Twenty-Six

IN THE BEDROOM across the hall, my grandmother was deep in a dream. In it she was back in Beauregard's Manhatine, in the apartment with the cracked porcelain kitchen sink and the bureau with the drawer where, once upon a time, baby Pierette had slept. Her three siblings sat waiting for her around the wooden table, their faces and bodies whole and intact—René's handsome face handsome yet again, Margaux's heart beating underneath her solid ribcage, Pierette fluffing her bright-yellow hair.

René stood and wrapped Emilienne in his arms, then picked her up from the ground with one easy lift and plunked her into the chair in between her sisters.

"We've been waiting for you." Margaux motioned at the two decks of cards sitting in the middle of the table. "None of us can remember how to play bezique."

"You can't play bezique with four players," Emilienne answered. "You're thinking of pinochle."

Pierette wrinkled her nose. "What's the difference?"

Emilienne shuffled the cards, marveling at the agility of her fingers, at the plump skin across her hands. Pausing in her card playing, she wrapped a curl of her thick hair around her finger, relishing the black color that the years had faded first to gray and then to white. On her feet were a pair of laced black shoes, and on her head, newly painted with red poppies, was the cloche hat.

"I never liked that hat," Pierette mused.

"I think I liked you more as a bird," Emilienne answered, and the four began to laugh.

Emilienne drifted back into consciousness. In the dark she could barely make out the shadowed shapes in her bedroom: the faded wedding picture propped up on the bedside table, the rose-colored chair with the cat hair matted to the side, and the man sitting in the chair, his handsome face as handsome as it once was.

"None of us can remember how to play bezique," René said.

"I think you mean pinochle." Emilienne pulled the metal string on the lamp near her bed, and the light cast a soft glow across the room.

"Do I?"

"Yes, I think you do." Emilienne rose from the bed and shook out her dark hair from the chignon she would no longer wear at the nape of her neck. She slid her hand into the crook of René's offered elbow and gave it a light squeeze with young agile fingers.

"We were hoping you'd be able to play us a tune on that harpsichord of yours," he said as he led her from the room.

"Oh? Well, I think that would be lovely."

I peered out into the hallway, startled to find it empty. Hadn't I heard someone out there? I crept past my doorway, each step announcing itself with a long wailing creak. I paused and listened to the night sounds of the house: the motorized purr of one of the cats asleep under my bed, the soft swishing of the long hair on Trouver's legs as the dog ran in his dreams. There was the distant hum of the refrigerator downstairs, my mother's soft breathing from the room across the hall.

A soft glow spilled into the hall from under my grandmother's door. I walked toward it. I turned the doorknob slowly. Blinking in the light, I saw Emilienne tucked in her four-poster bed. Her eyes were closed, her white hair spread out across the pillows, her lips slightly parted as if she were waiting to speak.

I leaned down and pressed my face close to hers, determined not to breathe until I felt my grandmother's breath on my cheek. After a few moments of struggling, I finally exhaled and leaned my forehead against her cold cheek.

No one had occupied the third floor of our house since the days of Fatima Inês. It was believed that the room upstairs had long ago belonged to her and that her ghost kept everyone away from that floor. I learned the truth behind this myth when I entered the room with cautious, shaky steps. It was not the ghost of Fatima Inês that greeted me.

Birds perched on the rafters, each tipping its head curiously as I made my way past the dilapidated canopy bed, the dresser, the rocking horse. Their nests rested along the beams; their droppings covered the floor. They called to one another in a language only they understood. I glanced around at these strange-looking birds with big black crow bodies and tiny white dove heads, noting that never before had I seen such a bird. Not in the sky above my house. Not in the trees in my yard. And not in Nathaniel Sorrows's front room. These were Fatima Inês's birds—the very descendants of the doves who had escaped from their hutches to breed with the crows. Somehow, they were more resilient than all the other birds in the neighborhood. This I found most heartening.

The birds fell silent when I opened the door to the rickety widow's walk and stepped outside. I could see all of Seattle glowing beneath a handful of stars. The full moon cast a shimmering silver light on the ground below. My bare feet began to burn from the cold, and I looked down at the house next door.

Marigold Pie's house sat abandoned and vacant. They'd found Marigold in one of the upstairs bedrooms looking a bit like a whale-size Sleeping Beauty with stale cookie crumbs scattered across the pillow. When she finally awoke, Marigold, who had no intention of losing weight, joined a circus traveling through Seattle. She spent the rest of her years as the carnival's beloved Fat Lady in a tent between the Human Pincushion and Errol, the cloven-hoofed boy. She often sent me postcards from her travels. Later, at the occasion of her death, Marigold willed me Nathaniel's journal—discovered in her yard the night of my attack. It took me years to open its pages, even longer to read them.

Stalks of tall purple herbs gradually claimed her yard. Now, in December, the honey-sweet scent of lavender was finally strong enough to cover the horrid stench of the birds found rotting throughout the house. All that remained of Nathaniel Sorrows was a permanent field of purple flowers, a black mark on the concrete, and a bitter taste in the back of the throat the very few times his name was mentioned.

A car turned onto Pinnacle Lane, and I watched as it made its way up the Coopers' driveway. Two shapes emerged from the car. The larger one was undeniably Zeb Cooper, which meant the other had to be Rowe.

I smiled then in spite of myself. I smiled past all of my misgivings and reservations, past all previous heartbreak and any future heartbreak, because Rowe had come back.

It was true, what he had written to me. Suddenly the weary burden of my attack didn't seem quite so heavy as I remembered something else he wrote.

You don't have to carry it by yourself.

"It is all right, now? Yes?"

I turned around to see a translucent figure moving among the birds. Wrapped around her was the hooded green cloak that once hid her thick eyebrows and chapped lips from suspicious neighbors; it was the same cloak I'd used to hide my wings from mine.

I nodded. Yes. It was all right.

And with that, the ghost of Fatima Inês waved goodbye to her birds and slowly faded into the night.

Chapter Twenty-Seven

AT THE EDGE of the town's reservoir, on the neighborhood's highest point—the hill at the end of Pinnacle Lane was a close second—stood a little white house. Hidden by a grove of maple trees, the house had once been occupied by an old man and his wife. They had spent their autumn days scooping five-pointed leaves of orange, gold, and red from its still waters and turned the radio up when young lovers visited the isolated place, smiling at one another as they closed the curtains against the night.

From the attic window of the little white house, one could see the whole neighborhood, which some say was the very reason Jack Griffith bought it. Standing underneath the eaves, Jack could peer across the calm reservoir waters to where Viviane Lavender had once watched the moon disappear, where months earlier a group of cynical teenagers had met the myth they'd never quite believed. From there, Jack could see all the contributions of little Fatima Inês de Dores and her ship captain brother: the post office, the drugstore, the brick elementary-school building, the Lutheran church. He could see Emilienne's bakery, where customers came to purchase a morning sticky bun from the American-Indian woman behind the counter, where the wafting scents of cinnamon and vanilla comforted even the surliest souls. He could see the new police station and the rows of identical houses that had sprung up after the war. And he could see, at the end of Pinnacle Lane, a house painted the color of faded periwinkles. It had a white wraparound porch and an onion-domed turret in the back. The second-floor bedrooms had giant bay windows. A widow's walk topped the house, its balcony turned toward Salmon Bay.

I like to think that when Jack Griffith looked up at that moment, he saw a figure on the balcony perched precariously on the widow's walk atop the Lavender house, surrounded by a flock of peculiar birds singing an unusual song only they seemed to understand. I like to think that he saw me, the loosened ends of my long bandages and the wispy tangled curls of my hair reaching out to the wind, the skirt of my nightgown billowing in melodic waves. I like to think that he watched as I climbed over the side of the rickety widow's walk, my toes perched on the ledge, my fingers clasped lightly to the railing behind me. Perhaps he noted, with quiet irony, that never before had anyone more resembled an angel. I like to think that he marveled at the mass of bandages that unraveled completely and tumbled to the ground, and at the pair of pure white wings that unfolded from my shoulder blades and arched, large and strong, over my head.

But, mostly, I like to think that Jack Griffith, my father, smiled as I let go of the railing behind me and, stretching my wings to that star-studded sky, soared into the night.

fin

ACKNOWLEDGMENTS

I feel incredibly fortunate to have the support of a group of people without whom this book would have been nothing more than a fictional world I visited during conversation lulls:

Bernadette Baker-Baughman, agent extraordinaire and literary super-goddess, who believed in Ava from the very beginning. There aren't enough words to describe how lucky I feel to have such a rock star for an agent.

My editor, Mary Lee Donovan, whose fathomless dedication and encouragement helped make this book into what it is today. I owe so much gratitude to the entire Candlewick and Walker Books family for their hard work — most especially Sherry Fatla, Gill Evans, Sarah Foster, Angela Van Den Belt, Tracy Miracle, and Angie Dombroski. A very special thank-you to Pier Gustafson for the incredible job on the family tree, and Matt Roeser for the book jacket and cover design. It is far more beautiful than anything I could have imagined. Also, many thanks to the extraordinary Chandler Crawford for helping introduce Ava to the world, as well as to Gretchen Stelter, Nick Harris, and Christine Munroe for their tireless enthusiasm and insight.

Of course, none of this would have been possible without the constant love and support of my family and friends. Many thanks to Andrea Paris for inviting me over to her dad's little white house on the reservoir when we were in eighth grade. The beauty of that place never left me. Thank you, David Seal, for telling me I was already a writer when I told you that was all I wanted to be, and Whitney Otto for believing this little book of mine was something worth reading. Liz Buelow, my first reader, for your brilliance, honesty, and all those late-night brainstorm sessions over sushi and sake.

Thank you to my girls—Anna, Annelise, Carissa, Duffy, Maren, Megan, Nova, Reba, Raquel, and Stephanie—who know me better than anyone and love me anyway. You are the strangest, most beautiful people I know, and I'm grateful for you every day. To my gorgeous students, thanks for making me laugh and for thinking I'm cool even though we all know I'm not. You're the lights of my life. To my parents, thank you for allowing me to grow into a very imaginative (if not slightly delusional) adult. It's served me well. My *irmã*, Nichele, thank you for always telling me like it is, and thanks as well to my three-year-old niece, Kaeloni, who'd never forgive her *tía* for not thanking her in her first book.

And finally, to my Good Luck Charm for being right all along. I can't remember exactly what it was you said, but I swear I remember everything else. *Tenho saudades tuas.*

LESLYE WALTON was born in the Pacific Northwest. Perhaps because of this, she has developed a strange kinship with the daffodil — she too can achieve beauty only after a long, cold sulk in the rain. Her debut novel, *The Strange and Beautiful Sorrows of Ava Lavender*, was inspired by a particularly long sulk in a particularly cold rainstorm during which she pondered the logic, or rather, the lack of logic, in love — the ways we coax ourselves to love, to continue loving, to leave love behind. Leslye Walton lives in Seattle. Find her on Twitter: @LeslyeWalton

2/3/15